THE BLUE CUP

And Other Stories

THE
BLUE CUP
And Other Stories

BY

B. J. CHUTE

E. P. Dutton and Company, Inc.

NEW YORK

INDIVIDUAL COPYRIGHT

LIBRARY OF CONGRESS CATALOG CARD NUMBER: 57–8955

For

MARY GRACE

TABLE OF CONTENTS

THE BLUE CUP

And Other Stories

THE YOUNG ONES

THE FIESTA

IT HAD never occurred to the small Charles to rebel, since there was nothing whatever for him to rebel against. At five his was the ordered, golden age of Nurse and Father and Mother, of licensed visits to the park with respectable little friends (not all children are respectable), of schooling so selective that the flowers blooming in the garden of *Kinder* never risked the dangerous pollen of crossbreeding.

He was Charles Robertson III, sprung from the loins of Charles the First and Charles the Second, secure in patronymic and in the use of Roman numerals endorsed by king and pope. The city that surrounded him was a city of docility, where doormen tipped their caps and called him Master Charles and where the great river, tidal and often dirty, lay beyond his window a distant silver.

There was really no need for Charles either to think or to plan for himself, and he was not encouraged to. He was a small and quiet child who had never given his nurse a pin of trouble, who rose and ate and slept on schedule, and who occasionally carried cocktails for his parents' guests as innocently as some well-brushed medieval pageboy might have carried a lute.

He showed an early fondness for books and was an alert student of *Winnie-the-Pooh* and *A Child's Garden of Verses*, from which he could recite whole rhymes. He liked pictures, but newspapers and magazines were kept from him, and when he evidenced a creeping intelligence toward stars his nurse read him a book about them, eliminating Virgo from the constellations on a point of delicacy.

He was not given an allowance, but he learned the forms of money early, and he liked its miscellaneous copper and nickel and silver, especially the kind, quiet face of Mr. Lincoln. The few pennies he owned in his own right, given for being charming, were installed in a circle at the base of the little lamp beside his bed, and they glowed gold and new-minted when the light was turned on.

This reduction of finances to *objets d'art* was perhaps characteristic of him, so that when he found the dollar bill under the coffee table in the living room, just before he was called to bed by his nurse, he collected it interestedly but only as a portrait of George Washington, a man dimly associated with cherry trees and with something called a Revolution.

When he heard Nurse calling, he put the dollar hastily into the pocket of his England-inspired gray shorts, secreting not money as such but the germs that might be on it, since he was not supposed to pick things up off the floor. At the time he was most certainly not aware that the money had any possibilities beyond the portrait. The possibilities came to him later, after he was in bed, tucked under the sheet and with the light turned off. The long dusk of July lay outside the window, and he had not played hard enough in the heat of the day (had not, indeed, been allowed to play hard enough) to tire himself for quick sleep.

He made a tent of his bedclothes and imagined a camel waiting just outside, but it was a poor night for camels, and this one left the room almost immediately. He was often subjected to this difficulty with conjured animals, because he had nothing to feed them on and they gave up rather easily. He thought of tomorrow and of visiting in the park, but it was not an interesting thought. He rolled over on his stomach and nibbled at the pillow, but he was not trained in taking liberties, and he knew it was bad for the pillowcase. He rolled back and hunched up his knees and turned his head to peer at the pennies around the lamp. They were dissolving in the last traces of daylight, but he knew how they looked and where they lay, and his mind jumped to the dollar bill.

Green, he thought, on one side but grayish on the other, where Mr. Washington looked out stiffly. He frowned, trying to reconstruct the green side. He sighed and wished he could see it, and it was a measure of his virtue that he waited nearly a quarter of an hour before the idea of not seeing it became insupportable.

He pushed back the sheet and climbed out of bed, standing there on the rug with one bare foot resting on the other and his toes curling tightly like snails, uncertain which direction to take. When he finally moved, it was toward the closet. His shorts hung neatly, and he had no difficulty locating the bill, crunched up and giving forth a pleasant crackle of sound.

He took it back to bed with him and smoothed it out. There was barely enough light to see what he wanted on the back of it: the eagle; the pyramid, which he was unable to identify, being unacquainted with Egypt (this may have accounted for his difficulty with camels); and, most amazing of all, a single eye above the pyramid looking at him fiercely. This eye he could understand. It was the All-Seeing one, and, being so good a child, he had always heard it well spoken of, but it was unsettling to find himself in bed with it.

He shook his head, trying to get rid of its fixed glare, and this defensive effort to evade Heaven's attention did a curious thing to the piece of paper in his hand. It reverted to size and took the form of money.

By daylight, having identified its consequence and value, he would have surrendered the dollar bill to Nurse at once, but in the soft, increasing dusk more than the room was becoming blurred and a quaint and curious magic was at work. He was no longer Charles, in pajamas, in bed. He had become a man of property.

He clutched the bill, first act of possession. The Eye must have winked a little as the paper creased.

It should not be said of Charles that he surrendered to the acquisition of wealth without a struggle, but the money cried out for action. Tomorrow, of course, lay at the other end of the night, but at the age of five tomorrow is too far away to be of any use. When he found himself standing again in the middle of the room, he was surprised but acquiescent.

Dressing was not easy, but he triumphed over it, patient with buttons, making a compromise with shoelaces. When he put his cap on, squared neatly above his fiercely concentrated eyebrows, and stepped at last into the hall, he took no precautions toward secrecy.

It was an hour before Nurse found that he had gone, and then of course it was too late.

No one saw Charles leave. He took the stairs instead of the elevator, and the doorman, who had a hard time accounting for it later, was at the back of the long lobby, smoking an unauthorized cigarette. On the street no one was interested in one more small boy, and a girl about ten, pigtailed and absorbed in a rhythmic game with a ball, looked at him and then through him, so that for a moment he had the delighted impression that he was invisible.

This deepened his sense of security, and he began to walk quite fast without any idea of where he was going. When he came to an avenue alive with trucks, he joined a group of people at the curb, apparently standing sensibly idle, only to discover that they were waiting for a bus. The bus, on arrival, was red and very large, and Charles followed his companions and climbed aboard.

The driver held out his hand as Charles passed him, and it became clear that he was going to have to surrender the Eye. For a moment the vanity of possession warred with adventure, but only for a moment. He submitted to an interior guide and gave up the bill tranquilly, receiving in exchange a great many coins of all shapes and colors. He started to poke through these, looking for familiar faces, but the driver reached out and took some of his treasure away, and the transaction appeared to satisfy whatever powers were in operation.

He took a seat by the window and twisted around to stare out, an action as delightful as it was unfamiliar, since he was discouraged from twisting about in moving vehicles (the family Cadillac, the taxicabs). He sat sober but alert, watching the avenue unwind like a long wool thread.

He had no plans for getting off the bus and would probably have gone to the end of the line, had not a sudden blare of music and dazzle of lights jerked him out of passivity and into what was either a brilliant dream or a world he had never suspected.

The avenue ahead had become an archway of jewels, lights strung from curb to curb in an endless glitter. Booths and tables marched its length, and the tangle of music that rose over it had the pleasing quality of being almost pure noise and not at all the kind of thing he was encouraged to listen to on the radio. His musical taste had been assiduously cultivated, and he possessed his own small phonograph with neat little madrigals and a very dashing song about a bear, but it was nothing like this.

The bus stopped, and he was decanted almost before he knew what had happened, slid into the stream of sound and wonder like a small minnow inserted among bright tropical fish. He stood wordlessly, transfixed. No one noticed him, no one spoke to him, and, when he was jostled, he was as casually set straight again by the touch of a hand on his shoulder. He looked up, half expecting Nurse, but the body that owned the hand had already swung out of his orbit.

He felt excitement pull against his natural caution, and he walked without direction, his head tipped back, his chin out and his hands in his pockets. He stopped before a table loaded with all kinds of food, brightly colored and open to the air, in a muddle of smells so strong and rich that they lay on his tongue and he could almost have chewed them.

He was a little shocked. Nurse would never let him have ice cream at any of the gay carts in the park, and he understood this to be because people were breathing germs all around them. He looked at the food worriedly, and after a second he stretched out his hand and replaced a piece of waxed paper that was flapping loose over what appeared to be a sort of hot salad, full of screaming reds and varnished greens. A voice said "Hey!" He looked up and found himself staring into the face of the man behind the counter, a large face, somewhat fierce but unaccountably lively. Charles patted the paper harmlessly and backed off a little.

The man said "Pizza?" and held out a limp orange slab. Charles thought it was an offering like the tiny hot pastries at his mother's cocktail parties; this was certainly a party of some sort. He accepted it politely.

"F'teen cents," said the man, and held out his hand again, empty, palm up like the bus driver's.

It took Charles a moment to realize that this was not quite like a party after all; this was like the carts in the park. He felt in his pocket and took out his small store of coins, extending them hopefully.

The man took two without comment, and Charles was sorry to see them go, but the pastry thing was hot in his hand, and he felt the early thrill of *quid pro quo*. He moved away, holding his purchase tight, and after a moment he bit at a corner of it. The taste in his mouth was extremely odd, and he would have spit it out, but such direct action was unthinkable. He chewed it resignedly, and on acquaintance it became rather interesting, durable and yet exotic. He took another bite, small, and then a larger bite, and in a moment he was one with the chewing crowd.

He began to look around him now, and up, and he observed that many of the faces were darker than the ones he was familiar with. These must belong to what his nurse called colored people, like the porter who waxed the floor in the hallway, and he could almost feel Nurse's hand jerking him away. For a moment he was really alarmed, but the people were uncommonly gay, and his fear dissolved as he watched a little boy about his own age suddenly begin to spin in a cheerful dance in the middle of the sidewalk. Spin and spin, while people eddied around him, and then sit down abruptly, chuckling like a brook, scrunched to a chuckling ball among all those moving feet.

He would have liked to try it himself, if only because it was so indefensible, but he might lose what remained of his pastry, and anyway he was already caught up in another wash of crowd, and he moved resistlessly with the tide.

The tide flowed now toward a center, and he found himself walking in the street instead of on the sidewalk, above him a glorious banner with words on it and a bright-colored, splendid picture of a lady in robes that surpassed the sunset or his crayons. He set himself solidly against the push of the crowd and stared up, trying to read the words, but they were too strenuous for anyone on a Pooh Bear diet, and he gave up and ate the last crumb of his pastry lingeringly.

When he came to a big building with people standing in orderly lines outside and its stairs hospitable with the going up and coming down of feet, he moved toward the sidewalk again, but a wooden barrier stopped him firmly. He leaned against it and stared absorbedly up into the building. It was full of light, and the glimpse he had of the ceiling through the open doors was astonishing, being a cloud-covered sky with large winged figures sailing around in it. His association with churches was mannerly and sabbatical, but he had once been taken to see *Peter*

Pan at a children's theatre, and, since that had been equally full of light and of people flying around, he identified this place to his own satisfaction and nodded to himself.

For *Peter Pan* it had been necessary to have tickets; he was sure of this because his mother had lost them and he had been worried that they might be turned away at the door. Here it would be necessary to have tickets too, and he stood for a while looking wistfully at the floating figures and the flying clouds and the fine blue sky cupped inside a building, and then he was saved from any more regret by a tremendous shout of music from down the street. It spun him around, an eager puppy following any leash that pulled.

The music was easy enough to trace. A bandstand in front of a big dark building was loaded with musicians, and a crowd stood staring up at it, swaying just a little to the sound like water rippled over with wind. Charles stationed himself next to a man eating a large slice of pink, dripping watermelon. As the man came to a seed, he chewed rhythmically for a moment, spit it out, bit and chewed again. Bite and chew and spit. Charles' absorbed respect must have penetrated. The man looked down and grinned. Charles smiled back cautiously ("Never talk to strangers") and the man said, "Lost your folks?"

He had no idea what "folks" might be, but he had not lost anything that he knew of, and so he shook his head wordlessly. The man shrugged and forgot him, giving him that wonderful anonymous feeling he had before.

Unnoticed, a baby star in an indifferent Milky Way, Charles swung in his universe. The music pushed through the pavement at his feet, making them quickstep, and the cover of lights pushed down on his head, making him dizzy and immortal. He saw a man with a parrot on his shoulder, gray-polled rose-breasted and sleek, with a fierce bill, but he could not get through the knot of people around it, and he promised himself he would find it again and went in innocent quest of water-melon. This search was not blessed, but he found instead a table spread with post cards in tinseled garish colors, painted brooches framing a lady's face, like his great-aunt's cameo, only livelier and not at all pale, and finally small statue groups consisting of a baby lying on the ground and figures bending over it and sometimes a small china lamb. This, of course, was the baby Jesus, and with great daring he stretched out a finger and stroked one of the little lambs.

That was when he saw, next to his own hand, a small paw flicker out and snatch. One moment a painted brooch lay in plain sight; the next moment it was gone. Charles sucked in his breath and glanced sideways. Next to him a small boy, face like a placid cherub, stared into his eyes for a moment, then winked.

He's a thief, thought Charles, and was shocked.

The boy, the thief, moved nearer him. Charles' gaze widened, fixed on the small hand touching and poking, but he did not move. His sense of property, of rigid mine and thine, lay spell-bound. An inward voice warned him to disassociate himself from the roving, prying fingers, but fascination held him tight. The hand flashed again, quivered like a leaf, and a gaudy post card joined the brooch.

There was a sudden bellow from behind the table. The snatching hand reached out and snatched again—not more treasure but Charles' own hand. He was seized and jerked around and pulled. "Run, run!" said the hand's owner in a voice of pure delight.

Charles ran, mindless, a young shooting star guided through space, tricked to a spasm of motion that carried his feet and ran along his spine and shot giddy rockets all through his head. The bellow became a roar, then suddenly dimmed behind them as the two refugees slipped, dodged, twisted in a mad hide-and-

seek around people's legs, under a barrier, past a flight of rainbow balloons, wild under the lights, dipping into a sudden darkness that closed over them.

The little thief, the runaway, the villain, crouched suddenly,
pulling Charles down beside him, a smothered spurt of laughter
welling up. Charles waited, his heart pounding. He didn't know
where they were, but it was dark and spacious, and the air,
which should certainly have been full of bats' wings and
witches' cats and the proper trappings of wickedness, was quick
and pure and wonderful to breathe.

"Be quiet," said the boy's voice.

The warning was not needed. Charles breathed deeply. His
heart righted itself like a cockleshell of a boat after the first
heady lurch of wind and storm. He was among devils, linked by
his fingers to a thief, and he had never in his life been so rap-
turous.

"Shhh."

No need. Over his head music flew up in a burst of sound,
and he knew now where he was. Crouched and bad and bold
and brave, just under the bandstand, surrounded by who knew
what dangers, quivering like the whiskers of a cat. It never
occurred to him to protest his position. The sin was certainly
no sin of his, he was not a thief, and the hand that stole had
dropped his hand. He could have crawled away, out the other
side of the stand, but the small good child, the dutiful Charles
III, had been sea-changed.

The dark got lighter, as his eyes grew used to it. Things began
to have edges. He could see the glint of his companion's white
teeth, the bright dark eyes alight with excitement. "You get
anything?" the boy said.

Charles shook his head.

"I thought you was going to," said the boy. "I thought you
was going to get a statue." He called it stachoo; it sounded
miraculous. "I never got one, not a statue."

Charles glowed, stroked by such praise as he had never known. This companion in the dark actually believed he shared the magic of fast fingers, of snatch and grab and dart away. The boy clutched suddenly at his arm, said "Look!" and pointed. Charles, staring, trying to pierce the darkness, saw only legs pass the uprights of the bandstand, stop, and turn again. Blue trousers, and black shoes that were well shined.

"Cop," said the boy.

"What?" said Charles, not knowing what "cop," a dangerous, sharp-sounding word, might mean.

"Cop—a policeman. Duck down."

Soft, soft, soft, a seed in an apple, a pit in a peach, a kernel in the night's fruit. The boy pulled him suddenly closer and spoke in his ear. "You go out that way," he said. "I'll go the other way." He gave him a little shake.

Charles gripped the boy's shirt. "Will I see you? Will I see you?"

"Sure. We gotta lie low." He sounded important and dramatic. "We hafta scatter. Here, you can have this." He pushed something into Charles' hand, the stolen picture card. Charles felt the gravelly tinsel under his thumb, knew from memory how the colors glittered. Clutching it, he scuttled, impelled by the urgent hand. Head down, crouching, bandy-legged like a little frog, he scrambled toward the open air, butting against the supports under the bandstand, groping his way past, until all at once he was out in the velvet night once more, the music and the boy behind him.

His pockets were too small to hold the post card, and he thrust it down inside his shirt. He wondered for a moment if he ought not to be running, and, if so, in what direction, and he tried to think what the boy would expect him to do. Hands in pockets, supernaturally casual, he decided to saunter. No one glanced at him, no one knew he was a cargo ship carrying stolen treasure. He began to feel extremely bold. He circled the

bandstand, and he was so sure that the boy would be there waiting for him at the far side that it was a shock to discover nothing
but people listening to the music. He hunted anxiously, searching for faces on his own level, for the now-familiar face. No
one. No one at all.

His boldness began to slip away. There was the parrot again,
numbers of small boys hanging about its brilliant feathers, but
not *the* boy. He wanted to call out, but whose name would he
call? He wanted to run to the nearest stranger and ask for help
in his search, but the crowd that before had made him feel so
wonderfully single was now a gigantic pushing mass hiding
his friend, and Charles could no longer sort it out into individuals.

When he found himself back at the bandstand again, he dived
under it without hesitating. It was familiar now, a black and
downy hole, friendlier than the streets, and he made his way
around under it, molelike, calling softly "You, you" because
he had no other name to call.

He came out at the other end as he had come before, but all
his early excitement was gone. He could not find the boy, he
could not. He felt a great emptiness inside him, and the backs
of his legs began to tremble with weariness. Never in his life had
he hunted for people he needed and not found them immediately there. Suddenly, awfully, he wanted his nurse's hand.

Now, for the first time, he realized the enormity of his
running away from home. The sense of sin, which must have
been lying jealously in wait for him, pounced. The All-Seeing
Eye glared.

He was no longer brave and wild, but only five and very lost.
He no longer believed that he had only to turn the next corner
to find the little thief, who would seize him by the hand and
run him swiftly and safely down all the streets. There was not
going to be any pirates' rendezvous.

The tears behind his eyelids began to slip down his cheeks.

He caught them on his tongue, hot and salty. He scrubbed at them and tried to fight them back, but new ones came along and suddenly he could not endure it any longer, all the aloneness to be borne alone, and he sat down on the sidewalk and put his head down on his knees and let grief and fright have their way.

Someone touched his shoulder, and he lifted his head. The face leaning over him was kind, wrinkled like a nut and heavy-mustached. The man sat down on his haunches in front of Charles and put a hand under Charles' chin.

"You lost?" said the man. "You lost and sad, huh? You can't find your mama?" The voice was a recognizable comfort, putting its arms around him, telling him everything would be all right. Charles snuffled, rubbing his nose with the back of his hand because he had no handkerchief. The man shrugged helplessly and spoke to someone. A woman's voice said sympathetically, "So he's lost. Hey, mister policeman, here's a kid what's lost hisself."

Policeman, cop, the sharp, dangerous word. A hand dropped on Charles' shoulder before he could run from this worst of perils. The visored cap with the bright shield on it came down on a level with his face. He made himself as small as a mouse.

"What's the matter, son? You lost your mother?"

The voice sounded safe enough. "Lie low," the little thief had said when the other cop passed too near, but the thief was gone and the runaway was no longer running away but very lost. The policeman was like policemen in the park where he walked with Nurse.

Charles looked up at him anxiously, and the policeman said, "All right, kid, nobody's going to eat you," and to the crowd, "I'll take him to the station house." He lifted Charles to his shoulder, and the people who had gathered interestedly from nowhere got out of the way, making approving sounds.

"Poor little thing," said the sympathetic woman's voice.

The policeman turned, the small mouse huddled against him, and they moved, the two of them, through the streets where Charles and the other little boy had raced. If the boy saw him now . . . .

Charles turned his head and hid his face against the broad blue shoulder, felt the sharp edge of the silver badge. He didn't want to be seen, but he didn't, now, want to leave the safety of the arms. He had been lost and now he was found, and for the moment he couldn't think beyond the considerable comfort.

"Feeling friendlier?" the cop asked. It was his only question.

As it turned out, there was no need for questions. The police alarm that had gone out for Charles Robertson III had blanketed the city. A small boy, a small wealthy boy of some importance, had disappeared from home. Brown hair, brown eyes, five years old, small for his age, quiet. His nurse, morassed in tears, had gone through his closet; the gray tailored shorts, the neat white shirt, were a part of the police record. Charles Robertson III; case closed.

His mother cried over him; she must have been crying all the way to the station house, racing uptown in the big Cadillac to redeem the little pledge from the legal pawnshop. She cried down the police captain's front, and his father swore valiantly and blew his nose and rushed around spreading thanks and shaking any hands that were willing to be shaken and then rushing back to Charles again.

They bundled him into the car, and he sat quite still for a moment, gazing at the familiar, respectful back of the chauffeur. Then he wriggled loose from his mother's arms and got onto his knees on the seat so that he could stare out the back window. His mother tried to pull him down beside her again, but he wouldn't come, and he stayed so, kneeling, watching, until the last gay light of the fiesta blinked, faded, and disappeared from sight.

He sighed then and turned around and sat properly. He had thought he might catch one glimpse of the small bright face. He would have liked so very much to wave goodbye.

All the rest of the way home he was quiet and docile. Nurse met them at the door of the apartment, a fountain of tears, and the family doctor was with her. Charles submitted to them both with the greatest politeness but the same intense quiet. The doctor, who was not a complicated man, said, "Put him to bed, he's sleepy. It's Mrs. Robertson who needs the sedative. Just put the boy to bed."

Nurse put the boy to bed. He only spoke once, and that was when she found the tinseled post card inside his shirt. She took it from him before he could stop her, and she said "Tcha!" with a sharp, clicking tongue, looking at the lady's face and the bright colors and the glitter. Then she tore it across, and he watched her drop the two pieces into the wastebasket. The basket had ponies on it, bright-green ponies following each other's tails. Charles spoke to himself and for himself exclusively. He said, "That's mine."

Nurse said, "What? What, precious baby? Oh, just to think—" and then she started to cry again, and then she dried her tears. Charles climbed into bed in clean pajamas, and the bed felt good. He lay and watched Nurse while she pulled up the sheet, turned out the light. He heard her moving around the room, sighing heavily, hoping to be comforted, but he lay quite still and withdrawn. He closed his eyes.

He heard his mother and father come into the room, knew they were standing over him, heard his mother say, "Oh, Charles, how awful if—" heard his father say, "There, there." He knew what they wanted. They wanted him to sit up and hold out his arms to be loved and forgiven. He held his breath.

His mother said, "It was so unlike him, so terribly naughty."

"He ought to be punished." The father voice had no special conviction.

"Oh, Charles, he's been punished enough. He was so frightened he couldn't even speak." She sighed like Nurse, but the faintest, the most delicate tremor, not Nurse's heave. "My baby boy. He won't do it again."

"I should think not," said Charles' father comfortably.

He heard them tiptoe out, and the room was quiet in the dark July night. He lay silent until he knew he was safe, and then he got out of bed. He went straight to the wastebasket and took out the two torn pieces of post card, the glittering gift of the boy he had run with, wild, through the dark-bright streets, the boy he would never see again.

He climbed back into bed, small and grave and self-contained.

Nothing was changed, and everything was changed. Clutching the two pieces of pasteboard, he lay on his back, remembering the fiesta. Remembering it fiercely, dangerously, lovingly, with the golden light of liberty in his eyes.

THE CHRISTMAS DOLL

IT WAS three days to Christmas, and the ice skates and the hockey stick for Miss Martha Jones lay on the top shelf of the front closet, pushed well back and cunningly camouflaged by her father's raincoat.

Marty moved the coat only just enough to assure herself that what lay underneath was what she had ordered, or, rather, requested. She was not a bossy child, although at nine her skinned-back pigtails, round freckled face and solid body gave her a look of confidence which intimidated nervous adults.

Satisfied now that it was safe to boast about what she was getting, Marty climbed down and went into the kitchen where she had left her ski jacket and an apple, then shouted into space that she was going sliding.

Her mother, upstairs with a mouthful of pins, shouted back with muffled good temper that this plan was acceptable and would she please get home in time for dinner.

"What's dessert?" yelled Marty, weighing her answer.

"Apple pie."

Marty paused in the act of inserting herself into her jacket and contemplated her apple. There would be one apple fewer in the pie, but that was life. "I'll be back in puh-lenty of time," she shouted reassuringly. "Where's my mittens?"

"In your pocket."

This turned out to be quite true, and one of them in fact was fortuitously wedded to a half-sucked sourball. Marty worried it loose and stuck it in her mouth. "Well, g'bye," said Marty briskly and shot out the door.

She paused to collect her sled and then, performing *Hark the Herr-uld Angels Sing* at the top of her lungs, she bounced euphorically toward Hudson Hill. It was perfect sliding weather, just cold enough, and she could see her breath puffing importantly before her into bright clear air that smelled of snow and Christmas.

The hill, when she arrived, was swarming with that deceptively aimless activity peculiar to anthills, subway crowds and children at play. Marty lifted her sled and clutched it firmly to her middle. She then gave a loud cry, somewhat reminiscent of one of the Valkyries on a good day, and shot off recklessly downhill.

The cold air blew in her face and rushed down her throat, her mouth being open to shout "Hallelujah! Hallelujah!" which was happily appropriate to the holiday season and made very good shouting. For a moment she owned the hill, the town and the whole world, all in one burst of dizzy white speed. No one could fly so fast or so far as Marty Jones, except maybe God's angels. "Hallelujah!" shouted Marty, addressing the angels with hearty reverence. "Hallelu—"

She broke off in mid-glory, her mouth ajar. The unthinkable had happened. A sled and rider rocketed past her at breakneck speed. Marty gave a violent heave and pressed herself flatter, urging her sled to take wings and meet the challenge, but it was too late although it was a willing sled and would die game.

She arrived at the base of the hill a good two yards behind her competitor and came to a stop by dragging both feet, duck-style. The owner of the rival sled rose from his chariot, glistening red and yellow, and stood looking down at her, his hands in his pockets.

He was a new boy she had never seen before—about her own age, chunky, with a button nose and a cowlick of brown hair plastered to his forehead with damp from the flying snow. He said "Ya-ah" hostilely.

"Yah yourself," said Marty. "Bet you can't steer as good as I can."

"I c'n steer rings around you with both hands tied behind my back," he informed her and, to further show his superiority, he spit grandly through a gap in his front teeth.

She eyed him jealously. "You lose a tooth?"

"Got knocked out in a fight."

This was an advantage beyond all argument. Marty herself had never qualified for a fist fight, since males were always checked by some primeval sense of etiquette, probably batted into them by their mothers, and females refused to fight at all. Marty returned to the attack. "What's your name?"

"Rodney," he said and added "Anderson" after a pause.

"Rodney's a fatheaded name," said Marty pleasantly. "Mine's Marty Jones."

"Fathead yourself," said Rodney.

The amenities dealt with, they fell into a brief silence. At this moment, a third sled put in a sudden appearance, and its rider fell off into the snow with a resigned cry. It was Tommy Egan and he always fell off, some inscrutable Providence having shaped him like a butterball without any adhesive surfaces. Like the White Knight, he had acquired a fine ability for talking upside down, whether in a winter snowdrift or a summer blackberry thicket. What he was announcing this time was that Rodney was his cousin.

"Ho," said Marty gratefully, as this explained Rodney. He was visiting. She whacked snow off Tommy's rear with a brisk mitten and gave him to understand that she and Rodney had already met.

"I beat her coming down the hill," said Rodney.

"You did *not*," said Marty, spirited if inaccurate.

Rodney eyed her distantly. "I'm going to get a new sled for Christmas," he said.

"*My* parents," said Marty loftily, "are giving me ice skates and a hockey stick."

"Like fun they are," said Rodney. "Girls can't play hockey."

"Marty can," said Tommy with his beautiful rotund loyalty.

Rodney grunted. It was one of those superior masculine grunts that are calculated to drive an independent female mad. It worked fine on Marty. "I'll show you exactly the kind of skates they're buying me," she said, inflating dangerously like a frog or balloon. "They're in the window at Grover's store and they've got rawhide laces and everything. And there's a hockey stick goes with 'em."

"Huh," said Rodney. "My parents would give me anything in your old store window that I wanted, I guess."

"So would mine," said Marty quickly.

"They would not."

"They would so." Her pigtails were not actually sizzling at the ends, but they gave that effect.

Tommy, who had a pacific nature, said, "You can show him the skates on the way home, Marty. We can go round by Grover's."

"I'll just do that little thing," said Marty and gave herself and sled a flounce that faced them uphill. "Betcha don't dare go down the other side of the hill."

Tommy looked at her anxiously. "Through the trees?"

"Sure, through the trees." She poked a finger at Rodney. "You don't dare."

"I dare anything once."

"Yah, cowardy custard," said Marty. "*I* dare anything twice." She started uphill, her sled following her faithfully. Rodney glared and girded himself for battle.

By the end of an hour, they had arrived at a stalemate. Marty had a wilder way with tree trunks and overhanging branches, but Rodney had a system all his own of streaking straight for peril and then hauling his sled back on its tail like a plunging mustang. Tommy was aghast. Each downhill flight convinced him that it would be their last, and he had carted them off to hospital and broken the sad news to their parents so many times that at last even his fertile imagination tired and he sat quietly on his sled like a small, stout and sympathetic snowman.

It was Rodney who, with calm superiority, said he guessed Marty must be tired by now, being a girl. Marty's chin jutted dangerously. Tommy reminded them they were going to stop by Grover's. Marty grunted, jerked her sled around and led the way, while in her vigorous mind's eye she skated victoriously to some distant goal line, wielding her Christmas hockey stick as Rodney labored to catch up, his ankles sagging.

Grover's store shone out at them through the early December twilight. Even from a distance, they could see the Christmas tree in the big plate-glass window, brave with lights and dripping tinsel, the mysterious red-ribboned packages clustered at its base and that wonderful, star-dust, plum-pudding, carol-chanting look of anticipation that is both wild and holy and not possible to any other month or any other tree.

Marty inhaled the richness. The skates would be lying near the tree, their glittering runners reflected in its fat red balls. She tasted the flavor of saying casually, "That's the kind I'm getting," then looked and gave a yelp of indignation. The skates were gone, and in their place, crowning frustration, there was a doll.

Marty's eyes, impervious to dolls, skimmed over it and lit on a catcher's mitt, newly introduced and indicating that Grover's was not lost to all sense of decency. If there had been less snow around, she might have coveted the mitt but her mind was on skates, and baseball could wait for spring. She muttered at the window and turned to scowl at the doll.

It was different from other dolls, being neither round, blonde nor vacuous. It had brown hair and a serene look, and it was wearing an old-fashioned dress dotted all over with tiny blue and pink roses. Black strapped slippers showed just below the ruffle of the hem.

After a minute, Tommy poked Marty with his elbow. "There's your skates," he said. "Under the tree."

"She's stuck on the doll," said Rodney.

Marty turned around and gave him a look of fury. "I am not! I was looking at the catcher's mitt." The mitt was right behind the doll; it could have been true. It should have been true because Marty despised dolls. She pointed firmly to the skates. "Those are mine," she said.

Rodney admitted grudgingly that they weren't bad.

Marty didn't hear him. She was staring into the window again, and, after a moment, she pulled one of her braids around and began to chew fiercely at the end. Something inside her was stretching out its arms to the doll, and she felt a dreadful melting-down sensation. She said gruffly, "What'd they want to put a silly old doll in the window for?" and knew in the same instant that she had hurt the doll's feelings.

Dolls didn't have feelings. She must be crazy.

Marty gave a sudden blood-curdling whoop, whirled her sled around and announced to the world that the last one back to her house was a black-eared baboon. Tommy said, "Gee whizz, Marty—" with no more hope of a successful protest than a corporal reasoning with a general, but Rodney had already leaped into action. Marty, who could give two jumps to a jack-rabbit, caught him up at the first lamppost and cut in front of him so neatly with her sled that he fell into a snowbank.

The incident reconstructed her morale and cleared her head of fuzzy emotions so that she forgot the doll. Greatly cheered, she went into the house which was blooming with lights and the good hot smell of cinnamon and apple.

Her father accepted her large hug placidly and pulled a pigtail. Her mother, apprehended in the kitchen, observed that she was trailing melted snow all over the house and shooed her upstairs. With a comfortable sense of being extremely welcome, Marty shucked off her snowpants in the middle of her room, started to pull off her sweater and paused on the fourth button.

The doll was back, tugging at her thoughts.

Still unbuttoning vaguely, she went over and sat on the bed. Her room was messy but austere, and there was no place whatever for a brown-haired doll in a rose-sprigged dress.

Well, it could go on top of the bed. It wasn't absolutely necessary to have a life preserver marked "S.S. Algonquin" on her pillow. The life preserver could go under the bed, and the doll could——

"Oh yah!" said Marty furiously to the empty room. "Yah, yah, yah!" What would everyone think if it got out that Marty Jones was hankering for a doll? That little pipsqueak of a Janie

Darrow had told her once to act more ladylike, and Marty had kicked her, hard, right in the rear of her fancy pink dress. Suppose Janie Darrow saw her with a doll?

She didn't want a doll. *She didn't want a doll!* She wanted her skates and her hockey stick.

Comforted by her mounting passions, Marty flopped down on the bed. Tonight they would decorate the tree and, on Christmas Eve, the package with her skates in it would go under the wide branches. With a card, with her name on it. No Santa Claus nonsense. Marty had mistrusted his whiskers from the crisp age of two.

In her mind's eye she began to undo the skates. The red ribbon unwound, the tissue paper pushed aside crackling, the white shiny cardboard of the lid waiting to be lifted . . . She lifted it.

Inside was the doll.

Marty sat up with a terrible snort and smacked her feet down on the floor. Fugitive from dreams, she hurled herself at her closet, snatched a pair of grubby overalls off a hook and proceeded to dress herself wrathfully. They were the toughest looking things she owned and she felt a vast need for toughness.

She didn't want the doll. She never had wanted a doll, and she never would want a doll. That settled that.

She clattered downstairs to dinner, and the overalls proved their worthiness at dessert time when the apple pie burst its bounds. Mr. Jones gazed at his daughter in a kind of awe. "What did you do all day, squirt?"

"Coasted," said Marty in a pie-crusted voice. "Tommy Egan's cousin is visiting him. He *really* stinks."

"Marty." The upward inflection in her mother's voice was a comment on the choice of words.

"Smells," said Marty with refinement. "His name is Rodney, and he thinks he can beat me sliding."

"Ah." Mr. Jones nodded comprehension.

"We came back past Grover's," said Marty, acting under compulsion. "They've put a *doll* in the window."

"Dolls," said Mr. Jones broadmindedly, "are not essentially vicious."

Marty thought of the brown hair to be stroked, the pink and blue roses and the tiny strapped shoes. "Dolls sti——"

"Marty!"

"I don't like dolls."

"Very sad," said her father. "We bought you one for Christmas."

For just a second Marty's heart gave a magnificent leap, then she realized her father was teasing. She subsided into a second piece of pie. It wouldn't have been *the* doll anyway.

"Marty, you'll bust."

"Are we going to trim the tree tonight?"

"As soon as the dishes are done."

There was always something in the world, postponing the ideal. The silverware was lucky to get put away at all, and the moment the drawer closed on it and the dishtowel hit the rack, Marty dragged her parents into the living room.

"First, the star," said Marty ritualistically. "The star on top." She held it up with reverence. It was five-pointed and silver and sprinkled with bits of tinsel. It was a Wise Man's star, fit to be stationary in a sky of great importance on a night of great light, and Marty always felt a little holy when it finally got into place on top of the tall green tree.

The red balls came next, then the blue, the silver, and, last, the gold, trembling and bowing at the tips of the branches. Then the special ornaments—a woollen Santa Claus that Marty didn't like but that had been on Marty's mother's tree when she was a baby and therefore had seniority rights; an angel with gold wings, a halo and an expression of impressive vacuity; a peacock-like bird of great dignity and poor balance, and, finally, Marty's favorite, a rainbow ball caged in glittering silver and powdered with gold.

"'S gorgeous," said Marty approvingly. "Now the big hunks of tinsel—"

"Hanks," said her father.

"Hanks?"

He translated. "Ropes."

"Hanks," said Marty, always pleased to meet up with a new word. By the time tinsel hung in glittering loops from star to carpet, the whole room was lit up with Christmas. "Every year we do it better," she said solemnly.

She sat down on the floor, hugging her knees and contemplating the star-crowned achievement. On Christmas Eve, her parents would put their present for her under the tree, and she would be allowed to poke it. Even though she knew what was inside, there would be that pleasantly tingling feeling of anticipation. You could get that feeling just looking at the space under the tree where the package would be.

She looked at the space hopefully, and nothing happened. This was one of the best moments of Christmas, and nothing happened at all. Marty rested her chin unhappily on her knees. It wasn't just because she knew beforehand what her present would be; she almost always knew that. And she wanted the skates, she wanted them terribly. Only this morning, she had been in a passion of joy.

She got to her feet, walked over to the tree and touched a red ball with one finger. It danced, and she gave it another poke and this time it nearly fell off. She backed away and wandered across the room to the sofa.

The doll rose uninvited in her mind, lovable beyond any reasonable dream. Marty closed her eyes and said "Nebuchadnezzar" under her breath, exorcising it with strong words, but the doll clung.

She opened her eyes. All her life she had been all of a piece, and now there was a stranger inside her, a stranger who wanted a doll.

"Darling," said Marty softly, making the doll welcome, ashamed to be saying it and helpless not to.

Someone tapped at the window. She whirled around and saw the tip of a round nose pressed hard against the pane. Armed in the righteousness of invaded privacy, Marty stalked to the front door and yanked it open.

"Hello," said Tommy sociably. "We're going to the store for ice cream. Can you come along?"

"Nope," said Marty, "it's too late. I wouldn't be allowed."

Rodney waded up off the snow-banked lawn and eyed her loftily. "She's not old enough to go out by herself," he explained to Tommy.

"I'm as old as you are!"

"You're a girl."

"Is that so?" said Marty ragingly. "I can beat you running, I can beat you sliding, I can beat you at anything."

Rodney said, "I'm going skiing tomorrow. I'm going down Hudson Hill on skis."

Without stopping to think about it, Marty said, "So'm I."

Rodney briskly told her not to be silly. "You can't ski."

"I can so."

"You can not. Tommy says you don't know how."

"Tommy doesn't know everything," said Marty darkly, implying that she had led a life of great danger in the Alps.

"It just happens," said Rodney casually, "that I'm going to ski down the *other* side of the hill."

Tommy gave a sudden piteous bleat. It had begun to dawn on him that these two were a bad influence on each other. "Don't pay any attention to him, Marty," he said earnestly. "He's kidding."

"Who's kidding?" said Rodney. "I'm not scared of any old hill."

"I'm not either," Marty said quickly. "Anything you can ski down, I can too."

"Huh. You haven't even got skis."

This was true, but her father had a pair. They were in the basement, near the collection corner where she kept various things such as the large bone which her father generously thought might have belonged to a dinosaur.

"I'll take my father's skis," said Marty grandly.

In technical possession of the field, she swaggered back into the house and started upstairs, looking over her shoulder for just a moment at the tree with its trembling shower of tinselled light and the bright glitter of the Christmas balls, reflecting the room in endless enchanting miniatures.

She took the stairs two at a time and sang her way into her pajamas. A general feeling of good will, based soundly on the routing of Rodney, enveloped her. Her father's skis would undoubtedly be too large, but that hardly mattered . . .

Her father's skis.

About to leap heartily into bed, Marty paused and sat down conservatively on its edge. After a moment, she drew her feet in, pulled the covers over her and, hunching up, stared at the opposite wall.

She must have been crazy to tell Rodney she would take her father's skis. Suppose she busted them? It was perfectly possible, since she'd never been on skis before. It wasn't going to be much use trying to explain to her father that Rodney had dared her.

What on earth had gotten into her? She'd never done a silly thing like that before, trying to throw her weight around by bragging she could do something when she knew she couldn't. Marty Jones' self-confidence had never needed that kind of bolstering.

There must be something wrong with her, some awful kind of thing happening so that she wasn't Marty Jones any longer, but a stranger. The old Marty might have bragged a little, but not this stupid way.

She curled up tight and buried her nose in the pillow.

The whole thing was the doll's fault. She'd only bragged to Rodney to prove to herself that she wasn't the kind of dope who wanted a doll.

She hated the old thing. Nothing had gone right since she had seen it in the store window. If she had it here now, she would smash its head.

The image of the doll rose behind her closed eyelids and looked at her pleadingly. Marty hardened her heart. She would have none of it; she would show it she didn't care. Tomorrow, first thing, she would go look into Grover's window, and the doll wouldn't interest her a particle. Not one tiny little measly bit. Deliberately, coldly, she pushed it out of her mind—the flower-sprigged dress, the white hands and the little feet, the brown hair . . .

After a moment, the destructive catalogue became quite easy, and she felt a sort of sleepy triumph. She would make the doll let go of her and, with the doll, the stranger inside would let go too. Rid of them both, she would be herself again.

Her mind drowsed, slid deliciously into a picture of herself on skis, flashing in and out of trees while Rodney stood by in amazement and chagrin. The whole problem began to fade, get misty at the edges, dissolve.

Marty gave a little growl of hope and comfort, rearranged herself, and slept.

There were muffins for breakfast the next morning, and the Christmas tree looked beautiful. Marty announced that she was going down to the village. "I hafta," she said firmly.

"Well, if you hafta, you hafta," her mother agreed. "Don't stuff yourself so, Marty, the muffins won't get away."

Marty had just pushed a buttery half into her mouth and at the same moment reached for reinforcements. She grinned amiably, impervious to etiquette, and when she left the house she had two emergency muffins in her pockets.

The good crisp air pleased her. She felt strong and confident and superior, last night's optimism and this morning's muffins making a firm foundation inside her. She was Marty Jones with no invisible fidgets.

Grover's came in sight. She put her hands nonchalantly into her pockets, hit a muffin on each side and pulled one out. Chewing like some calm cow, she advanced on the window. Her eyes swept it with cool detachment and came to rest immediately on the doll, skirts spread, hands neatly folded on rose-sprigged lap.

Marty's heart turned over. She clutched her muffin in helpless love. She pressed her nose against the glass of the window and, through the frosty O of her breath, the doll's beauty shone steadfastly.

She, who had thought she would never want to see the doll again, could have howled from pure frustration and longing.

A voice said "Hullo, Marty," and she spun around, choking down adoration and muffin. It was Tommy and Rodney, of course; they were following her around. In silent savagery, she began chewing on her second muffin.

"What you doing?" said Tommy.

Marty said distantly, "I had an errand. At the grocery store." She hated them both. They were always making her tell fibs.

"What were you looking at?"

"Nothing," said Marty.

Tommy, who liked speculation, waved an inclusive hand. "If you could have anything you wanted in the window, what would you take?"

It was generally a good game, but this time it wasn't. The doll looked at Marty in a waiting sort of way.

"The catcher's mitt," said Marty stoically. It was like hitting a kitten across its nose, and it was no good telling herself that the doll didn't have any feelings. She glared at Rodney.

He spit through the gap in his front teeth in a businesslike way. "When you going to take your father's skis?"

"Right now," said Marty, hating him. She turned on her heel.

"See you at the hill," said Rodney.

Instead of going in shouting by the back door, Marty let herself quietly in through the basement. Completely unadjusted to secrecy she was clumsy about it, but she had no choice since, if her mother saw her taking the skis, there would be considerable trouble. Marty did not approve of having trouble with parents. They were right in general, and in this case they would be right in particular. It would be hopeless to try to explain.

The skis were heavy, and her feet dragged, taking her to the hill. Maybe Rodney had changed his mind.

He hadn't. He was already there, waiting for her, with Tommy a faithful shadow. The three of them made a silent procession to the other side of the hill. Marty, with Tommy's help, laid her skis out funereally. "They're too big for you," said Tommy.

Marty nodded. The fact seemed like a reproach, a reminder that the skis were not for her. She turned them carefully toward the brow of the hill before she put them on. Rodney kept eying her impatiently, but it was all right for him. His skis fitted.

Safely mounted, she took her first real look at the hill. Sled-borne, she knew every twist and turn of it, and the trees were no more than a bright challenge. From skis, it looked altogether different. The sudden coldness in her hands was not winter's. She caught her breath and took a quick look at Rodney.

"Scared?" he said.

"In a pig's eye," said Marty, using a frowned-upon expression to stiffen her knees.

"Well, go ahead then."

"Go ahead yourself."

"You don't know how to ski," Rodney pointed out. "I don't want you running into me from behind."

Tommy said, "I don't see why either of you has to go down," but his was a lost cause.

Marty swallowed hard. She shuffled her feet forward and found her knees trembling so they would hardly support her. It was because she was afraid she might damage her father's skis . . .

She knew hopelessly that it wasn't that way at all. She was just plain scared, the way any sissy would be. The way Janie Darrow would be, or any silly girl who played with dolls. It was bad enough to have shown off by taking a stupid dare in the first place, but to be frightened now was unforgivable.

She was face to face with the true Marty Jones at last, and it was not to be endured. At least, no one was ever going to know that she was scared!

With a fierce cry, Marty thrust herself forward over the brow of the hill.

She heard Rodney's shout. Or it might have been Tommy's. And she saw the tree coming at her, distant and black and narrow for an astonishingly long time, and then suddenly so close that the deep-ridged bark was like a map with rivers on it.

If she had been on her sled, she would have known just how to twist and scrape lightly past. But the skis refused to turn, no matter how her feet wrenched at them. The tree refused to move. The map with its rivers became bigger than the sky.

Marty yelled and tried madly to kick off her father's skis so they wouldn't break. The rivers rose up spectacularly. A big bright black star exploded with a crash and split itself into a million comets.

The world spun itself quiet.

"Abrasions, contusions and lacerations," said Dr. Crosby cheerfully.

Even from a great dreamy distance, Marty recognized his voice and then her mother's saying anxiously, "Is she all right, doctor?"

"My dear Mrs. Jones," said Dr. Crosby, "children are indestructible. Where did you come from, baby dear? Out of the rockpile into the here." He started to make packing-up noises. Marty moved a cautious eyelid. "Stop peering at me, Marty," he said sternly. "Your mother's worried about you. Sit up and show her you're all right."

She sat up and she was all right, except for her head which swam. He put a nice large cool hand on it and smiled unexpectedly. "All right, Tarzan, lie back again.—I'll drop by in the evening, Mrs. Jones. Keep her in bed. If necessary, tie her down."

Mrs. Jones smiled. The doctor departed. After a moment, Marty said, "Mum" in a small voice. "What happened to the skis?"

"One of them broke."

Marty smoothed the top of her sheet with infinite care over the blanket. "It wasn't a very good idea my taking them, was it?"

"I've heard better ideas." However, she gave the blanket a pat, and the blanket included Marty. "Go to sleep now. I'll pull the shades."

Marty slid down against the pillow, closed her eyes and slept instantly. She woke to a twilit room, sat up in bed and yelled "Moth-er!"

Her mother put her head around the door and diagnosed acute recovery. "You've got visitors, Marty. Rodney and Tommy. Do you want to see them?"

"Sure, send 'em in," said Marty regally and assumed a consciously heroic pose. When the door opened again, it was Tommy who sidled around the edge, his round face expressing concern. After him came Rodney. Rodney's expression was glum, and he was carrying a box.

Marty eyed it with curiosity. Rodney said, "My aunt says I shouldn't have dared you to go down that hill. She says to tell you I'm sorry."

" 'S all right," said Marty, languid, queenlike.

"I brought you a present," said Rodney, still glum, and shoved the box toward her. The word "Grover's Department Store" showed on its lid.

The catcher's mitt, thought Marty. It was Rodney who maintained that girls couldn't play baseball. Triumph tasted sweet in her mouth. She broke the string and lifted the box cover.

The doll stared up at her.

It was dearer, more lovely even than she had remembered it. It lay in its nest of tissue paper, smiling gently and with its arms reaching out in the serene confidence of being welcome.

Marty's hands followed her heart and reached out too, and then her hands stopped. She couldn't let them go to the doll. Not in front of Rodney.

She pushed the box away from her, not rudely but just enough to show how little she cared. The doll still smiled.

And, all of a sudden, something inside Marty stretched and grew tall. She knew that she loved the doll and that the doll loved her. There were more important things than having people admire you. Who cared what Rodney thought?

She took the doll firmly out of its box and, holding it close to her, she looked at Rodney over its head. Her mouth was a tight line and her chin stuck out. Silently, she dared him to jeer at her.

Rodney said, "My aunt picked it out for you. I told her you'd rather have had the catcher's mitt, but she said no." His face was no more scornful than the doll's. "Would you rather have had the catcher's mitt, Marty?"

Marty shook her head. "I like the doll," she said. "I like the doll a whole lot."

He looked puzzled but relieved, and she decided there was no use trying to explain. She loved the doll and, when she got her skates on Christmas morning, under the star-tipped shiny tree, she would love them too.

Loving a doll was simply a new part of herself that she hadn't met before. Marty felt a warm interest in the discovery. It was like opening a package. Sometimes you knew what was inside, and sometimes you were surprised. It was all rather unexpected, like Christmas itself, but, like Christmas too, it was very rich and secure.

She held the doll tight in her arms and bent her head to impress a kiss on the round, sweet cheek. The kiss, however, was interrupted by a novel sensation.

Marty raised her head. "Hey, you know what!" she said happily. "I think I must've knocked a front tooth loose. I'll be able to spit."

She knew her friends would be very happy for her, her with a loose tooth and a new doll on the same day.

BIRTHDAY GIFT

"Doggone knife just chews the wood," said Jimmy aggrievedly, running a dissatisfied thumb along the blade. The knife had cost him fifty-nine cents originally at the Variety Store and it had seen better days.

Henry, who was sandpapering the shaped edge of a wing with loving delicacy, glanced up and said, "What we going to use for rubber for the motor?"

Jimmy grunted, the professional grunt of the model plane builder. "Simpson's pile," he said. The place back of Simpson's Garage where they were working might not be the most elegant place in town, but it was protected from too many visitors by a swaybacked board fence and it was highly convenient to Simpson's really beautiful rubbish pile.

Henry nodded and returned to his wing.

After a minute Jimmy said regretfully, "Pretty soon I've got to get home. It's getting late."

"Only takes you five minutes."

"That's for getting there. I've got to wash before dinner." He said this in the tones of a man betrayed, and added, without resentment, "You're lucky. Dirt doesn't show on you. That's an advantage you've got."

Henry gave this his serious consideration. "I can't always get dirt that matches," he pointed out. "This is all right here, but you take that light clay on the river bank—it matches you better'n it does me."

"Well, I'm not on the river bank now," Jimmy grumbled, "and I've got to be clean for dinner." He put his wood down, humped his knees up and rested his chin on them, overcome by a mood of dark foreboding. "Maybe I'll even have to take a bath."

Henry, moved by this somber prospect, gave one last loving scrub with the sandpaper and put the wing down on the grass beside him. "Okay. We'll go."

Jimmy gave a satisfied sigh. It was things like this that united him and Henry so securely. Henry had dinner later, and he could have stayed on, sandpapering with the sunset for company, but he resigned the privilege, recognizing that it would drive Jimmy wild with envy. Henry was a good sort of friend.

Jimmy gazed at him for a moment with pleased affection, then stood up, pushing his hands down into his pockets and creating a perilous separation between his shirt and shorts. "Well,

I'll be seeing you tomorrow," he said, and added, in rather pointed reminder, "at my birthday party." Not being one to cheat himself out of possible presents, he was apt to throw a tactful memorandum into any conversation that touched on his birthday.

Henry got to his feet. "You sure it's all right, Jim? Your folks know I'm coming?"

"Said I could ask who I wanted," Jimmy nodded, having extended his hospitality carefully because his mother had limited him to eight at the table. "I guess the cake will be chocolate all right."

Henry sighed a loving "Oh, man," and rubbed contentedly at the short tight hair of his head.

"Well—" said Jimmy and picked up his knife, closed it and slid it into his pocket, marking the end of another afternoon's work.

"Well—" said Henry.

Together, and with great tranquillity, they skirted the rubbish pile, climbed the fence and walked up the road.

Having characteristically underestimated the time, Jimmy found that his rather vague plans about a bath had to be abandoned. With great presence of mind, he scrubbed his face and hands to an impressive state of cleanness and put on a jacket so that anything above the wrist line would be invisible to his mother. He figured that, with any luck at all, his knees would get by.

This was a false hope. His mother came out of the kitchen just as he ambled into the dining room and she said exactly what he had expected her to say. "Oh, Jimmy—your knees!" He could have given it back to her, quite uncritically, with her precise inflection.

He gazed at her plaintively. She had a kind of shining way of looking neat that he admired and would have been happy to duplicate, but nature always opposed him. "They'll be under the table, Mum," he offered.

His father turned around in his chair, studied him and gave a snort of pure amusement. "It's a free country, Ann," he said.

Jimmy grinned back in relief, pulled his own chair out from the table and sat down hastily, unfurling his napkin. He reached contentedly for a piece of bread and began to think about his birthday.

He had definite hopes of getting a set of tools from his father, which he needed badly, and while he was not one to conduct illegal investigations, the fact remained that his father had come home the night before with a package that was a very promising shape. His mother, he feared, was going to give him some new shirts. She liked him to look nice and she knew that he would labor to keep his birthday shirts clean, so in a way it was rather underhanded of her, but in another way it was a compliment. Anyhow, they would look kind of elegant in his bureau drawer. He had already, very thoughtfully, cleared a place for them.

"All set for tomorrow, son?"

Jimmy came out of the bureau drawer. "Yes, sir. Everybody's coming."

"Who's everybody?"

His mother answered for him. "Seven of his friends, dear. I left it to him whom he wanted to have."

He drew a deep breath and launched on specifications. "Bill and Spud and Joe 'n' Jim Egan and Henry and Pete and Mickey." He then added meditatively, "I know what Pete's going to give me for a present. It's a necktie and he said he didn't think I'd like it much, but his mother bought it for him to give me."

His father said mildly, "Don't be so commercial."

His mother was looking at him and there was a little frown

line between her eyebrows. "Henry, Jimmy? Which one is Henry?"

"Henry Wilson. Will you please pass the jam, if it's strawberry?"

It was strawberry. After a moment his father passed it. His mother was looking sort of anxious about something. Jimmy found an unsquashed strawberry and put it in the middle of his piece of bread and then began to drip the runny part of the jam lovingly around the edges.

"Jimmy."

He looked at her. "Yes'm?" He really knew that you weren't supposed to spread jam that way and he put his butter knife down obediently.

It hadn't been the jam that his mother was thinking about. She said, "Jimmy, isn't Henry Wilson the little black boy?"

He gave this question his sober consideration. Henry was half a head taller than he was, but he knew that when grown-ups said "little" all they meant was that you were still in grade school. He ignored that part of her question and answered the rest of it. "He isn't black, Mum. Just sort of dark brown."

Across the table, their eyes meeting on a level above his head, his mother and father looked at each other. He knew the look very well. His last report card had inspired it and the time he had gone off and played baseball when he'd known very well his aunt was coming, and also the very difficult time when he'd got hold of a thoroughly dull book that he wasn't supposed to read.

But this time there didn't seem to be any reason why they should be looking at each other like that. "Mum?" he said after a minute.

She kept on looking across the table at his father and she might just as well have said out loud, "You handle this, Mark." Jimmy knew that look so well, he could almost hear the tone of her voice. His father cleared his throat and moved heavily in his chair. Jimmy put his hands on his lap under the table and waited, staring hard at his bread and jam.

His father said, "I'll tell you, son— It's a little difficult—" It was apparently very difficult. He picked up his spoon and began to trace a slow pattern on the tablecloth. "You play with Henry quite a bit, Jim?"

His mother interrupted. "The Wilsons only moved into town about six weeks ago, Mark. I don't believe—"

She didn't know about the model airplane that he and Henry were building, but it wasn't exactly a secret anyhow, so he told her. "We work back of Simpson's Garage," he said, "on account of it's very handy."

They didn't seem much interested in his project.

His father said, "I—see. I didn't know—" His chair creaked a little. "Jim, there are a lot of things that are hard for you to understand now, that you'll know more about when you're older. Social differences. I mean, it's one thing, the acquaintances you have at school—and then at home it's something else again." He smiled at Jimmy apologetically. "I suppose it's hard for you to understand, but, well—I think it would be a good thing if you asked someone else to your party instead of Henry, Jim."

Jimmy shook his head. "I've already asked him."

"Yes, I know. I realize that." He looked across the table helplessly.

Jimmy's mother said, "It would only embarrass the boy, Mark. He's probably never been invited to a—a white home before. He'd only feel awkward."

On surer ground, Jimmy interrupted cheerfully. "No, he won't, Mum. His house is pretty much like ours, so that's all right."

His mother's voice was unexpectedly sharp. "It's not all right, Jimmy. You'll just have to believe your father and me, and do what we tell you to. Henry will understand."

Incredulously Jimmy turned to his father.

His father nodded unhappily. "Your mother's right, Jim."

"You mean, I can't have Henry?"

For a second it seemed as though they were going to start explaining things again, and then they didn't after all. His father said, flatly and definitely, "No, son, I'm sorry."

He knew that tone of voice and there was no appeal from its decisions. It was law. Jimmy looked down at the strawberry sitting in the middle of his bread and butter. "Yes, sir," he said.

Right after dinner he went over to the Wilsons to tell Henry that he couldn't come to the party. He walked over very slowly, with a hollow feeling inside himself because he didn't know what he was going to say. His feet dragged up the front steps to the porch, and his finger had no wish to press the perfectly familiar doorbell.

He heard the bell ring inside the house and then voices and then steps. Mr. Wilson opened the door, remonstrating gently with the catch, which had a tendency to stick. "Evening, Jimmy. Come on inside."

He was a big grave black man and Jimmy liked him a great deal, but just at the moment he felt like turning around and running home. He gulped, nodded and followed Mr. Wilson into the living room.

It was roomy and cheerful, with good places to settle down in. Mrs. Wilson was sewing in a circle of light and Henry was humped up in the middle of the floor on his knees and elbows with his chin on his fists, reading the funny paper. He glanced up, said, "Hi" companionably and moved over to make room. Mrs. Wilson, who was very small and brisk and light-colored, smiled at Jimmy and bit off a piece of thread.

Jimmy just stood, gazing longingly at the funny page and feeling miserable. Then he drew a deep breath and said what he had to say, all in a rush. "Dad asked me to come over," he said. "He figured Henry'd rather not come to the party."

Mr. and Mrs. Wilson looked at each other. It was peculiar the way parents had of looking at each other. Jimmy waited helplessly for someone to say something, then he glanced down at Henry. Henry was sitting on the floor with his feet out in front of him and he was very carefully tearing bits of paper off the edge of the funny page and making a neat little stack on the rug beside him.

Jimmy stared at the top of Henry's head and then turned despairingly to Mr. Wilson.

Mr. Wilson said quickly, "It's all right, Jimmy, it's quite all right. We understand."

Jimmy gazed back at him and sucked in his lower lip. He wanted to say something, but he didn't know what to say.

There was a moment of silence stretched tight and then Mr. Wilson spoke to his wife. His voice was very gentle. "There any cookies in the house, Jen?"

"There's a few ginger ones in the jar. Henry—"

Jimmy said abruptly, "I've just had my dinner," and then he was sorry he'd said it because, although he didn't feel like eating, it wasn't very polite to refuse. But Mrs. Wilson seemed to understand that a person might not want cookies right after dinner and she just nodded and picked up her sewing again.

Henry got to his feet suddenly. "Mom, did you find that piece of ribbon?"

She shook her head. "I was going to look for it tonight. I don't think Jimmy will mind its just being string, dear."

Henry walked over to the mantelpiece. There was a big bronze clock on the narrow mantel ledge and next to the clock was a small package, wrapped in tissue paper and tied with green string. He took it down in both hands and brought it over to Jimmy. "This is yours, Jim," he said. "I meant for it to have ribbon on it, but if you—if I'm not—I'd better give it to you now."

He handed it to Jimmy and Jimmy took it mechanically.

He had obeyed the law. He had said what he came to say.

Now all he had to do was go. "Well," he said, "I'll be seeing you."

Henry nodded. "Sure. I'll be seeing you."

"Well— Good night, everybody."

"Good night, Jim."

He took himself to the door and out on the porch and down the steps. His fingers were so tight around the little package Henry had given him that the knot on the string bit into the palm of his hand. Carefully he put his gift into the pocket of his coat and then he walked home fast.

His father was in the living room, reading the evening paper, and he looked up when Jimmy came in. His mother came out of the kitchen, wiping her hands on a dish towel, and she stood in the doorway looking at both of them.

Jimmy said, "I told Henry."

His father folded the two sections of the paper together neatly and leaned over to put them on the floor beside his chair. "What did he say?"

"Nothing much." There was a short stiff silence and then he turned to go out of the room.

"Jim."

"Yes, sir?"

"Where you going?"

"To do my homework," Jimmy said.

"Oh. That's all right." His father leaned over and picked up the newspaper he had just folded so carefully.

Jimmy went on upstairs. Behind him he heard their voices and then he heard his mother go back to the kitchen. He went into his own room and shut the door and stood looking around him. Then he took his math book off the top of his desk, along with some paper and a pencil, and sat down, opening the book to the problems that had been assigned.

The first math problem seemed to be even stupider than math

problems usually were, but it wasn't particularly hard. He wondered if Henry was going to have trouble with it. It was the kind that usually set Henry to glaring because it was full of fractions that would never have come up at all if the man in the problem had just been willing to work an extra quarter of an hour.

He sat for a moment looking at the math book and then suddenly he put his arms across it and laid his head down on top of them.

When the door opened and his mother came in, he straightened up quickly. She stood in the doorway, looking at him, and then she said, "Don't stay up too late, will you, dear?"

"No, Mum."

"Good night, Jimmy."

"Good night."

She turned to go, and then, with her hand on the doorknob, she hesitated. "Is everything all right, Jimmy?"

He said yes and she went out.

He sat for a while, heavy with depression and poking his pencil into the desk blotter. Then he pushed his chair back suddenly and stood up.

He couldn't do anything about what had happened. He had better forget it.

Empty and restless, he began to undress. He took off his coat and his hand encountered a bulge that was Henry's present in his pocket. He took it out and looked at it, and then he put it very formally in the middle of his bureau, flanked on one side by his brush and comb and on the other by a cigar box which had been given to him by his Uncle George and in which he kept tacks, bits of string and anything else he might need suddenly.

After that, he dug his pajamas out of his closet where they were unaccountably resting on the floor, and finished undressing. Washing was a lengthy process. First the soap slid out of his hands while he was staring at the bubbles on it and nested behind the radiator. And then he lost the cap of his toothpaste tube down the drain pipe. It seemed very important to get it back and he spent a long time correcting this domestic complication with infinite patience and a long piece of wire from the cigar box.

Eventually he ran out of legitimate delays, opened the window reluctantly, turned out the light and crawled into bed.

He lay on his back in the dark for a little while and then he heaved a woolly sigh and turned over on his side, curling his knees up toward his chin. He had hoped to fall asleep, promptly and comfortably, the way he always did, but the margins of sleep stayed just out of reach. After a minute he rolled over in the other direction and the bedsprings protested sharply.

He shut his eyes tight and in the dark, behind his closed lids, the picture of the little package on his bureau formed, neat and sharp. He began to wonder what was in it. It couldn't be very much, because Henry's allowance was as small as his own, but it would probably be something he wanted. It might, for instance, be a box of drawing pencils or some good chalk or any one of a number of things Henry knew he needed.

He sat up in bed, switched on the light and looked at the bureau.

It was really a very small package and its smallness decided him. He pushed back the covers, swung his legs over the side of the bed and padded across to the bureau, then climbed back into bed again, sitting up and clutching his present.

He poked at it inquiringly before he began to untie the green string, but because it was a box there was nothing to be deduced from its shape. The string he rolled carefully around his finger and put on one side. Then, as tenderly, he unwrapped and folded the tissue paper.

The box was the color of oatmeal and had "Jackson's Hardware" stamped on it in blue letters. Jimmy drew a deep anticipating breath and lifted the lid. Inside, lying on a piece of cardboard, was a penknife.

He took it out and snapped it open. The blade was neat, wicked and sharp. It would carve initials deeply on trees, it would strip the smooth bitter bark from willow branches, it would shape the ailerons of the model plane. It was a beautiful knife and he felt the rich excitement of ownership.

Jackson's was the best hardware store in town and their things cost money. Henry must have been planning the present for a long time.

Jimmy lay back on the bed and, gazing at his new knife, began to think back. There was the time Henry had said firmly that an ice cream cone would spoil his dinner. There was the way he had been using saved-up paper to write assignments on, instead of a lavish notebook from the school store. There was the time Henry had talked him into walking out to the ball park instead of taking the trolley.

It took a lot of nickels and dimes to buy a knife.

Jimmy rubbed his thumb lovingly along the smooth narrow handle. First thing in the morning, he would go over and thank Henry—

It was like having a familiar welcoming door slammed in his face.

He went suddenly rigid and dug his heels into the bed, his shoulder blades pressing against the pillow until he could feel the head board pushing at his back.

He couldn't just go to the Wilsons now and say "thank you" to Henry. He didn't even know if they wanted him there any more, after what had happened.

For a long moment he stayed still, gazing blindly across the room. Then he shivered suddenly, reached out his hand and snapped off the light, sliding down under the covers for warmth and pulling them up to his chin. In the darkness his alarm clock began to tick very loudly.

Maybe it wasn't ever going to be again the way it had been.

He rolled over in bed, the bedclothes boiling around him, and pressed his face into the squashy comfort of his pillow. Inside of him was an unhappiness that even spoiled the new knife. He lay there in bed, feeling that unhappiness hurt, and the room filled up and choked with the sound of the ticking clock.

He pulled his pillow down against him, with his arms wound tight around it and his hand clutching his knife, and tiredly and desperately he began to cry.

After a while he stopped crying, because he had to think.

The birthday party was at noon.

At eleven-fifteen Jimmy went into the kitchen, planted the kitchen stool in front of the high cupboard over the sink, climbed onto it and reached down the round red and white cakebox. There was nothing secret at all about his movements. If his mother had come into the kitchen then, he would have explained what he was doing. But she didn't come in and he didn't have to explain.

He lifted the tin cover carefully off the box and looked inside. The birthday cake was chocolate with white frosting, and across the frosting there were daffodil-yellow letters that said, "Happy Birthday to Jimmy."

He got down off the stool, hugging the box to his chest, and put it on the table, then took a bread knife out of the table drawer and cut two thick pieces very neatly with the edges tidy. Then he wrapped them up in waxed paper and went and got his school lunchbox from its place on top of the refrigerator. He put the cake inside and got two apples and put them with the cake. After that, he put the stool back in its corner, leaving the cakebox out on the table.

It took a little hunting to find where his mother had put the extras for the party, but he finally located them all together in a box on the cupboard shelf, hidden behind the electric toaster. Out of the box he took two fat yellow candles, two gaily decorated red paper crackers, and two paper napkins that had "Birthday Greetings" across the corners. There was a box of candy mints with them, and he hesitated in his choice, then finally selected six, two of each color, and put them into his lunchbox along with the rest of the things. Last, he took three kitchen matches out of the metal container over the stove and dropped them into his pocket.

He looked around the kitchen, decided he had everything and let himself out the back door, the lunchbox in his hand. In his pocket, along with the matches, was the knife that Henry had given him.

He walked through the back yard, turned right and walked on down the road with the box in his hand, as he might do any school morning. Only this was Saturday and he wasn't going to school. He was going to their place back of Simpson's Garage.

Henry was there. He was sitting up against the fence, studying a strip of blackened rubber tubing that he had taken out of the rubbish pile, and when he heard Jimmy's steps he looked up quickly and his face went surprised.

"Hello," said Jimmy.

He set his lunchbox down on the ground and squatted beside it. First, he took out the paper napkins and spread them carefully on a clean piece of earth, and then he put an apple in the middle of each one to hold it down against the small breeze that was weaving around.

Next he took out the pieces of cake, unwrapped them and set them up on their own waxed paper, planting a candle on top of each. Beside them, he laid a red paper cracker and three candy mints.

Last of all, he pulled one of his matches out of his pocket and lit the two fat little candles. They flickered for a moment, with his hand cupped shelteringly around them, and then they flared up, pale in the sunshine but pleasingly bright. He looked at his party. It had a transplanted look, but it was extremely festive.

"There," said Jimmy.

He realized suddenly that Henry was being awfully quiet and for the first time he turned around to look at him.

Henry was still sitting up against the fence, with his feet sticking out in front of him. He was staring hard at the party laid out so carefully on the ground and for one awful moment Jimmy thought that his guest was going to cry.

He grabbed up one of the red paper crackers and shoved it at him. "Here," he said. "We have to pull these first."

Henry gave a loud sort of sniff, but it was a reassuring sniff. It was expectant, like hitching up your trousers before you got down to work.

"Pull," said Jimmy, relieved, holding out the cracker.

Solemnly, one on each end, they pulled and were rewarded by a tiny explosion of sound and a green tissue-paper cap. Then they pulled the other one and the cap was orange. Jimmy put his on his head, and after a moment Henry put his on too, and the party became a real party.

Jimmy waved a hostly hand at the food and leaned over to blow out the candle on his own piece of cake.

Henry forestalled him. "You want to wish on your candle," he said. "It's your birthday cake and you can wish on it."

This was true and he had almost forgotten about the important ritual. The chance of getting your wish when there was only one candle to blow out was practically perfect. He closed his eyes tight and said rapidly inside himself, "I wish for everything to be just the way it was before." Then he puffed and the tiny flame expired instantly.

He opened his eyes and Henry was grinning at him. Jimmy grinned back widely, took the candle out of his cake, licked the frosting off the end and laid it next to his apple.

Silence fell across them as they alternated, lingeringly, between large bites of juicy apple and thickly frosted cake. After
a while, his mouth pleasingly full, Jimmy said, "It's a swell
knife."

Henry nodded.

"You can use it any time you want to."

"Thanks."

It ended the conversation and mutual absorption in crumbs
ended the cake. Stuffed at last, Jimmy pointed to the candy
mints. "If you suck 'em," he said practically, "they last longer."

They sucked them and they lasted admirably. Jimmy sighed
and eased his belt. "You find some good rubber?" he inquired.

Henry nodded, reached down in the thin grass beside him and
handed over the piece of tubing. It was a long strip with a good
stretch to it. Jimmy gave a nod and passed it back. "You want
to use my old knife to cut it up?" he said. "It isn't very sharp,
but you can keep it if you'd like to have it."

Henry accepted the gift, looking happy. It was a nice thing,
thought Jimmy, that he had happened to bring it along. He took
his own birthday knife out of his pocket and opened it, looking
around for a good piece of wood to test it on. Wordlessly,
Henry handed over a piece they had been saving, because it was
flat and smooth-grained with a delicate flying look.

He began to whittle. Sun dipped through the leaves and a
sparrow came nearer to check on the waxed paper that was
lying on the ground. There were no crumbs, and it hopped
away, disappointed. The comfortable mutual silence of shared
work settled down on them.

Jimmy began to hum gently under his breath, his piece of
wood absorbing all his attention.

A shadow fell suddenly across it and he looked up. His father
was standing over him. There was a moment's silence and then
his father said sharply, "Come on, Jim. Your guests are waiting
for you."

Jimmy got very slowly to his feet. Henry stayed still where he was, in the grass.

Jimmy's father looked at Henry and then down at the ground. There wasn't very much there to see. There was the lunchbox, and the waxed paper and the napkins with "Birthday Greetings" in the corners. There was his split red paper cracker and Henry's. And the apple cores.

Jimmy said uncertainly, "We had my birthday party."

"I see you did." His father was staring at what was left of their party as if he were memorizing it, as if everything that was lying on the ground was very important. Then he said suddenly, "I see you did, Jimmy. But we'd better go home now. Your guests—your other guests are waiting for you."

Jimmy nodded, picked up the lunchbox and began to put the remains of the party into it. Even though it was a rubbish pile they were next to, it was Simpson's rubbish pile and Mr. Simpson wouldn't necessarily want birthday napkins on it.

His father and Henry watched him while he cleaned up carefully. Last of all, he picked up the piece of wood he had been working on, gazed at it for a moment lovingly and then handed it to his friend. "You work on this if you want to," he said. "We'll finish up the wings tomorrow."

Jimmy's father looked down at Henry. After a moment he said, "Looks like you're going to have a nice airplane there," and then he stretched out his hand to his son.

Jimmy put his hand in his father's and they went home together.

IRENE said, "You're not being fair to the child, George. You're only thinking of yourself."

George Ashe looked up to meet his sister's hard kindly stare and shook his head. "I don't think I'm that single-minded," he said. "I don't mean to be."

"Of course you don't mean to be," she told him. "Nobody ever *means* to be anything. But a man your age can't be expected to understand anything at all about a fourteen-year-old girl. It's a woman's job."

He didn't say anything. Marjorie's mother had died when Marjorie was eight, leaving him their small intrepid child as a reason for living. He had needed a reason very badly. In a moment Irene would say that it had been six years ago. After six years you were entitled to scars, but not to pain. He waited and she said it. "It's been six years, George."

He said shortly, "I know that."

Irene went on. "It's chiefly Marjorie I'm thinking of. The child has no real social life at all."

"Depends on what you call a social life," George said. "Marjorie has plenty of friends."

"You know very well what I mean by a social life." She shifted in her chair and replanted her feet. She was not so much stout as of a geometric persuasion, with solid cubed corners. "When other girls are going to proms, Marjorie's home with her nose in a book. She reads too much. She's a lot worse than you ever were."

"I survived it. Marjorie likes books."

"That's not the point. Really, George, you're much too detached about things. I suppose it's being a professor but when Eleanor was alive you were a lot more human."

His mind warned her silently, talk about anyone else.

Luckily she did. "You say Marjorie has plenty of friends and I don't doubt it at all. She's a nice child. But that's not what I'm talking about, George. I'm talking about the kind of thing any normal girl wants—you know, going to dances and having boys cut in all the time." She gave him a sharp look. "Marjorie doesn't even have a dance frock, does she?"

He shook his head. "She doesn't care for dances."

"You mean she never gets asked," his sister said. "She's shy, George, she always has been. That's why she needs help right now."

George frowned. This picture of his daughter gave him a sudden inward wrench for which he was not prepared and against which he had no defenses. It was true that Marjorie was a shy, solemn child but she had always been shy and solemn, even when her mother was alive, although she had been subject to abrupt personal fits of delight when she would stalk the house from basement to attic, filling it with her hoarse triumphant chants. He had assumed that now, at fourteen, she was as contented and well adjusted as she seemed to be. He preferred not to believe that her admirable and selective young mind was really bemused by a picture of herself in a frilly dress, stamping the stag line.

He sighed. Perhaps he was too much the detached professor, impatient of all these meaningless social patterns. Perhaps, to Marjorie, they were not meaningless at all but very wonderful.

Irene went on, her voice suddenly more gentle. "If Eleanor were alive, George, I wouldn't say anything. Eleanor could give the child what she needs. It's hard for a man to see it."

She had caught him on his most vulnerable point and it was out of a sense of his own inadequacy that he said, "What do you suggest, Irene?"

She told him promptly. "Have a talk with Anita Marshall. That pretty little daughter of hers is a tremendous hit. The boys are crazy about Lee."

George stirred uneasily. He liked Anita very much and her husband was a good friend of his, but the idea of Lee as a butterfly example for his daughter irritated him. He hedged. "I don't think I ought to impose on Anita—"

"Nonsense. She'd be delighted. After all, Lee's about the same age as Marjorie and that makes everything so much simpler. She must have at least one extra boy on her string that she wouldn't mind lending."

It sounded like a friendly exchange of polo ponies and he almost choked on it.

"I could speak to Anita, I suppose," he said reluctantly.

Irene rose. "I already have. She'll be expecting to hear from you." She looked at him with approval. "I'm glad to see you getting some sense, George."

It seemed unanswerable.

After she had gone, he went out into the kitchen. Mrs. Dolan, his small sparrowlike housekeeper, was peeling apples at the sink, the waxy green spirals falling back from her knife. She glanced at him and went on with her work.

"Marjorie not home yet?" he asked.

"Any time now, Mr. Ashe."

"Apple cobbler?"

She nodded. He watched her hands moving deftly and wished he could ask her what she thought about Marjorie but of course he couldn't. At that moment the back door opened and Marjorie came in.

He looked at her with what he told himself was implacable objectivity, as if she were anybody's child. It was the first time that he had realized she wasn't pretty. She had a square pale face, given a Celtic look by the heavy black eyebrows drawn straight over gray eyes. Her dark hair was pulled back by a ribbon and wind-tangled so that the uncompromising bangs looked like a Shetland pony's. She had a rather stocky figure and her hands were exceedingly capable. He could not, for the life of him, imagine those hands patting a masculine coat sleeve.

Her sweater and skirt outfit seemed all right. He said, "Hello, darling."

Economical of words, she smiled at him and put her pile of books on the table. He picked up the top one and glanced at the title. *Madame Bovary*. Flaubert seemed an odd choice at fourteen. "Is this required reading?"

Marjorie shook her head.

"Isn't it rather heavy going for you?"

"No." The Shetland shake of the head again. "She was a stupid woman, wasn't she? It's awful the way he knows everything about her."

He agreed, rather pleased. A lot of adults encountered Emma Bovary's pitiful vacancy without the faintest recognition of the awful brilliance (*awful* was exactly the word) that had created her.

Mrs. Dolan, speaking to the apples, said, "You read too much."

"I suppose." Marjorie accepted this as an apparently inescapable fact and picked up her books. George followed her out of the kitchen and she asked him over her shoulder about the plans for his lecture course.

"I finished the outline this morning."

"Daddy! That's the hardest part."

He would have liked nothing better than to tell her all about it but there was his promise to Irene. He sat down on the sofa and pulled Marjorie down beside him. "I want to talk to you, honey," he said. "Your aunt was here a little while ago." He waited a moment, got no assistance and went on. "She's worried about you, Margie."

"Me?" She seemed surprised.

"Yes. She doesn't feel you're getting any social life."

She traced the pattern of a rose on the carpet with a scuffed toe. "You mean dances—and things?" she said carefully.

He nodded. "Dances and things."

There was quite a long silence and she did the rose counter-clockwise. She was, perhaps, too used to being honest with him so that he was very afraid of forcing her. When she finally got the words shaped up in her mind, they came out sounding as if they had been pushed. She said, "I don't get asked, Daddy."

He had not wanted this admission at all, since it confirmed what Irene told him. He had wanted to be assured that dances and things didn't interest his daughter, that she was independent. Now he had to admit with a pang of real discomfort that Irene was entirely right, that Marjorie was missing something she really wanted. He waited unhappily for her to go on.

She made a funny little movement with her shoulders. "I never seem to know what to talk about, for one thing."

"Just what interests you, honey."

"Oh, no." She looked at him then. "I know that much about it, Daddy. You're supposed to talk about what interests *them* but that's part of the trouble. I don't know what does. And if they do want to talk about what I want to talk about, that means they're what the other girls call drips and it's really better not to go to a dance at all than to go with a drip."

This was a long speech for Marjorie and it opened up vistas that confounded him. He remembered Irene's dictum that this was a woman's job and, with a real effort, he committed himself. "Marjorie, your aunt suggested I have a talk with Mrs. Marshall."

"About me?"

He nodded and then, because this seemed a little crude, he added a stumbling statement about Aunt Irene's thinking Mrs. Marshall could help with, well, clothes and things.

There was no need for his earnest tact. Marjorie viewed the prospect with unexpected eagerness. "Do you really think she would, Daddy? She's awfully nice." She stared past him at the wall, her lips parted. "There's a big school dance next week. Maybe—"

He wanted her to be happy. He said, "Do you want me to—to talk with Mrs. Marshall, dear?"

For a moment he thought she was going to say no, that she was contented with things the way they were. Then she turned suddenly and buried her nose against the lapel of his coat, a small child trick of hers from years ago. "Would you, Daddy?" she said, muffled. "Dresses and things?"

And things.

He said yes, he would.

He wanted nothing less the next day than to call Anita, but he had no morning lecture and consequently no excuse for putting off the inevitable. Prepared for his call, she had already made her plans and said she would drop in on him that afternoon. "That way I can see Marjorie at the same time," she said, "and we can fix everything up."

He was a little alarmed because she sounded so executive but she was being extremely kind and he made the suitable sounds of gratitude. When Anita came, everything went very smoothly. She talked to him before Marjorie came home and she stamped on the anxious retina of his mind an extremely clear picture of herself as a helpful and wise woman. She told him how necessary a real social life was to a young girl and she made it very plain how satisfyingly well her own daughter had done in this respect. "Of course, it's no credit to me," said Anita disarmingly.

"Lee has a better example than Marjorie, I'm afraid."

She smiled at him forgivingly. "You *are* rather a hermit, George, but after all you can't be expected to know what the child needs. She ought to be taking it for granted that she'll go to dances."

"She doesn't seem to get invited," he said with difficulty,

feeling disloyal. "And I don't think she'd ever get around to just asking someone to take her. I suppose that wouldn't be protocol anyhow."

"Oh dear no!" She was amused by his innocence. "It's really just a matter of getting started. Men are such sheep about things like that and boys are even worse. If one asks a girl, the others will ask her."

"Well?" said George, not knowing how to set this desirable chain reaction going but anxious to be helpful.

Anita clasped her long-fingered hands together lightly. "I've arranged everything," she said reassuringly. "Lee has a cousin who'll be in town just in time for the dance. He's a charming boy and there's no reason on earth why Marjorie shouldn't have him. Lee will tell him she's fixed up a blind date and there you are." She smiled. "Mind you, George, it's very good of Lee. She had a picture of herself with two escorts, but we talked it over and I've promised her a new dress instead." The barter-and-trade quality of this transaction must have eluded her, because she went on serenely. "Marjorie will need a new dress too, of course. That's all right, isn't it?"

He said hastily that, of course, it was all right. And when Marjorie came in at last, everything was settled and all Anita had to do was tell her the plans.

He had thought his nice-mannered daughter would be suitably grateful but he had not expected her to glow. He was glad for her and he was also distressed. The occasion seemed too slight.

But the day Marjorie came home with her new dress, he knew that he was wrong and that a piece of happiness is a piece of happiness, whether for large cosmic reasons or small social ones. She came flying into the living room, clutching a shiny white box and chanting, "We bought it! We bought my dress." Her neat square hands wrestled with the string and she finally had to break it before she could lift the dress reverently out of its tissue-paper nest. "Lee's coming over tonight to see it. Daddy, isn't it lovely?"

It was a charming shade of blue and in obvious good taste. "It's beautiful," he said.

She sighed deeply. "I hope Lee likes it."

He was annoyed. If she liked it herself, what did Lee's opinion matter? But then he remembered that Lee's social success was assured and her judgment counted.

Fortunately, Lee did approve. She came over after dinner, melting with delicious charm for the benefit of Marjorie's quaint old daddy and making him feel every century of his forty-five years. "It's just sweet," she told Marjorie, stroking the delicate folds of blue, "and it's definitely your type. Can you manage the long skirt, honey?"

Marjorie said, too humbly, that she hoped she could. He looked at them, standing together, Lee graceful and cuddly and pretty as a kitten, Marjorie with her hands hanging at her sides, simply because her skirt had no pockets, and her face flushed with rather childish enthusiasm. He knew if he were a boy which one he would want to take to the dance, and he damned the whole race of males.

"Bob's a senior in high school, you know, Margie," Lee went on. "He's really sweet."

Marjorie said, "He sounds nice," and George saw she was stiff with foreknowledge of uncertainty and clumsiness and the agony of going out with a senior. But Bob was hers, for that night he was hers, and who knew what wonders might follow the first real dance, the first genuine escort?

He said heartily, "You'll have a fine time."

"I hope he'll like me," said Marjorie.

She spent so much of the next week taking her new dress out of its cover that George became concerned for its health, but she only laid it most tenderly on her bed or held it up to yearn over her mirrored reflection. She had new shoes too, with heels much higher than they should be, but twice he heard her talking to them on such a note of love that he never mentioned his conviction that they were unsuitable for a little girl.

Unused to prayer, he merely relayed a request to God to make it a happy evening for his daughter.

But the tragedy came anyway and it was a real tragedy, small only because it had no dignity. It was ignoble from the beginning, starting as a severe cold in the head of Lee's escort, Johnny Dayton. The Dayton doctor ordered the Dayton pride and joy to bed and Mrs. Dayton phoned Anita Marshall. Anita phoned George immediately.

She was terribly distressed, telling him about Johnny, much more distressed than the occasion seemed to warrant. There seemed to be no doubt of the young man's survival. "Lee's so upset," Anita said.

George said he was sorry and added, "Marjorie will be sorry too, but I'm sure she'll get along all right. Maybe it's better for her to be on her own."

There was a short silence. Then Anita's voice came over the wire again, and it had a curious, placating sound. "George, dear," she began, "I'm afraid—"

He waited, faintly uneasy.

He could almost hear her draw the long necessary breath. "I don't think we can ask Lee to be the one to stay home," she said.

He looked at the telephone in his hand. It was an excellent instrument, suitable for perfect communication. He had not heard wrongly. "But, Anita—"

"I know. It's a dreadful shame." He could imagine her smiling, expecting him to understand. "Your dear child's been looking forward to it so, the new dress and everything. But Lee's on the dance committee and of course Bob's counted on having her there and—George, there'll be plenty of other times for Marjorie. I'll see that there are. It's just that—"

He said that he understood. He reassured her automatically

because she was talking so fast, almost distractedly. It was embarrassing for her, he understood that too. When he finally hung up she was still saying that she was so distressed, so really distressed . . .

Ahead of him was the task of telling Marjorie. All that morning his papers lay on his desk untouched.

In the end he didn't even try to explain. He just told her. Johnny Dayton was sick, Lee was going with Bob, there would be other dances. He looked at her anxiously, hoping that she wouldn't cry.

She didn't. She just stood quietly, accepting his words. After a while she said, "Well, I guess it's just one of those things. It's too bad about Johnny."

He looked at her helplessly, thinking that tears would almost have been a relief. After a moment, he thought he had better leave her alone.

It was just as he turned to go that he had his idea. It was the thought of the blue dress and the foolish little shoes that gave it to him. All she needed, surely, was an escort to take her to the dance. Once there, she could rely on Lee and the stag line and all the youngsters she must know.

Marjorie need an escort and Marjorie's father had a perfectly good dinner jacket. He would take her himself. He turned back. "Darling, I've got an idea. How would it be if *I* took you to the dance?"

She looked startled. "Oh, Daddy, I don't think—I mean, nobody ever—" She stopped.

He tried not to show his disappointment. It had seemed such a good idea. A little stiffly, he said, "Well, I just thought—"

She flung herself suddenly into his arms and hugged him tight. "It would be wonderful," she said. "Would you really take me?"

He kissed the top of her head, feeling delightfully expansive. It was all going to work out fine in spite of everything. . . .

George looked down at his daughter. The blue dress was certainly very charming and suitable but they had been standing there glued to the wall for ten minutes now, watching the dancers move past in their intricate routines, faces smooth and absorbed. No one in the stag line had given Marjorie so much as a second glance. The bored young eyes rested on her father in faint surprise, then passed on.

It was ridiculous for a middle-aged man to feel so lost and awkward. In this small jungle he should be an amused explorer, and instead he felt like a rather backward monkey. This bit of self-criticism cheered him considerably. He told himself they were only children after all and pressed Marjorie's cold hand.

"Want to dance?"

She nodded dumbly and he took her in his arms. She was such a square little thing, he thought, so compact and somehow so nice. They moved out onto the floor.

He had never been a good dancer but he had always managed to get by without actual damage to his partners. This music, however, with its nervous beat was new to him, and it never seemed to be doing quite what he was doing. Marjorie was stiff in his arms and he couldn't say that he blamed her. What she needed was one of those tall young men with their relaxed and casual steps, half dance, half walk. He noticed the way the other girls, dancing past the stag line, smiled at the boys in it. He looked down at Marjorie and found she was staring at his lapel with dreadful earnestness.

"You know any of the boys in the stag line?" he said.

She gave them a quick sideways look and shook her head. "Just by sight," she said. "One or two. I don't know many of these boys."

He gave her a small playful hug and missed a step. "They might remember you—by sight—if you'd smile at them, sweetheart. They don't bite."

"No," said Marjorie.

He felt a mild prick of impatience. The stag line was only there to be danced with but he could see they would at least have to feel that a girl was willing. He could also see what Anita meant when she said Marjorie had a lot to learn. Poor kitten. He pulled her close to him and looked out over her head. "There's Lee," he said suddenly.

"Where?"

"Over by the orchestra." Lee was radiant and, although the palm of his hand itched to smack her for her annexation of Marjorie's partner, he was still very glad to see someone who knew all the ropes. If that was Bob dancing with her, he was a good-looking youngster.

Marjorie said, "I guess that's Bob."

"I guess it is," said George and steered their way toward the orchestra. He knew a few ropes himself, he thought indignantly. When they bumped into Lee and Bob it was not unintentional.

"Why, Mr. Ashe! Marjorie!" The Marshall poise seemed to have forsaken Lee for a moment but its passing was brief and, almost at once, her voice was exactly like her mother's. "Of all people!" she drawled enchantedly. "Mr. Ashe, this is my cousin, Bob Wheeler, And Marjorie Ashe, Bobby—" Her hand made the correct social wave.

"Sir," said Bob and nodded to Marjorie. She gave him a small uncertain smile and her father felt again that dim annoyance. Surely, with her quick mind, she could think of something to say to the boy.

George sighed inwardly. He had brought her to the dance but apparently that wasn't going to be enough. He turned to Lee, said heartily, "How about finishing this dance with me, young lady?" and took her hand. She was surprised but most embraceable. There was nothing for Bob to do but turn to Marjorie, and George felt intensely relieved. Entranced by his own finesse, he moved away with Lee in his arms and found that he was dancing much better. He couldn't understand why she was so deliciously light and Marjorie so unmaneuverable; they had gone to the same dancing class as children.

He looked around for Marjorie and Bob and saw them, moving grim and wooden, unspeaking, glued together. A wave of honest anger swept over him with the knowledge that Bob was frankly sulking. Whatever they taught the exalted seniors in that young man's school, it was certainly not manners.

On the other hand, it was no use pretending that Marjorie had Lee's light touch. He wondered if it could be learned.

Lee said, with just the right blending of deference and admiration, "It was really sweet of you to bring Marjorie, Mr. Ashe. I know you think I was awfully bad but I couldn't have been more upset. I just *couldn't*."

"I'm afraid Marjorie isn't really socially minded," George said unhappily.

"Well, you were *sweet* to bring her," Lee said firmly. Someone tapped George's shoulder, and a tall boy said, "Sorry, sir."

George went back to the wall. He wasn't going to cut in on his own daughter. She had an official escort now and, whether she was happy or not, it looked all right from the sidelines.

Lee already had another change of partners. For the first time he understood the slight smugness in Anita's voice when she talked of her daughter. It would have been somehow so satisfying to see Marjorie whirl from one pair of arms to another. He only wanted it for her sake. If her mother were still alive, she would have known the things to tell Marjorie, the things a girl had to know for her own success and happiness. He sighed. Perhaps Anita—

The music ended in a crash. Marjorie and Bob stood in the middle of the floor, clapping. The orchestra leader lifted his baton for the next dance and, as the trumpet gave its first mewling wail, Bob took Marjorie by the elbow and steered her toward her father. Safe, stowing her within this paternal harbor, he muttered, "Lee'll be looking for me," and left them.

Marjorie said, "Thank you for the dance," to empty air. After a moment she said uncertainly, "I guess I was supposed to say that I enjoyed the dance, not thank him for it. The man is supposed to say thank you." She turned to her father. "I looked that up in an etiquette book at the library but then I forgot which way it went."

She had been reading etiquette books these days, then, not *Madame Bovary*. "It doesn't matter," George said.

Side by side, they waited for something to happen, someone to come. Finally, George held out his arms. "Dance, dear?" She nodded and they started out again. He was troubled because she was so quiet and her hands were still so cold, and then he began to be exasperated again. If she would only make some effort to attract the boys! Everyone was staring at them, father and daughter dancing interminably together, or at least it felt as if everyone was staring. When he looked around no one seemed even interested. Eyes were following the girls like Lee, casual and lovable, pressed against one faultless tuxedo after another. It wasn't a jungle really; it was more like an exclusive club and he couldn't get his daughter into it.

"Margie," said George.

She looked up at him and they both missed a step. He felt infernally clumsy. "Sweetheart," he said hopefully, "if you dance with Bob again, try to find out what he likes to talk about. He probably plays fullback or shortstop or something."

"He plays center on the basketball team and he's captain of the baseball team," said Marjorie, "and he's president of the dramatic society."

This was cheering news. "He told you all that?"

"I found out from Lee."

"Oh," said George.

They passed Lee at that moment, arm in arm with her current escort in a strolling dance-step. Her dress frothed out around her, and she smiled when George caught her eye. On an impulse, he spun Marjorie around so they were shoulder to shoulder. "Having fun, Lee?" he said casually.

She looked at him in surprise. "Wonderful," she said.

Deliberately, weighing the words so she would be sure to get the point, he said, "I must remember to give your mother a report on you, my dear."

A very pretty archness overlaid a slight uneasiness. "I hope it's a good report, Mr. Ashe," said Anita's daughter.

"I hope so," said Marjorie's father and moved away. When the dance ended, Lee turned up, admirably prompt, with a boy in tow. George beamed upon her, gently congratulating himself on the success of his social blackmail.

"Margie," said Lee, with something of the efficient kindliness of a very worldly aunt, "this is Dick Peterson. He's on the refreshment committee so he hasn't danced a step tonight, but he's just dying to." She smiled at the pink-cheeked representative of refreshments, then looked to George for approval. See? her look said. Tell Mother how good I've been, bringing boys around.

She left them and Dick gazed after her with the melting eyes of a cocker spaniel, then turned to Marjorie. "I didn't plan to dance tonight," he said. "I'm not much good at it but if you'd like to—"

George's heart warmed toward him. The youngster was half a head shorter than Marjorie and looked as if he belonged in grade school but any partner was better than none.

Marjorie smiled anxiously and the two moved off together. George lost some of his good cheer. Dick had understated the case against his dancing. Their feet, moving, collided. They tried again but the music was sharp and exact and unsympathetic. An earnest dew appeared on Dick's forehead, and Marjorie's smile was starched.

Her father felt suddenly irritated with the child. Everyone was doing everything they could for her. He had brought her to the dance himself, Lee had found her a partner, poor young Dick was struggling along as best he could. If she got mixed up with the dance steps, the least she could do was to make an effort and be charming to the boy, say something gay and amusing.

The dance stumbled to a close. The couples stood, politely clapping, waiting for the music to start again. The orchestra leader lifted his baton, and Dick turned to Marjorie with a dreadful virtue. George's heart ached for him, martyr to his own good manners.

But unexpectedly, Marjorie was backing out of the reluctant grasp. "I have to powder my nose," she said fiercely, loud enough for George and nearly everyone else to hear and, picking up her long blue skirt, she fled across the floor.

Dick watched her go, relief and distress almost equal on his pink face.

George stayed where he was. He stayed there during the playing of two dances and he had just begun to be really worried when Marjorie reappeared. She looked very tidy and completely controlled, unlike the little girl who had run off the floor. She smiled at him and he drew her hand through the crook of his arm. "Want to go home, honey?"

"No, thank you," said Marjorie.

"Want to dance with me some more?"

"Please," said Marjorie.

They stayed on to the end and then Marjorie went and got her coat. Lee and Bob were on the steps outside and for a moment George thought of offering them a lift home, but reconsidered. He wasn't sure how Marjorie was feeling although she had seemed quite happy during the last dances with him. Maybe it hadn't been such a bad evening for her. After all, she had no previous standards to measure the dance by.

They drove home in silence. He wanted to ask her straight out, for his own reassurance, but all he could do was hope. When they got into the house he took off his coat and hat, laid them over a chair and then turned uncertainly to look at his daughter.

She was smiling, a really happy smile. It lit up her eyes. "Thank you for taking me," she said and suddenly she put her arms up and gave him a swift tight hug. "Oh, Daddy, I had the most *beautiful* time." She turned and ran up the stairs.

"Well!" said George. The whole dreadful weight of the evening rolled off him.

And that was the moment when the phone rang.

He almost didn't answer it because it was far too late to talk to anyone and then he hurried to it, realizing the call might be urgent.

"George?" said Anita's voice.

Good Lord, he thought, but he said, "Hello there," very cheerfully because here was someone who could share his relief and pleasure.

Anita said, "George, Lee just got home. She told me all about it—about your taking Marjorie." She sounded terribly wrought up. "George, how *could* you?"

"How could I what?"

"Take that child to a dance that way!" It was a moment before he realized she was accusing him. "Oh, I know you meant well but, good heavens—! Why didn't you phone first and ask me? I could have told you."

"But, Anita, I don't see what—"

"Lee said that everyone was laughing at her. Marjorie's not a fool, George, she must have known. A girl doesn't go to a dance like that. With her *father*. Like a baby. You might at least have considered her feelings." She must have realized that she sounded too sharp. Her voice smoothed out. "It's not that I'm blaming you, George. It's—"

"But, Anita— Marjorie said she had a beautiful time. She said—"

Suddenly his voice trailed off. He stood there, staring at the telephone in his hand. Dismay and a sense of shock held him for a moment, and then he did something he had never done to anyone before in his life. He hung up, without apology, without explanation.

He turned and walked upstairs and he was barely halfway up before the phone started ringing again. He let it ring.

He walked to Marjorie's room, and the door was closed. He leaned against it, listening, and he heard what he had known he would hear from the moment he hung up the telephone.

He heard his daughter crying.

She wasn't noisy. They were long deep slow sobs, muffled against the pillow. They had a controlled quality about them. If he knocked on the door, they would stop at once.

He turned very slowly and walked downstairs. The phone had stopped ringing. He went into the living room and stood, hands in pockets, staring at the furniture. He and Eleanor had planned the room together, a long time ago now, and he hadn't changed anything.

It was Eleanor's daughter who was crying upstairs on her bed.

George knew what he wanted to do. He wanted to turn and go back to Marjorie. He wanted to take her in his arms and stroke her hair and comfort her. He wanted to tell his daughter that none of this mattered, that the flimsy world of social success wasn't what counted, that there were other values, infinitely more important—

He stopped himself.

Marjorie already knew what was important, knew it better than he did. It was Eleanor's daughter who was crying upstairs on her bed, but it was also Eleanor's daughter who had put her arms around his neck and said, "Oh, Daddy, I had the most beautiful time."

The evening had hurt her. She would not let it hurt her father too.

Dismayed, he realized how completely he had failed her. He

had wanted to see his daughter shine, he had been impatient with her inability to attract partners. He had wanted Marjorie to be successful as Lee was successful. He had admired Lee with her pretty ways, and he had been humiliatingly willing for Marjorie to learn from them.

He was ashamed of himself.

His daughter was crying upstairs now because she had been a failure in the world where Lee did everything so well. Eventually, he knew, she would stop her tears. She would blow her nose and go sensibly to bed. Tonight's world had been Lee's, not hers. Her enchanted hopes for it were all gone, and she would just accept that now, this grown-up child of his, and let them go. There were other worlds. In the end, she would possess something that Lee could never hope for.

Meantime, she was crying, and he would be very careful never to let her know that he had stood outside her door and listened.

He walked upstairs to his bedroom. It was a lonely place, but tonight it was not quite so lonely as usual. Eleanor was less far away than she had ever been, and George Ashe was thinking of the very lucky man who would, some day, marry Eleanor's daughter.

THE IN-BETWEENS

THE JUKEBOX AND THE KALLIKAKS

THEIR real name was Callinan, not Kallikak; but on Misery Road, titles are apt to wander, and Misery Road itself had once been Missouri Road.

The Callinan name had survived five years of the Road, four babies, and innumerable clashes between Pa and the Town Board of Larkspur. But when the fifth baby had no more discretion than to turn out to be twins, the chairman of the Board rose in his wrath and, with unintentional permanence, rechristened the entire family.

The crux of the matter was that twins were going to mean a double ration of milk. Double rations of milk came out of the Welfare Fund, and the Welfare Fund came out of the pockets of the taxpayers, while Misery Road infants caroused like baby bacchanals.

Sorely tried on this occasion, the chairman of the Board pounded both fists on the table and gave tongue. "Callinans!" he roared. "Kallikaks is what they are. Next thing you know, we'll have the Jukes on relief here, too!"

As he had majored in sociology in college and had studied the two notorious families, he felt the witticism was both apt and distinguished, and his temper improved noticeably. Most of Larkspur, however, had never heard of either Jukes or Kallikaks, so it was the name that lingered in their minds rather than the chairman's educational background, and in a short time it was more or less accepted that the Kallikaks lived on Misery Road. The point was negligible, since neither Pa nor Ma could read or write, and in any case they were involved in their own name calling, the twins being boys and the Kallikaks having got used to girls, as evidenced by Amanda, Sarah, Dolly, and Hester.

The new babies lay in a packing box, bursting with health and that excellent Larkspur milk which must have tasted so deliciously of taxpayers, and they beamed at their parents.

"We've gotta call 'em something," Ma pointed out reasonably, leaning over the infant nest, her hair coming down, Hester sociably in her arms, and Amanda clutching a fistful of skirt.

"Mark," said Pa, inspired to sudden firmness. "And this un's Jeb."

His wife looked at him with open admiration. "Mark 'n' Jeb," she repeated approvingly. "Mark's eyes is slantier and Jeb's nose points higher, and that'll do to tell 'em apart."

In the eighteen years following the twins' arrival, these were the only factors that remained unchanged. Mark's eyes continued to slant and Jeb's nose to tilt, while the twins themselves grew strong and tall, dark-haired and dark-eyed, with their mother's unplanned charm, their father's aimlessness, and a sturdy love for each other, like twin birches.

Time, not content with turning sprouts into saplings, had further outraged the Town Board by producing more Kallikaks, in the endearing shapes of Ella-Lou, Jeremiah, Caroline, and the baby, Tad, who had been something of a surprise. However, the ranks had been reduced by Amanda's marriage and by the departure of Sarah to the city, where she worked off her ambitions in a department store and sometimes cried at night for Misery Road.

Baby Tad slept in the packing box that had cuddled his kinfolk, and the only change in the house was caused by the acquisition of a massive gasoline lamp, promoted by one of Pa's more intricate trades and presented to his wife on the occasion of their tenth anniversary. The lamp was regarded as dangerous, and it was never used, but it had pink roses and blue forget-me-nots on its bulging milk-white curves, and it received a great deal of respect. Mark and Jeb particularly yearned over it, as it had come into their lives when they were five years old, that age of delicate impressions, and their father had spun them a dream tale of a golden-haired, flower-eyed princess who apparently always traveled around in a perfect welter of roses and forget-me-nots.

The twins lived in a home that was full of drafts and affection, and they shared with their family a passion for all lovely sounds, whether originating from a red-winged blackbird or Pa's guitar. The latter they were occasionally allowed to play, but not often, since it had been handed down from Pa's own father and had been heard humming to itself nights in a melancholy and romantic way.

Rich in each other's company, they were no more concerned with the world outside than was the whippoorwill that sang witlessly in the swamp.

It is written (and documented) that even a whippoorwill is susceptible and that love can be a sword. Between Jeb and Mark, there fell the shadow of Corinne.

They saw her first on one of those glimmery days in mid-spring when the sun is as warm and soft as a kitten's paw and the sky is as blue as an angel's eyes. Misery Road and the path along Cover-Me-Up Creek were latticed with hawthorn bloom, the wild crabapple trees were putting out pink and creamy buds, and the grass along the roadside was golden green, sprinkled with dandelions and all drunk with dew.

It was, in fact, a day so outlandishly beautiful that it put both Jeb and Mark in mind of the gasoline lamp and the fairy-tale princess, but Jeb only remarked comfortably that it was real nice out, and Mark said it would be hot come midday. Neither of them spoke of the princess, but they jumped the creek, circled a ring of birch trees, stepped out into a flower-caught meadow, and there she was.

Mark, who had been whistling, swallowed his closing notes and nearly choked on that spasm of the heart which is caused by beauty. Jeb, with no whistling to stop, stopped breathing.

Her hair was as bright as the sun, her eyes were fringed gentians, and her mouth was a redbird's wing. She was wearing a green dress that clung to her in curves that were like the curves of a cloud, and her little feet were in bright-green slippers with heels so magically high that they looked absurd in the tangle of meadowsweet and cuckoo-flowers.

A little sighing wind ran over the tall grass and counted all the clover tops. It blew a lock of hair across the vision's face, and when she put up her hand to push it back, two bright bracelets, as real gold as dandelions, jangled music on her wrist.

Jeb and Mark stared, and she gave them an encouraging smile. "Ain't you two never seen a girl before?" she inquired.

Jeb turned bright pink. "I'm s-sorry," he said, stumbling over three syllables he had known since extreme youth, having been a scrupulous baby. "We didn't expect to find no one here."

She shrugged. "Meadow's free, so far as I know. What's your names?"

"Jeb," said Jeb shyly.

"Mark," said Mark.

"Mine's Corinne." They weren't the kind of young men she was used to, but they were real cute and much more interesting than all this meadow and sky. "Corinne Porter," she added, becoming autobiographical.

Mark said, "We're Kallikaks."

"Come again?"

"Kallikak. It was somethin' else once, but we don't rightly

remember what." Mark had always had an easier tongue than Jeb. "Corinne's a real pretty name."

She smiled again, this time just for Mark. Something moved in Jeb's heart, emerald-eyed and unlovable. It took a great deal of beauty from the day, but none from Corinne.

Mark was smiling back. "Where'd you come from, Corinne? I ain't never seen you in these parts before."

"We're just looking around. We ain't settled on staying." It seemed an unnecessary detail to add that her father had left the last town by request, three orthodox jumps ahead of the sheriff. These abrupt changes of climate were occasionally advisable. "We took a house up there aways," she said coolly, jerking her thumb vaguely northward.

The twins nodded. That would be the old house at Cat's Corner, which had been abandoned years ago. It had holes in its roof, where the stars shone through, and squirrels, field mice and people were continually moving their families in and out.

A long silence fell, and Corinne began to suspect that the meadow and the sky were not much duller than the twins. Still, their masculine admiration was very gratifying, and she gave them her smile again, causing the whole meadow to glitter and spin. "Ma'll raise hell if I don't get home," she remarked, turned in a whirl of skirts and left them.

They watched her go, yearning to be the ground under her little feet but not knowing how to attain this useful ambition. When a twist in the landscape swallowed her up, they sighed, deep-hearted, and set their own feet on the path toward home.

There was a difference in their silence now. It was no longer companionable.

When Jeb awoke at midnight, it was to a feeling of emptiness. This was not caused by an appreciable void in the Kallikak house, since Pa and Ma were in the bed, Tad was nesting in the packing box, Dolly, Hester, Ella-Lou and Caroline were clustered like dahlia petals in the lean-to, and Jeremiah and a visiting dog named Sam were lying across Jeb's legs. There was not so much an absence of life as a superfluity of it, but to Jeb there was one sleep-wrapped breathing too few.

He slid out from under Jeremiah and Sam, dragged on Pa's shirt and his own trousers, and took another look at the spot where Mark should have been sleeping. There was only pale moonlight, and a finger of it stole up the wall and pointed out that something else was missing.

Pa's guitar.

Jeb caught his breath, torn between the perfidiousness of the crime and the wish that he had thought of it first, and then he plunged out into the night, heading furiously for Cat's Corner.

Arrived there, he slowed down and listened. Dimly there came to his ears the faintest humming, as of orchestral bees dipping into honey pots. This was Mark's prelude to song, and in better moments, one of Jeb's favorite noises.

This was not one of his better moments. He went around the side of the decayed old house, and there was Mark, cradling the guitar. Corinne was nowhere in sight.

"That's Pa's guitar," said Jeb accusingly, ignoring the real issue and taking the unethical path of moral rectitude, which would indicate that love is not as ennobling as some people think.

Mark, recovering from the sight of his brother stalking out of the moonlight, said with dignity, "Pa lended it to me."

"He never," said Jeb with conviction.

"He would if I'd asked him."

"He wouldn't," said Jeb.

The fact that Jeb was right gave him an unfair advantage in this exchange of thoughts. Mark gazed at him hostilely for a moment, then suddenly swept his fingers across the strings of the guitar. It was a beautiful chord, but love, noble or not, is stronger than musical appreciation.

Jeb snatched the guitar from him and hurled it into a bed of nettles.

War was thus openly declared. Mark's fist caught Jeb high on the cheekbone; Jeb drove his elbow into Mark's ribs. Mark gave a grunt and went backwards, and they rolled together on the cold, wet grass, wrestling, biting and kicking.

When a heavy hand landed on them, they were too busy to pay attention, and it was not until they were jerked sharply apart that they stopped fighting long enough to discover a large, red-faced man glowering down on them.

There was nobody else it could be but Corinne's pa. Jeb blushed and Mark paled, nicely balancing between them the classic reactions of affected hearts. Their host gave no indication of sharing any such tender emotions. "Start talking," he invited grimly. "What you doing prowling around in the middle of the night, interfering with decent folks' sleep?"

Jeb and Mark got to their feet with as much dignity as they could manage. Mark walked over to the nettle patch and retrieved the guitar. "We're real sorry we woke you up, Mr. Porter," he said. This was a hard man to warm to, but he was Corinne's father and entitled to courtesy. "I just came to play this here for your daughter, and maybe sing a little."

It had the ring of truth in it. Porter was aware that Corinne had a very persuasive influence on young men, although he never remembered such a downy pair as this. He gave a short bark of laughter. "You sure come calling on the wrong girl!"

"Ain't Corinne your daughter?"

"She's mine, all right. But she ain't the moonlight-and-guitar type of a dame. Corinne's strictly a jukebox girl."

"A what?"

"A jukebox girl. Cripes, you know what a jukebox is!"

They shook their heads, and he stared at them, finding a certain morbid fascination in such ignorance. "It's like a big red icebox," he said finally. "You put in a nickel, and the music comes out. Folks dance to it, and Corinne's real crazy about dancing. There was a jukebox near where we stayed in Tipton, and she mighty near got engaged to a guy who took her dancing there."

"Tipton," said Jeb, sorting out the one relevant fact. Tipton was a long way off, but if it had a jukebox, he would go and see this thing his princess loved. He shot a quick look at Mark, and his heart sank. Clear as daylight, Mark was thinking the same thing.

Porter suddenly remembered his interrupted sleep. "You two come lallygagging around here again," he said briskly, "I'll knock your ears off." He turned back toward the house, added "Beat it!" over his shoulder, and would have slammed the door behind him except that there had been no doors at Cat's Corner in ten years.

The twins stood still for a moment where he had left them. Then Jeb drew in his breath, forgetting their feud. "Mark," he said anxiously, "you really believe they's such a thing as red iceboxes with music in 'em?"

For a moment, the old family love nearly rose up and smothered the new love for Corinne. Then the thought of her, hair all glittery and mouth like wild strawberries, hardened Mark's heart. "You keep on y'r side of the fence, Jeb Kallikak," he said, "and I'll keep on mine."

The next morning, Jeb and Mark, having hastily absorbed breakfasts of mush and drippings, departed in opposite directions.

Their elaborate precautions, taken to conceal the fact that each was hitchhiking to Tipton, were completely nullified by the discovery that there was only one jukebox in that unprogressive town. This was lodged in the shadowy confines of a small bar and grill (E. Affelt, Proprietor), and Mark was already there when Jeb arrived, panting.

Mark eyed his brother coldly and without any sign of recognition. E. Affelt, troubled by a strong sense of ditto marks, looked at them anxiously and rubbed the back of his head in a gesture so habitual it had given him a bald spot. "You brothers?" he said finally, having worked it out.

They scowled at him, and Mark said, "I ain't here to discuss who's kin to who. You got a jukebox?"

Their host admitted he had and inquired brightly, "You want to see it?" He was not feeling bright, but he had to start somewhere. The twins nodded, and he led them to the back of his establishment. There, among the tables and chairs, pushed against a wall and flanked by a potted palm that was unwell, stood the jukebox.

They gazed at it in silent awe. Not only was it red, as Mr. Porter had promised, but it was gold and green, too, and there were lights shining out richly through a glass porthole, and scrawly gilt letters danced across its front. It was as big as an emperor's throne and more gorgeous than a sunset.

"Want to hear it play?" said Mr. Affelt. They nodded respectfully and he held out his hand, palm up. "Takes a nickel, you know."

They did know, because Corinne's father had told them. Jeb's ears turned pink. Mark dug deep into his pockets in the absolutely unfounded hope that some furtive hen might have laid a nest egg there.

"Broke," said Mr. Affelt, who was good at symptoms. "Well, I'll loan you a nickel, and you can wash some glasses to make it up to me." He dipped into his pocket, produced the needed sum, and fed it delicately to the jukebox. A deep sigh swelled up from its interior.

"Does that," said Mr. Affelt. "It's getting pretty old."

The sigh gave way to a rumbling, the rumbling to a hiccup. And then—loud and clear and fierce and fine and free—a burst of music swept the room in a vast wave of sound. The dead palm fronds stirred under the breeze, and the beer glasses jostled one another.

"Cheerful, ain't it?" said Mr. Affelt.

This was like saying that the streets of heaven were nice and bright.

Jeb and Mark, their mouths ajar with wonder, listened raptly from the first blast of inhaling woodwinds down to the last glutted sob of the trombone. The jukebox coughed, the final ineffable rag of sound wavered away. There was silence.

Jeb and Mark sighed together. First the gasoline lamp. Then Corinne. And now this.

Jeb gave Mr. Affelt a velvety look and said, "That was beautiful." This surprised Mr. Affelt, who had said hard words in his day about the jukebox. "Make it do it again," said Jeb.

"That's two nickels you owe me," the proprietor warned, touched by their wonder, but not that touched. He pushed another coin into the slot. The music surged up again, and a cowboy tenor lamented hoarsely under a Texas moon, came to a bad end and sang posthumous regrets with admirable vitality.

When it finished, the twins turned to their host in double trustfulness. Mr. Affelt shook a bewildered head, found three more nickels in his pocket, and lined them up on a table. "That's two bits' worth of washing up you owe me," he said sternly, "and when you finish those three nickels, that's all you get. I got ears same as anybody else, and that thing squawks at me all night. Can't stand it in the daytime, too."

He paddled off to the bar, muttering. Three songs later, dazzled and drunk with sound, his guests found him there and accepted their dish towels meekly, putting such a high, dreamy gloss on each glass that Mr. Affelt cordially invited them to come again.

Jeb shook his head. "We live out Larkspur way."

Mr. Affelt leaned over the bar and stared at him incredulously. "Mean to say you come all that distance just to hear an old broken-down jukebox?"

"It's what Corinne likes," Jeb said simply. "I had to know what my girl likes."

"*My* girl," Mark warned. There was a moment's silence, then he added casually, " 'Course, I don't know why I can't learn to play and sing them dance tunes just as good as a jukebox. If that's what Corinne likes," he said virtuously, "that's what she ought to have."

"I c'n sing, too," said Jeb desperately.

"Ho!" said Mark. "Like a foghorn you c'n sing. Like a old bullfrog on a lily pad. Who'd listen to you?"

"I'll tell Pa if you take his guitar."

"No you won't," said Mark with simple faith. "You won't never tell."

There was no answer to that. Jeb spun on his heel and headed for the door. When he finally got back to Larkspur, via two trucks and a tired delivery cart, he found that Mark had arrived ahead of him, first even in the matter of transportation, and was already telling Caroline, Jeremiah and Tad of the wonder he had seen.

Naturally, they understood perfectly well that it was a fairy tale, but they warmly appreciated his inventing such a splendid thing.

Next evening Pa was sitting up with a sick deck of cards, and when Mark took the guitar down off the wall, Ma merely said, "Lovey, that's Pa's," in mild reproof. She then went back to helping Baby Tad wash the dog Sam with an old bar of laundry soap. Baby Tad must have been a throwback of some sort; no other member of the family had ever felt this warm attachment to soap.

"I know, Ma," said Mark politely, and soft-stepped out the door, hoping to get to Cat's Corner before Jeb did. Actually, he caught him up at Endwise Hollow, and they concluded their pilgrimage together with their silence a wall between them.

Corinne was sitting on the front stoop, her chin in her hands and a scowl drawing her eyebrows together.

"Corinne," said Mark, just breathing her name.

She turned, straightened her back and rearranged her legs. They were good-looking young men, all right; she wondered if they had the price of a beer between them, decided they didn't, and sighed.

Jeb felt the answering twist in his heart like a knife. "What's the trouble, Corinne?"

She frowned at her little green slippers, their sharp heels digging into the grass. "I'm good and sick of this place," said Corinne crossly. "Sometimes I get so bored I could scream."

Mark pulled the guitar up close to his heart and drew a deep breath. The tunes he'd heard on the jukebox had been caged in his head since yesterday, and he knew he could coax them out of the strings. "I'll sing for you, Corinne," he said.

Jeb swallowed hard. It wasn't true that he was an old bullfrog on a lily pad. Maybe he couldn't keep a tune, but he was very sincere.

Corinne said, "Who wants to sit and listen to songs?"

"It's a special one," Mark said wistfully. "I learned it off a jukebox."

She gave him her sudden interest. "What do you know about jukeboxes?"

"They're just like heaven," said Mark promptly, in the tones of a man who had studied jukeboxes since childhood.

Corinne gazed at him speculatively. She wouldn't have picked Mark for the jukebox type, but it was a very deceiving world. Anyway, there must be something jingling in his pockets, because jukeboxes needed nickels. "You like to dance, Mark?"

she asked, melting appreciably. "You go for bright lights and lots of noise?"

"I like anything you like, Corinne."

Jeb, listening, clenched his fists. It wasn't fair. He had seen the jukebox too and loved it with all his heart. It wasn't fair for Mark to woo her with what Jeb had seen. "Corinne," he said.

She turned to him.

"*I'll* take you dancin', Corinne," he said eagerly. "I'll take you to places where they's a hundred jukeboxes. You'll be wearin' gold slippers and you'll dance on red velvet." Not for a moment did he doubt his ability to give her this or anything else. "You be my girl, Corinne, and you c'n have whatever in the world you ask for."

Mark said, "Where'll you get the money, Jeb Kallikak?"

Precisely this thought had passed through Corinne's mind. In her experience, which was extensive, she had found that the bigger they talked, the less they had. It began to look as if Mark was more her type. She turned toward him and away from Jeb.

Mark reached out his hand to her.

His intention had been to help her up from the stoop, a most innocent and reverent gesture. Jeb, however, in a fevered and quite inaccurate flash of intuition, instantly visioned his brother pulling Corinne into his arms. His imagination then catapulted him toward their inevitable kiss. It was not to be borne.

For the second time in eighteen years, Jeb struck his brother.

Mark hit back. Corinne screamed.

There was an explosion from the house like a Roman candle, and Corinne's father burst out the door, madder than a scalded cat and spitting oaths. "Them two back again!" howled Mr. Porter apoplectically. "Hell on wheels, Corinne, I thought you'd at least been bit by a sheriff!"

He yanked the twins apart. "Git!" he said. "Git the blazes out of here!"

"Pa!" said Corinne, suddenly realizing that the shortage of young men was about to become even more acute.

"Shut your mouth!" said Porter furiously.

"I won't shut my mouth!" said Corinne. She could be twice as furious, and besides, she was a female. "It's your own fault we're stuck out here halfway to nowhere. Don't you start knocking my boy friends around!"

"I'm sick of finding 'em fighting all over the yard," Porter said bitterly.

"Some yard!" said his daughter. "Anyway, it only happens because there's two of them and they get mad at each other."

"Well, then, choose one," Porter growled. "Choose one, and tell the other to git out."

Corinne bit her lip and looked at the twins. They were pleasing to look at, and she would have much preferred to keep them both, but she knew her father could be pushed just so far.

Mark stepped forward. "You're my girl, Corinne," he said. "Don't you forget it."

Jeb said, "You're mine."

There was a distant rumble as of thunder. That was Corinne's father warming up again. Corinne offered up a brisk prayer for inspiration. It came, and a pussy-cat smile curved the corners of her mouth. "I know what to do," she announced with satisfaction.

The thunder receded. "About time," said Porter.

Corinne turned to Jeb and Mark, who had given up breathing. She eyed them quite affectionately. At least, if she was going to be denied fifty percent of her suitors, she was not going to be denied adequate compensation. "Whichever one of you gives me the nicest present," said Corinne in a voice like clear water, "that's whose girl I'll be."

They stared at her. Porter gave a short laugh. "Bet they can't scratch up a plugged nickel between the two of 'em!"

The pussy-cat smile stayed in place. "Don't be silly, Pa," said Corinne purely. "They can earn it, can't they? I'll give them a whole week." She jangled the bracelets on her arm. "In a week, I should think, a man could earn enough for a pretty nice present."

Her father looked at her with real respect. She touched his arm. "Come on, Pa. You leave 'em alone now." She turned back to the twins for a moment, spinning on her spike heels. "Remember, you've got a whole week," she said, and left them.

Jeb sighed heavily.

Mark dug his fists into pockets that always seemed to be empty and scowled. "You keep out of my way is all."

Jeb nodded, feeling the cold breeze of solitude. Always before, they'd made their plans together. He and Mark were walking different roads now, for sure, and it was like having a year when the Lord had left out the summer.

It was quite impossible to conceal Corinne's ultimatum from the Kallikak family. Jeremiah and Caroline tracked Mark to old Mrs. Peters' garden the next day, confirmed with their own eyes a rumor that their brother was weeding the pansy bed and rushed home to report the revolutionary tidings.

Pa Kallikak was sincerely shocked. He didn't like to hear such things about a son of his, and he wandered uneasily over to Mrs. Peters' house and leaned over the fence. "Earnin' money, son?" he inquired. "What you plannin' to buy?"

Mark didn't want to call Pa nosy, but he sure was persistent, and if he didn't get an answer now, he'd put Ma on the problem. "I'm buyin' a gift for Corinne," Mark said reluctantly.

Pa nodded. "We figured you was sweet on that girl. What's happened to Jeb?"

"I ain't seen him."

Pa said sadly, "You two boys ain't livin' in the same pod together no more."

"I guess not," said Mark. After a moment, Pa's question caught up with him, and he said sharply, "Ain't you seen him neither? Ain't he workin' somewheres?"

"Carrie and Jeremiah says no."

That settled it. You couldn't hide a beetle in a hedgehog nest without Carrie and Jeremiah knowing. Mark frowned and jerked at a weed.

Pa looked at him with honest concern. "You'll burn yourself out in the prime of y'r youth," said Pa warningly and ambled off, shaking his head.

Mark sat back on his heels. After Mrs. Peters' garden, there was the doctor's driveway and then Miss Hill's rock garden. But when he got through, Mark was heading for the Elite Jewelry Store, and there he would put his money down on a ring with a stone in it that had lights like the stars over Larkspur in wintertime. By the end of the week, he'd have earned enough money to own it, and then he could march up to Corinne and put it on her finger, and she'd never think of Jeb again.

Mark pulled up a pansy by mistake and had to stuff it back into the damp ground extremely fast. It was fretting about Jeb that got him doing things like that, he thought crossly. Because if Jeb wasn't out earning money in Larkspur, what was he up to?

Jeb got home that night an hour after sundown, and he looked as cheerful as a bee in clover.

Mark was in a mixed mood. He had made his down payment on the ring but on the other hand, Miss Hill's idea of planting a rock garden was to try each rock in twenty different places, and she wanted him back tomorrow. He regarded his twin's briskness without enthusiasm. "Where you been all day?"

"Out," said Jeb.

"Out where?"

"Just out."

It was a most unsatisfactory conversation and carried no useful clues whatever. "You ain't been workin'," Mark accused. "*I* been workin' like a horse."

"Who says I ain't been workin'?" said Jeb mildly.

"No one in Larkspur's seen you all day, and Carrie and Jeremiah hunted all over."

"Larkspur ain't the whole world," Jeb remarked.

He seemed maddeningly pleased with himself, and Mark gave him a hard look. "I s'pose you went out in the woods and shot a squirrel," he said caustically. "Goin' to give it to Corinne so's she can make herself a fur coat, I guess."

A faraway look came into Jeb's eyes. "What I got f'r Corinne," he said softly, "is gonna be so beautiful—" He broke off, looked at his twin with forgiving pity and walked on into the house.

Mark kicked a puffball, exploding it, started to kick a juniper bush and just missed Carrie, who was crouched down behind it. He dragged her out and held her up at arm's length, but her pigtails stuck out so charmingly and she looked so docile that he put her down. "Allus creepin' around behind things," he grunted, his mind already on other matters.

"I was very int'rested," said Carrie with dignity. "Mark, when you and Jeb give Corinne her presents, kin I come 'n' watch? I and Jeremiah?"

He remembered the jewelry-store ring with all the fires leaping in it, and a great wave of cheefulness swept over him. "Whole world c'n come and watch for all I care," Mark said generously. "The whole world and all his kinfolk."

It was not perhaps the whole world that turned out for Corinne's gift day, but it was certainly all the Kallikaks.

They arrived in battalions, Carrie and Jeremiah first, since they were always first at important occasions and their family recognized and respected their rights. Once this priority was established, Dolly, Hester, Ella-Lou, Tad and the dog Sam put in their appearance and ranged themselves neatly in the Cat's Corner yard.

Corinne, who had been waiting with considerable impatience to see how her investment was going to work out, regarded her uninvited guests with very negative enthusiasm. They stared back, steadfast and admiring, weak-hearted wherever beauty was concerned.

The arrival of Pa and Ma Kallikak rounded out the audience. Pa identified Corinne by the simple process of deducting her from his own family, and he gave her a very courtly bow of sincere welcome. Ma said, "Where's your folks, lovey?" smiling because Corinne was so pretty.

Corinne shrugged.

"You mean they ain't comin'?" Ma shook her head in real distress, feeling that only a matter of grave urgency could have kept the Porters away. Kallikaks assembled by instinct. When Baby Tad fell down the woodchuck hole that time, there were eight rescuers to pull him out and comfort his wails, not counting the woodchuck who had taken a slightly different attitude.

Pa gave his wife a gentle punch with his elbow. "Here's Mark," he said proudly. He had every reason to be proud. Mark was as brushed and neat as a member of the Town Board, and he was carrying a package that was very small but beautifully wrapped in tissue paper and shiny ribbon.

The package seemed to be about a good size for a jeweler's box. Corinne touched her lips hopefully with the tip of her pink tongue.

Pa said, "Where's Jeb, boy? Ain't seen him all day."

"Ain't he here?" Mark looked uneasy. "We'd better wait."

"I'll open your package first," said Corinne, holding out her hand.

Mark shook his head. There wasn't any satisfaction unless she opened it when Jeb was there. "I don't want—" he began, and broke off.

Jeb was coming, running down the road. He was empty-handed.

"Where you been? said Mark.

"Where's my present?"said Corinne.

"Down the road." Jeb looked as pleased with himself as a rooster that's just crowed the sun out of bed. "I'll bring it up, Corinne, soon's you've opened Mark's." He nodded toward the package in his twin's hand.

It wasn't like Jeb to be so almighty sure of himself. Mark clutched the ring a little more tightly. "Let's see yours first."

"Can't," said Jeb sunnily. "It ain't wrapped, so it ain't fair for me to show mine first."

"What's that got to do with it?"

Corinne gave a small sputter of impatience. They were capable of standing there arguing until the stars came out. There was a flutter of skirt, a quick grab like a pigeon going after a kernel of corn, and Mark's package changed hands. "It's mine," said Corinne, forestalling any further argument. "I can open it when I want to."

Mark scowled, and she took a second out from opening the gift to give him a smile that turned his heart to butter. He decided it didn't matter which she opened first; his would be the best, anyway. Only he wished she wouldn't rip off the paper. The man at the shop had done the wrapping with great tenderness, and it ought to be unfolded slowly, like a bud that was fixing to be a blossom.

The little blue velvet box surrendered itself to Corinne's hands, and she snatched off the lid. The ring winked up at the sky like a dewdrop, like a star, like a tiny baby icicle with the sun shining through it. A little tinkle of wonder ran up and down the line of Kallikaks.

Corinne caught her breath. "Gee, Mark, it's really something,"she said and slipped it on, stretching her hand out to admire it, the way women have done ever since Eve first put her finger through a sunbeam.

Mark looked pleased and modest, cast a quick, triumphant look at Jeb and got the shock of a lifetime. Jeb's face completely failed in its duty to register defeat. "It's real pretty, Mark," Jeb said kindly. "Too bad it just ain't pretty enough."

Corinne looked up from the glitter on her hand. "What's yours, Jeb?" she demanded. "Hurry up and show me." Things were going a lot better than she had expected; maybe she would get a necklace, too.

"I'll show you," Jeb assured her. "Just stay where you are." He turned and left them, walking with his shoulders swinging.

Mark watched him go, wild with curiosity to know what had made his twin so cocksure.

He had only a minute to wait.

Jeb came back up the road, leading a battered old horse with a straw hat falling over its brow and long ears waving through. Behind the horse, a tipsy-looking wagon lurched and grumbled. Mark got one good look at what was in the wagon, and then his mouth fell wide open.

Big and red and shiny and beautiful, a jukebox rode in state to the Porters' door. Like a king, like an emperor.

"Jehoshaphat!" said Pa. A shiver of delight ran over the Kallikak kids, the way wind runs over a wheat field.

Mark felt his heart sink like a bird falling out of the sky. The jukebox was a gift beyond all mortal dreams. He had lost Corinne. He looked at Jeb hopelessly and said, "How'd you get it?"

"It's Mr. Affelt's," Jeb told him proudly. "He's buyin' a

new one, and he said I c'd have this if I'd work it out at his place. All I gotta do is hitchhike to Tipton every day, and by the end of the summer everything's evened up." No shadow crossed his face at the thought of a lost season of blossom. He looked adoringly at Corinne. "It's worth it," he said.

They all turned to gaze respectfully at the recipient of this magnificent, this priceless gift. Mark's heart ached all the way through.

Corinne stood staring back at them. Her face was a vivid shade of pink, and she seemed to be struggling for words. Speechlessness was something the Kallikaks could appreciate under the circumstances.

And then she exploded.

"You silly fool, Jeb Kallikak!" She threw the words at him, almost screaming. "What's the use of a jukebox in a place where they ain't even any electricity to play it with!"

It took her two steps to get to Mark. She put her arms up around his neck, and the ring on her hand shone like a diamond. "I love my ring, Mark honey," Corinne said.

The landscape froze for a long moment in time. There was Mark, the girl he had won wrapped around his neck. There was a row of Kallikaks, holding their breaths.

Very slowly, Mark undid Corinne's fingers. He said, "You c'n keep the ring, Corinne."

She looked up at him, puzzled. "Of course I can keep the ring, Mark. I'm your girl now, like I promised."

"You ain't no girl of mine," said Mark Kallikak hoarsely.

"What do you mean?" she asked in amazement.

Mark told her in terms that were exact and scornful. "No woman who ain't got the sense to know that a jukebox is the most beautiful present in the world," said Mark, "is goin' to spend her days hangin' around my neck."

"But, Mark! It's not my fault Jeb's such a dumb ox he forgot about not having electricity around here. It's not my fault—"

"I didn't forget," said Jeb miserably. "I just figgered it didn't matter."

"It don't matter," said Mark.

Corinne blazed out resentfully. "What good's a jukebox you can't play?"

All the Kallikaks turned grave eyes on her, pondering the incomprehensible question. The gasoline lamp with the roses and forget-me-nots had never been lighted. You didn't have to wash in Cover-Me-Up Creek to appreciate its wonderful wetness. You didn't have to eat the apples off a tree just because you had stared at its baby blossoms against a blue sky.

The Kallikak court stood in judgment. Corinne was beautiful and the jukebox was beautiful and they were, both of them, dumb. But deep down in the heart of the jukebox, there was music. And deep down in the heart of Corinne, there was just Corinne.

"C'mon, Jebby," said Mark.

"Where to?" said Jeb heavily. And then, all at once, he felt a whole lot warmer. It was a long time since Mark had called him Jebby.

"Home," Mark told him. "We're goin' to move that jukebox in alongside the lamp, and you 'n' me is goin' to Tipton and work for Mr. Affelt together. That way, it'll only take half the summer. And anyway," he said, "some things is worth workin' for."

Pa Kallikak, trailing his sons home in the gathering twilight, considered this statement with some anxiety. It might be true, but he just hoped he would never get himself in a position where he would have to find out.

ROOKIE COP

JOE MASON tightened his belt, feeling the buckle flat against his middle and the good official drag of the holstered gun against his hip. The visor of his uniform cap was squarely between his eyebrows, regulation dead center, and the gold and gray patch on his left shoulder said, CITY OF NEW YORK POLICE ACADEMY.

A couple of teen-age girls turned on the sidewalk to take another look at him, and he grinned and pulled his shoulders back, the shield on his chest catching the light from a street lamp. Wait till he got into the official blue of the Finest, then he'd really look good. Wait a few weeks, ladies.

His feet came down smartly on the pavement, and he whistled, owning the town, his eyes alert and a little self-conscious. The whistle went up a few cheerful degrees, and he put the words to it:

> *"My father he kept the Eddystone light,*
> *He married a mermaid late one night——"*

Where in heck had he picked that number up? A man walking a spaniel glanced at him curiously, and Joe's face did a hasty rearrangement of itself into the solemn planes suitable to the Law. The song went on again inside his head, decorously, *My father he kept the Eddystone light——*

Up ahead, the solid bulk on the edge of the sidewalk was Patrolman Ryan, the cop that Joe was assigned to for a four-hour patrol. Ryan stood with his hands behind his back, his night stick swinging, and a look as if they'd carved him out of the concrete.

Good cop, Ryan, but —— Twenty-six years in the job, fifteen on the same beat. He was really an old-timer.

Joe shook his head, and his eyes traveled appraisingly over Ryan's back. He was shorter than Joe and thicker through, and his shoulders had the settled slope that came from the endless standing and walking, walking and standing.

Joe's own wide shoulders straightened a little more. His uniform, when he got it, wouldn't show that shapeless wrinkle across the back or the bulge of gun against hip under the tunic.

Twenty-six years on post, and never moving up. Not for him, thank you. Smart cops got promoted, and Joe Mason was going to be a smart cop. Spare-time study, and the sergeants' list in five years. More study, more up. He had it planned, knew where he was heading.

He said, "Evening, sir," and saluted.

Ryan turned around. "Hello, son. I've been waiting for you."

"Anything doing?" Joe tried to make his voice sound crisp and respectful at the same time.

"Quieter'n a wake."

"It's a quiet post, isn't it?"

"I s'pose." Ryan gave his tunic a tug down, and the buttons strained a little. "All set?"

"Yes, sir." He matched his step to Ryan's, which was heavy and not so long as his own. His gun nudged his hip, and he could feel the square corners of his memo book in his back pocket. Everything regulation had sharp edges.

A youngish man, rather bald, in a belted gray topcoat, passed them, raised a friendly hand, then stopped. "Evening, Tom. How's the family?"

Ryan's square Irish-eyed face warmed into creases. "Can't complain," he said.

"Good. By the way, I got my watch back."

"I figured you would, sir."

The man smiled faintly. "Glory of the Department, h'mm? Well, I don't ask questions."

Ryan sounded sad. "It only means they picked up the dip,

sir. You gotta watch yourself on a crowded subway, any day."

"H'mm. You're the crime-prevention committee, Tom, not me." He glanced sharply at Joe. "What's this? A new one?"

Joe didn't like being an indefinite pronoun. He said, "Police Academy," rather stiffly.

The man nodded and said, "So you're going to be a flatfoot. Well, good luck, youngster." He sketched a goodbye and went on down the street.

There was a short silence, then Joe said, "Likes himself, doesn't he?"

Ryan grunted. "You'll get called worse things than flatfoot, son."

"I don't have to like it."

"Well ——"

The monosyllable sounded as if maybe you had to like what you got. Joe wasn't having any, but after a minute his fists uncurled. He wouldn't be pounding a beat any longer than he could help. He wasn't going to be another Ryan.

After a while, making conversation, Joe said, "How big is your family, sir?"

Ryan left him for a moment, crossed to a dark store entrance and checked the lock before he answered. "My wife and two boys. . . . You got to try doors like that one. I've known Sol Zivic not even to snap the lock." He stood back on the sidewalk and looked the store over carefully. The lettering on the window said "Novelties and Toys." The stuff in the window was junk.

Joe shrugged impatiently. Trying doors was old stuff; they pounded it into you at the Academy.

Ryan's face warmed up again. "My oldest kid's in college."

"What one?"

"N.Y.U."

Joe looked interested. "That's where I went."

"You a college man?" Ryan gazed at him respectfully.

"That's nice. Book study'll be coming easy to you then."

"Yep."

Ryan sighed. "I took the sergeants' exam twice, but I never made the list. You've gotta have a head. I've got one of those thick skulls that have to study out loud. I used to go down cellar nights and read to the furnace, but neither of us learned much." He turned his head quickly toward the line of flats on their left. Someone had thrown a first-floor window up, and Ryan caught the sound before Joe did.

A frizzled head came out of the square of light, and a soprano whine said, "Mr. Ryan? Is that you, Mr. Ryan?"

Ryan said it was, and moved to the window. Joe gave the dame a quick once-over. She was too old and scrawny for that much paint, and her thin, purplish-tipped fingers kept clawing at the grimy lace top of her wrapper, pushing it up in a kind of caricature of modesty.

Ryan touched his visor. "Can I do something for you, Mrs. Lemmon?"

For Pete's sake. "Can I do something for you, Mrs. Lemmon?" Joe scowled. She wanted company, an old hag like that.

She leaned confidentially over the sill, her bony elbows sticking out of sleazy baby-blue rayon. "I've been watching for you, Mr. Ryan. I'm worrying. I read the papers and I can't sleep nights and I worry. It's this burglar that I've been reading about. Creeping in and taking things from decent people." She shivered elaborately. "I don't sleep."

Ryan rubbed his jaw thoughtfully. Joe's shoulders twitched. Cripes! The guy she was bawling about worked the west side, just a medium smart operator that a cub reporter had played up. *Tell her to pull a pillow over her head, Officer Ryan.*

Ryan said mildly. "I don't think he's in this district, ma'am, but we're keeping our eyes open. He'll be picked up."

Her voice turned doubtful, then submissive. "Well, if I know you're watching——"

"That's what I'm here for, ma'am. I wouldn't worry if I was you."

She smiled suddenly. Her teeth were yellow under the thin red line of lipstick. "Well, I wanted you to know," she said. "I'm all alone." She reached up to pull the window down, and Joe could see her thin claws scrabbling at the sash.

He waited till it was closed tight, and then he looked at Ryan and said, "Cranks!" explosively.

Ryan shook his head slowly. "Maybe. She's getting old. And she lost her son in Korea. He was growing up kind of mean, but he was her boy." His jaw jutted a little. "They'd just moved onto the block when I got this post. That was fifteen years ago, and she wasn't a bad-looking woman. Happy, kind of. She had a husband, then, and a kid. People go to seed, and a cop stands around and watches it happen. You can't do much." He glanced at his watch, crossed to the signal box and opened it up to call the precinct.

Joe leaned against a lamppost, watching idly and thinking that, in those fifteen years, Ryan had gone a little to seed himself. He wondered what the patrolman had looked like when he'd first come into the Department. Not so thick in the middle, hair a good deal darker, more snap in his walk. Probably a pretty good figure of a cop then. Joe squared his shoulders. The physical exam they gave you now was really rugged; nothing less than perfection pleased the Police Surgeons. He felt a pleasant superiority, and began humming about the Eddystone light again.

Ryan hung up and grinned at him. "The lieut wants to know how you're doing. I didn't tell him what you're singing about."

Joe stopped humming. "I only know a couple of bars. I don't even know where I got it from."

"Art Slezak, probably. Safety man. He knows about twenty verses."

"Oh. How's it go?"

Ryan's grin spread. "You're too young to know." He looked down the street, and Joe's eyes followed his. It was long and dark and quiet. Manhattan, dead and laid out. They turned toward the river, and it got progressively darker. A warehouse showed a small light at one window. A sign swayed and creaked in a puff of wind. A taffy cat prowled past, then sat on a grating to watch them coldly, its eyes metallic.

Ryan said, "Getting cooler. We're likely to——" He broke off as a car turned the corner. Ryan stepped out into the street with a hand held up and signaled the driver to the curb. The driver was not pleased and he stuck his head out of the window like an exasperated turtle. "Now, what the hell have I done?" he wanted to know.

"One of your headlights isn't working." Ryan put a foot on the running board. "And the other's pretty dim. You'll have to get that fixed, sir. It isn't safe driving." Joe noticed that his hand was convenient to his gun, and he stiffened a little, wondering what Ryan knew that he didn't.

There was a low mutter from the driver, with the word "officious" somewhere in it. The patrolman's eyes got a little hard, and he walked around to the back of the car, took down the number and came front again. "There's a garage four blocks down and east two. It's called Charlie's."

The man's face flickered. "Friend of yours?"

Ryan said, "That'll do. You aren't knocking any kids down on my post."

"All right, officer. I'm sorry." He kicked the starter, and the motor coughed and caught. "Charlie's, huh?"

"Four down and two over. And go there direct before you take that crate anywhere else."

They looked at each other for a moment, then the man said, "All right, all right. I said I was sorry." He looked smaller than when he'd stopped. Joe felt a spasm of amusement.

Ryan came back to his side, grunting. "Ordinary citizen," he said.

Joe, remembering the hovering gun hand, said, "You think it was something else?"

"You don't take chances at night." Ryan paused. "If it's a hot car, they don't give a cop any breaks."

Joe felt a funny little thrill of regret. If it had been hot, there might have been a gun battle. He saw himself, tense and quick, reaching for his hip. He was handy with his gun, and it would look all right on the records. That was what made the high-ups notice you. Quick and smart and handy. A rookie too. He came back to earth, flushing a little. It was just that everything was so damn routine.

For a while, they walked without talking. Night had closed down, fitting tight, seeping into the dead-walled buildings, spreading over asphalt, dulling the edges of sound. The beat took them out of the warehouse district, back to people and lights, then away from them again and back once more. A bar and grill, with its jukebox squawking, got Ryan's quick check. The bartender greeted him like a longlost brother, leaning over the wet-ringed counter. "How's the kids?"

Ryan held up his hand, finger and thumb circled to an O.K. "Yours?"

"They ain't been hung yet." The man's voice was stuffed like a sofa pillow with his pride.

"Give 'em time. They're only young." Ryan jerked his thumb toward a corner. "Keep the lid on the noise, will you, Dan?"

"Sure thing." The bartender slid his bulk out from behind the counter. He was built like a pyramid; his shoulders were narrow, but his belt had given up trying.

Ryan nodded and backed out, satisfied. Joe sighed. Geez, it was dull. And this went on, night after night. He looked at Ryan curiously. "You know everybody on this beat?"

"I ought to." They turned again, walking the route. Ryan started to say something, changed his mind and then said it anyway. "I'm getting out."

Joe was startled. "You're what?"

"Getting out. I've put in my papers. Seven days more, and I turn in my shield."

Joe shrugged. Well, it was the sensible thing for Ryan to do. He wasn't getting anywhere, and he had his time in for his pension.

Ryan was talking slowly. "We can manage now," he said. "Tommy's working his way through college, and young Bud will be all right. You have to wait until the kids are on their own."

Joe nodded. But —— Nothing to show for it all. A living, and not too much of that. Twenty-six years added up to a lot of walking post. He felt a sort of contemptuous pity, and he said what he shouldn't have said. "You can get ahead in the Department."

Ryan's voice sounded a little stiff. "Sure. I guess you will, all right."

"You can say that again." He rubbed his hands together and grinned. "I'm going to be right up with the other head-hunters, once I make the sergeants' list." He thought of Ryan sitting there, lonely, with the furnace and studying the Manual, the Rules and Regulations, the city ordinances, the state criminal code. Reading them out loud to a banked fire, dogged and stubborn, and after twenty-six years still whacking his feet down on the pavement. Only, why be sorry for him? Some men got ahead in the world and did things. Some men didn't.

Joe said, "Well, it's been a living for you, I suppose. It's a job."

"It's my job."

Then they both stopped. A kid was galloping down the street toward them, a pasty-faced, bony little squirt with his freckles popping from excitement. He skittered to a stop in front of them.

"Mister, hey!" His ears were flapping with importance. "They's a fight, mister, they's a fight! Ma sent me after you! They're yellin' somep'n beautiful!"

Ryan's hand came down, quiet and steady on the scrawny little shoulder. "Who's fighting, Jimmy?"

"The Olsons again. Boy, c'n he swear!" He wriggled all over like a puppy.

"All right, kid. Beat it back to your ma. We'll take over." Ryan didn't ask where the Olsons lived. He jerked his head toward Joe and started back the way they'd come. He didn't seem to be moving fast, but Joe almost lost him when he turned into a doorway, muttering. "Holy saints," said Ryan, "fifth floor. Why can't the ground floors ever fight?"

By the time they got to the third landing, they didn't need to be told there was a battle on. There was enough yelling for Madison Square Garden on a big night.

On the fifth floor you could sort out the shouting. There was a man roaring like a bull. A foreign language, but good ripe cursing sounded the same in any nationality. And there was a woman's voice, thin and high and scared and yelping something over and over and over, like a phonograph record with a stuck needle.

Ryan put his shoulder against the door panel and turned the knob. The door squawked on its hinges and opened, giving them a view of the room. The woman was backed up against the wall with a chair held in front of her like a shield. She was a shapeless, sagging thing, and her mousy hair had come out of its bun in back and was sticking out straight like a tail. She had a bright red mark high on one cheekbone, and when she saw a blue uniform come through the door, she began to yell.

"You arrest him, officer!" she screamed. "He hit me! You arrest him quick!" And then she began to cry.

Joe looked away hastily, and at the man. He was big and beefy, and he stood there with his face purple and his big hands lumped into fists. If he turned on them, there'd be real trouble, but so far, he didn't even seem to know there was anyone else in the room. You could see and smell the red haze of liquor that kept him glaring at her and bellowing and shaking all over.

Joe rubbed his hands down along his hips, feeling sweat on the palms. He tried to figure out quick what he'd do if this was his beat and he was alone on it. At a desk in the Academy, the answer would have been right there on his tongue, quick and accurate. Only this was different, thinking on your feet. He suddenly realized that he didn't know what the score was, and he looked at Ryan helplessly.

Ryan was back of the man, his hands out, but not touching anything. If the drunk made a quick move, his elbows would be pinned back and, for all his bigness, he couldn't fight.

Ryan said, "What'd he hit you with, Mrs. Olson?"

Joe pulled in his breath, remembering. He'd hit her. It was simple assault, and on simple assault you could make a summary arrest. They'd book the big hulk at the station house and lock him up overnight to cool off. Or —— Oh, geez, could you always arrest on simple assault? His mind stumbled back into the intricacies of laws and ordinances.

"What'd he hit you with?" Ryan said again, not moving.

Her voice was scratchy and shrill, and the tears kept on rolling down her face, which was getting puffy. "It was his fist. He hit me with his fist. What you think he hit me with? You arrest him, and you lock him up! Go on! Arrest him!" She was getting hysterical.

Ryan shook his head. "He didn't hit you with a dangerous weapon. But you can make the arrest yourself if you want to, as a private citizen, and I'll take him in." He paused. "Only then you'll have to come along to the station house and make the complaint, and be in court tomorrow morning."

She stared at him, gulping tears. "Me?"

"Yeah. He——No, you don't!" Ryan moved quick.

A great, gathering roar had broken suddenly from the man's thick throat, and he plunged forward. Ryan's waiting hands clamped mercilessly on his elbows, dragging them backwards, and at the same moment he shoved his knee forward behind the drunk's knee. The big hulk staggered, then sagged. Joe stepped in and caught him.

Ryan, not breathing extra hard, said again, "You want to make the arrest, Mrs. Olson?"

Her laugh was a kind of shrill yelp. "Me? My own husband? What do you think you coppers are for? I gotta arrest my own man?"

"That's right, ma'am." Ryan looked down at her own man. He was just a limp suit of clothes on the floor now. Over the sledge-hammer stuff, and into the sniveling stage. Joe felt a crawling disgust. Drunks!

There was a moment when nobody did anything. Then all of a sudden Mrs. Olson came out of her corner, darting like a cat, and flopped down on her knees alongside her husband's slack body. Her horrible little mews of pity were like a cat, too, and the way her voice suddenly spat out at Ryan.

"You big bum!" she said.

Ryan sighed, looked at Joe and shrugged his shoulders. "They're all right now," he said. "Help me get him on the bed, Joe."

"Yes, sir." Joe took his feet.

Ryan stooped, shouldering the woman out of his way, and slid his hands under the dragging shoulders. They lifted him and dropped him down easy, and the bedsprings cussed them for his dead weight. His woman didn't get up. She slid along on her knees to the side of the bed, got her arm under his neck and started crooning at him.

Ryan took a look around the room, shook his head and

crooked his thumb at Joe. "Okay. We can't do nothing here now." He led the way out of the room, shutting the door carefully behind him. On the last landing, he turned and said, "She'll be all right. There aren't any kids."

Joe said something back in his throat. He didn't feel good any more, the way he had coming up the stairs. There was a kind of tearing pity inside him, and he didn't want to talk.

They went out on the street, both silent. Ryan dragged out his memo book and began to enter the incident. Joe hitched his belt up and stared into space. After a moment, he realized Ryan had put his book back and was looking at him. He was smiling a little. He said, "Women are funny."

Joe nodded.

"I remember one arrest I made," Ryan said. "There were kids in the flat and the guy had a knife. His wife threw a pail of slops at me, and I scraped off potato peels all the way to the station house." He clapped his hand against his hip pocket where he'd put the memo book. "A pail of slops over a man makes him feel thoughtful."

Joe nodded again. Ryan started up the street, and Joe fell into step, his eyes fixed on his shoes. At the corner, they met the radio car going its rounds. The sergeant stuck his head out the window and bawled cheerfully at Ryan, and the young cop who was driving peered over the sergeant's shoulder and waved an amiable paw.

"Everything okay?"

"Sure."

The sergeant took in Joe. "How you doing, kid?"

Joe said doubtfully, "All right, I guess."

The young cop said hopefully, "Bet your feet hurt," and put the car in low gear. It pulled away and left them standing, watching its tail light.

Ryan said suddenly, "That sergeant. He used to have the next post. Everything happened to him. He used to claim I brushed the crooks off my post and onto his." He made a pleased reminiscent sound deep in his throat.

Joe, who had noticed the gleam of enamel and a bronze star against the uniform blue, nodded. "He got a Commendation, huh?"

"Yeah. He's a good cop."

Ryan said it like it meant something. It did, of course. Commendations counted for a guy on his record—handy things to have, only you had to be in the right place at the right time. They gave those little bars for personal bravery, and, according to the Academy, bravery was something a cop was supposed to carry around with him in his pants pocket, like his memo book or his summonses.

They were back at the river again, and everything was as peaceful and dark as a coal bin. Times Square would just be coming awake. Columbus Circle would be full of voices. Lights on Flatbush Avenue and the Grand Concourse would be cheering the sky up. Down here the sky wasn't interested in anybody.

Ryan stopped suddenly, his fingers digging into Joe's arm. He was staring up at a building. Joe stared too, but there wasn't anything to see. It was pitch dark, like the rest of the street.

Ryan said softly, "No lights."

It didn't make sense. There weren't supposed to be lights. And then he remembered. On the last round there had been one, a small yellow eye glaring out at the street. He looked sideways at Ryan, and a cold finger of anticipation ran down his spine.

He said softly, "What do they keep in there?"

"Furs, mostly. Some secondhand stuff." Ryan's voice was hard. "Guy's too tight to put in a decent alarm system. Says what does he pay the city for? Could be the light's burned out."

Joe nodded, looking down the street. "There's no car waiting."

"They could enter from the other side. The building runs through to the next post." He crossed the street, and Joe went with him, shoulders touching. Ryan bent and examined the lock, frowned and shook his head. Not broken. He looked up at the window again, at the light that wasn't there.

"I'll get hell from the owner if I enter and there's nothing wrong," he said. "It means busting a window." He pulled off his coat. "Well."

He did a neat job. The coat laid against the window, deadening sound, and a tap of his night stick in the right place. The pane gave silently, and Ryan's hand reached through to release the catch. Wood snarled against wood as he pushed the sash up.

Ryan's shoulders blacked the window out as he heaved his heavy frame through. Joe slid in after him. If the street had been dead, the building was embalmed. Its silence and emptiness were like a blow in the face. Ryan's gun was out and in his hand. Joe eased his own out of its holster.

Ryan's voice, close to Joe's ear, said, "Better not use flashlights until we know what's up. Stay behind me."

Joe nodded, and then thought it was a silly thing to have done, when he couldn't even see his own hand in front of his face. He whispered, "Okay," and tightened his fingers around the grip of his gun.

They groped their way slowly toward the back of the yawningly empty room, and gradually their eyes got accustomed to the darkness, so that the walls came forward and the ceiling was a lid. There was an elevator shaft at the back, and near it a narrow flight of stairs, the treads hollowed with wear.

They went up slowly, guiding their way along the railing, and the darkness moved and stalked them. At the top, Ryan turned, gazing around him. There wasn't anything to see. More darkness, more stairs. Like he'd said, the light had probably burned itself out. Joe drew air into his lungs, and relief.

That was when the sound came from overhead. Not much of a sound—a heavy dragging, like a box being pulled across bare floor boards.

"Ah-h-h-h." That was Ryan, a soft explosion of held breath. He moved forward soundlessly along the uneven floor, then on up the stairs, his gun arm extended and lying across the railing, sliding ahead of him like a rifle, his fingers curved around the grip, the trigger not touched.

Joe's heart began to hammer. This was it, this was the real thing. He heard Ryan's voice, so soft that it was only words laid against air. "Move easy, son."

Joe moved easy, holding himself like glass. Up ahead was silence and the dark. Maybe that dragging sound hadn't been anything. Maybe it was rats.

Ryan stopped moving.

It wasn't rats. Just ahead, from under a door that didn't fit, where the darkness should have padded and prowled alone, there was a faint confirming wedge of light. Rats didn't pull electric switches.

Joe waited, hearing his own heart. He wasn't scared. He was just waiting to see what Ryan would do. Ryan moved forward, and Joe moved again with him. His foot, for all he had put it down so carefully, hit something. A loose board. There was a sharp crack of sound, magnified in silence. Joe stopped with his other foot midway between step and step.

In the closed room, someone moved. The wedge of light under the door was blotted out suddenly. Behind the panels, something lay and waited. Whatever was inside the room wasn't sure, with only the sound of danger to judge from, just the crack of a loose board. They'd have guns, whoever they were. They'd have guns. Joe looked at Ryan's back, and it was like granite. He had a sudden crazy desire to yell at him. *Get out of it, cop, get out of it. You've only got seven more days on the Force, and there's guns on the other side of that door. Get out!*

Fear caught him suddenly, its cold hand at his throat closing off his breath. A knot of ice in his stomach, and hands shaking on the butt of his gun. What was Ryan thinking, standing there so near that Joe only had to reach out a hand to touch him? *Flatfoot. What are you thinking, flatfoot, with guns waiting for you on the other side of a closed door? You thinking about your kids and your wife, about that shield you're going to turn in so soon?*

Ryan's voice, cold and hard and loud. Loud enough to kill the creeping silence. "All right, in there!" Ryan's voice, ordering. "Come out with your hands up! You're covered!"

For a second there wasn't any sound except Joe's own slow and suffocating breath. Then there was movement, quick and panting. A window thrown up. Ryan's voice again, "Fire-escape!" and then Ryan's big body charging the door.

He had one second's advantage, the advantage of eyes already accustomed to the dark. His gun roared, and the silence fell apart, crashing around them into tumbling bricks of sound. There were two men at the window, and they fell back as the flash of powder cut off their escape. One of them cursed, and another shot answered Ryan's.

A hand on Joe's shoulder threw him to the floor and safety. Packing boxes for shields. There were boxes everywhere. Ryan was flat beside him now, and the crooks' only exit was cut off. *Find them somehow in the crawling darkness. Officer, make an arrest.*

Joe felt an arm around his shoulder and his head drawn down. He could barely hear the patrolman's whisper, "Draw their fire, kid. I'm going after them from behind." He moved away from Joe, his bigness incredibly silent.

Make your arrest, officer. Don't think about your family. Don't remember safety, only a week away. You're keeping a town safe for people to sleep in. You're keeping New York peaceful at night.

From across the room, a gun spat pale flame, dividing and tracing the darkness. Joe steadied his revolver with the palm of his left hand under his right one. He pulled the trigger, heard the heavy smash of a bullet going into wood and a hoarse voice cursing.

He lay there flat in the dark and waited, then threw another slug in the space between window and box pile. Four more shots in his gun, and twelve cartridges in his belt. The return of fire came from exactly the same place. Joe's breath whistled between his set teeth. That could mean there was only one gun between the two of them.

He strained to listen. Somewhere in that room, creeping along the wall, solid and doing his job, was Ryan. Would they hear him, those two unseen men crouched behind shelter? Would that invisible gun be turned on a good cop, who wasn't a good cop to them, but a natural enemy and someone to plant a bullet in?

Hate coiled inside Joe, hate that he couldn't do anything about except try to keep his gun hand steady. Hate that killed the sick fear he had for himself. He was only scared now for Ryan. Ryan, that good cop, edging forward into gunfire, taking safety where he could find it behind the thin protection of wood and, where he couldn't find it, going ahead anyhow. They called it doing your duty. A nice easy, tidy phrase, and the tax-payers paid you for it. Twenty-six years of doing your duty, and at the end of it the privilege of crawling forward under gunfire.

There was a faint sound from the wall where Ryan was. Joe pulled the trigger of his gun again as fast as his finger could crook around it, but the shot that came back wasn't aimed at him. It was aimed at the wall. Joe's shoulders came up convulsively and he closed his eyes, wincing against the desperate fear that struck deep and hard inside him. *Don't let them. Don't let them.*

There wasn't any sound. Had that last shot got Ryan? He fired again, a prayer riding the bullet.

There was a kind of sobbing grunt from behind one of the

boxes. Joe moistened his lips, and his hand went to his belt, feeling for the reassurance of extra cartridges. Two more shots in his gun. He could reload in the dark in twenty seconds. You learned that in the Academy. You learned everything in the Academy, except the one thing that no one could teach you. The thing that was helping Ryan crawl along that wall now, when the odds were against him.

He squeezed the trigger again. The answer wasn't for him; it was aimed for wherever Ryan was. The other gun was sure, now that the pattern of attack had broken, that danger was coming closer and closer in the dark. The roof of Joe's mouth was like sandpaper. He fired the last shot in his gun, then grabbed for his belt.

From across the room, there was a sharp click. The click of a firing pin striking an empty cartridge. Joe stopped, his hand hovering. Everything stopped. The room and the darkness and all movement. His mouth was trembling, and he clamped his lower lip between his teeth. He prayed.

A gun roared in explosion. There was a yelp of sound, and then Ryan's voice with a command to reach for the ceiling.

Joe leaped to his feet and sprinted across the room, wild to get to Ryan's side. Behind the defense of boxes, there was one guy sprawled on the floor, and another at Ryan's throat. Joe dived for his legs. Ryan's fist came up and landed on the point of a jaw. The man went down without a sound.

"Okay," said Ryan, his voice satisfied.

There was a moment of flat silence. Then Ryan said, "Get to the light switch, will you, Joe?"

Joe obeyed, and the room leaped into focus. There were two guys on the floor, and two standing. The packing boxes were just packing boxes. Ryan and Joe looked at each other, and they both said the same thing at the same time. "You all right?"

Then Ryan said, "Get outside, Joe, and call the station house. We'll need the wagon."

Joe nodded, but for a moment he just stood there, not moving. He wanted to say something. He didn't know what he wanted to say.

Ryan reached out and touched Joe's shoulder. "You did all right, kid. Beat it now and call the lieutenant."

Joe nodded again, then he turned and went out the door and down the stairs. His heartbeat was back to normal, and his shoulders felt broad again under the gray shirt. One of these days, soon, he'd be exchanging this uniform for the blue one. But he wasn't thinking any more about how good it would look on him. He was just hoping, rather humbly, that he would do it credit.

THE BLUE CUP

THE apartment was beautiful. If she hadn't been so tired, Jessie would have done what she used to do when she came to a new place to work. She'd have gone around, touching things gently with the tip of a finger, pretending that the ones she liked best belonged to her.

She didn't have time for that now. Mrs. Mitchell had gone off in a hurry, quick and polite, but very firm in her directions and obviously not pleased at having to leave the new cleaning woman alone among her things. She'd meant to be there to supervise, and when she said, "Jessie, I've been called out. If I could have reached you by phone, I'd have asked you to come tomorrow," you could see what she was thinking. She was thinking that it would have been better to get someone through a regular agency.

Still, the references had been all right, except that they were nearly two years old now, and, besides, she cost less than anyone an agency would send. That probably helped.

Mrs. Mitchell had stood there this morning, pulling on her gloves and looking around the room. "I'll get back about three," she said. "You'll find enough for lunch in the refrigerator." She looked inside her bag and then closed it with a snap. "I've told the doorman you're here—he might look in. In case you need anything," she added.

Jessie understood. The doorman would be checking up on her. That was all right. You couldn't blame Mrs. Mitchell, who owned all these pretty things. She said, "Yes, ma'am," and Mrs. Mitchell went out, looking attractive in her nice black suit with the soft fur falling off one shoulder. The little gold mirror on the satin-striped wall of the foyer shut its face on the closing door.

After a minute, Jessie went over and stared into its cool surface. She thought, *I look stringy,* and she pushed her hair back and then turned away, because what a mirror told her didn't matter any more, and maybe it was never going to matter again. So long as her face and the old print dress looked clean and respectable.

She drew in her breath, and the corners of her mouth folded up tight and she felt steadier. Folding her lips like that pinched up her face, but the weight she'd lost in the hospital had done that anyway, and tight lips kept a person's chin steady.

The kitchen was the best place to start. There were the breakfast dishes to be done and the "few little things" that Mrs. Mitchell had left to be rinsed out and ironed, the lingerie and blouses.

If you worked through an agency, you weren't expected to do extras and you got paid better. But she'd tried one place and it had scared her, making her feel that she might never get a job at all, especially when the lady who did the interviewing had glanced at her sharply through steel-rimmed glasses and said, "You don't look very strong." Jessie had shaken her head and said she was very strong really, just thin, and that she didn't mind hard work, but that was all she'd said, and, when the lady had started asking more questions, she'd dried up completely. The references being old ones hadn't helped, and it was natural they'd want her to fill in the blank two years. Only she didn't want to, and maybe that hadn't sounded so good.

They had said they would let her know if anything turned up, but Jessie had known that nothing would, and the next day she'd answered Mrs. Mitchell's ad and she'd been lucky. From now on, what she had to do was to go on being lucky, and maybe this job would lead to others, and Mrs. Mitchell would give her a good reference.

That was the only thing that mattered now—some kind of steady work. Then she could get a decent room to live in and take Dorothy out of the Shelter. It would still mean working out all day, but there were day nurseries and she could have the baby with her nights. For all they were so kind at the Shelter, and Dorothy had grown fat and learned to giggle, a mother ought to have her baby with her and take care of it herself.

It was one thing Jessie had always been sure of—a family should keep together, close and safe, giving its own warmth, no matter what happened.

She couldn't see, even now, how Dave could have walked out on the two of them. Emptying his pockets onto the dresser, taking only a couple of dollars to start him off to nowhere, holding on tight even then to the idea that he was taking care of them a little, he had written the only letter she had ever had from him. He had written that they would be better off without him.

If she hadn't cried so that last night he came home, maybe he'd have stayed. If she'd told him that it didn't matter, losing another job, that they'd make out. If she'd been kind instead of right. But he'd lost the job again because of the quick little drinks he'd been taking, and his answer to that had been more drinks.

She should have made him black coffee, taken his shoes off, helped him lie back against the pillow, but instead she'd cried. He'd stood looking down at her, sitting there on the edge of the bed, until at last he'd said, "Don't, Jess. Jess, don't," and put his hand on her shoulder.

He was her husband that she loved and, if she'd helped him then, he might have stayed. But she hadn't helped him. She had lain down on the bed and pulled the blanket up over her. A long time later she'd slept as if she'd been drugged, and when she finally woke, there was his letter, and he was gone.

She hadn't cried then, and she hadn't cried since. The tears had dried up.

She stood now, with her hands on Mrs. Mitchell's kitchen sink, and, after a while, the unremembering parts of her mind came together and reminded her of the dishes to be done, the fluffy pastel things to be washed and ironed and the apartment to be cleaned. If only she wasn't so bone-tired all the time; if only she could make herself believe it was worthwhile going on, that the days ahead held any kind of promise.

Jessie reached out her hand and jerked on the faucet, and the water, running so hot, splashed and scalded her wrist. She shook off the clinging drops and reached for a dish towel. Thinking about Dave wouldn't bring him back.

It was a good thing the water was so hot, because the dishes almost dried themselves, and now she would have to hurry. Two years ago, when she'd worked out regularly in different homes, her ladies had praised her for her quickness. Even when she was falling in love with Dave, even when she was bemused like a bee in honey, her hands had been alive and quick. Not like they were now.

She put the dishes away carefully, trying to find the right

place for each one to go, and then she ran warm water into the laundry tub next to the sink. The right kind of soap flakes didn't seem to be in the kitchen cupboard, and she went into the bathroom and found them there in a green-and-white box. The bathroom had green mermaids and little dolphins on the walls, and there were dolphins on the shower curtains.

Back in the kitchen, she remembered how Dave had always talked about giving her pretty things someday and how luxuriously she had listened to him. Maybe that was what had been wrong; maybe he'd carried to work every day the picture of the two dingy rooms they lived in, alongside the bright rooms they talked about. Maybe he'd felt restless and hungry because he couldn't give them more, and the little drinks had dulled it.

The soap flakes foamed up in tiny iridescent bubbles of light. There was gold in them, and blue and green—peacock colors, prettier than dolphins and mermaids. Soap was cheap. She could have told Dave she thought soap bubbles were prettier than anything else. If he was back now, she could tell him that.

She dropped the pieces of lingerie one by one into the tub, and they floated on the surface like clouds, filling slowly with water. The lacy parts sagged first, and the blue and the pink and the honey colors billowed up above the suds before they filled too and sank. She put her hands down deep among them and they were soft and lovely to feel, but not any softer or lovelier than Dorothy's hair with the little duck tails behind.

If she'd told Dave that? If he hadn't thought they should have more money than he could make?

A man couldn't do a trucking job and keep taking quick drinks. You couldn't blame his boss for not trusting him, for not even giving him a second chance. The person to give Dave a second chance was his wife. She shouldn't have cried that night. She should have loved him.

She squeeezed the soft fabrics out, holding them above the water. Her wrists felt heavy, and her back ached in a spasm of warning that it would ache more if she kept on bending over.

The doctor had told her not to go back to work too **soon,** knowing perfectly well that she didn't have any choice. The sickness had put her so far behind and left her so listless. She'd fought it off too long, and that hadn't helped. The little sewing job that she had been doing, because it was the only kind of work she could get to do at home, had suddenly become great and insurmountable. She could remember her needle moving through silk as if it had been a nail through canvas, and she had had a wild thought that she was making a sail for a boat to fly before the wind, and then she must have fallen forward with her head on the pile of clothes, because that was the way they had found her. A neighbor had heard Dorothy crying.

When the clothes were rinsed, she squeezed them as dry as she could and shook them out. While they were drying, she could start cleaning the apartment.

Trying to move faster, she hung some of the things over the towel rack and then took the others into the bathroom. They'd dry quicker than she could clean, and the blouses ought to be ironed damp. If she could remember they were hanging there, she could save having to sprinkle them.

The vacuum cleaner would probably be in the hall closet where most ladies kept them. She found it there, pushed way in against the wall, and then started back to the kitchen to get a mop.

It was on her way back that she saw the cup.

It stood on a hanging wall bracket, along with a Dresden shepherdess and a white china cat playing with a ball. The cup was rather small, with a deep saucer and a flared rim. The gold handle sprang delicately from its side with a gleam like luster, but it was the color of the cup that held Jessie. The edge was so blue it was midnight, and from that first rich deep streak of sky the colors spread, sensuous and delicate, paling to cobalt, to delft, to the sunny blue that spring clouds ride against, and finally, at the very bottom, to a blue so soft that it was almost no color at all but the faintest milky white.

She drew in her breath like a child. She shouldn't touch it, but to hold the sky in your own two hands. . . .

She reached out and picked it up, the saucer in her left hand and the cup in her right, and then she set the cup on the saucer and, holding it like a bird, she turned it, ever so little, just by moving her wrists. The colors glowed in the light from the window. It was such a lovely thing.

Behind her the telephone rang.

The sudden and mechanical ring, so close, startled her, and the cup and saucer jumped in her hands. She clutched at air, trying to save them both, but she was too late. They struck the floor, missing the safety of the carpet by inches, and broke together, the cup slivering out into petals of china like an opening flower.

The phone rang again.

Jessie said, "Oh, please," staring down at the pieces of sky, begging the fragile vulnerable pieces to come together, begging the thing not to have happened. The colors glowed as richly as when the cup was whole.

After a long moment, she turned away from it, answering the summons of the bell. It was a lady wanting Mrs. Mitchell, a lady with a fresh breathless voice, and Jessie took down the name and telephone number, closing her mind to the broken cup, shaping each letter as she wrote it on the pad with a painful carefulness.

When she hung up, it was a full minute before she turned around. The childish trick of a tired mind almost persuaded her that nothing had really happened, that the cup would be back in its place, translucent as a jewel.

Damage didn't undo itself. Time didn't turn backward.

She knelt down on the carpet and picked up the largest piece of china. It lay on the palm of her hand like a sapphire, like blue velvet, like a butterfly's wing. She began to cry. All the tears that hadn't come when Dave left her, or later when she lay in the hospital bed, came now, as hopeless and steady as rain on dead leaves.

Any hope she had let herself have lay smashed with the cup. The job with Mrs. Mitchell had been the only promise she'd had. It would have led her to other jobs, the money from them would have meant having Dorothy back.

Fear began to swell inside her. It could be even worse than just losing the job. The cup might be valuable, and Mrs. Mitchell would make her pay for it somehow. There were ways, in court, that a person could get a judgment against another person. She would go on paying for it forever, never getting free, just because of one moment of loving something beautiful, one moment of being careless.

Suddenly, and with a terrible desolation, she wanted Dave. He wouldn't have blamed her. He would have just let her hold onto him until she got over being frightened, and then he would have worked something out. There must be a way, some kind of second chance.

When the doorbell rang, it was like having the silence in the room slit up with a knife. It couldn't be Mrs. Mitchell back so early. Maybe it was the doorman who was supposed to come around and check up on her. If she didn't answer, he would know something was wrong, perhaps use a passkey and find her standing there beside the broken pieces.

The bell rang again. She scooped the bits together hastily and pushed them back of a vase, then wiped her hands down the sides of her dress as if they were soiled and went to the door, opening it a crack. A tall, bored-looking boy shoved a small package at her.

"Mitchell?"

She nodded. He plucked a pencil from behind his ear. "Sign f'r it."

Her hands were shaking a little. She hoped he wouldn't notice, and she signed, took the package and stepped back, closing the door. She could hear him going down the hall, whistling.

She put the package down on the table, next to the broken china. That was all it was now, just broken china, not a cup any more. If the pieces would only disappear completely, as if they had never been. . . .

She stood staring at them. Suppose they did disappear? Suppose she wrapped them up in paper and took them away with her? Mrs. Mitchell might not notice right away that the cup was missing, or notice it too late to connect it with her cleaning woman. There would be other people in the apartment, and she'd never know which one had taken it.

The hope fell apart. A pretty thing like that cup—its owner would notice if it was gone. There would be questions right away, and only one person had been in the apartment. Even the boy with the package had stayed outside, just on the threshold.

Jessie drew in her breath. The boy.

What if she said the boy had been alone in the living room for a moment while she went to look for something? Her mind darted like a frightened animal. There had to be some reason why she would have left him alone in the room, and for a moment she couldn't think of one. Then she remembered the pencil.

That would do. She had signed for the package, and she could pretend the boy hadn't had a pencil. Suppose she'd had to go back to the bedroom to find one?

The pencil next to the telephone lay there in full sight, beside the leather-covered pad. She went over and picked it up. It could easily have been somewhere else when the boy came. She could say that Mrs. Fields had phoned later on. Her mind began to construct her answers carefully. First, she had looked for a pencil on the telephone table, and it hadn't been there and she had gone into the bedroom, leaving the boy alone.

Holding the pencil that was going to save her job for her, she walked to the bedroom and stood on the soft gray rug, looking around her. It was a lovely room, done in rose and gray, and something about it hardened inside her the feeling that she was doing what she had a right to do. It wasn't fair that the Mitchells should have all this luxury, and she have nothing. Less than nothing now.

There was a desk in the corner with dark satiny wood, and on the desk was a silver pencil. She put the pencil she had been carrying into the pocket of her dress. She would take it away with her, along with the bits of china. Half frightened and half excited, she took the silver pencil back into the living room and laid it beside the pad. This was now the pencil she had used to sign for the package.

She checked through everything in her mind with passionate carefulness. The boy had been alone in the room while she was looking for the pencil. She had come back, signed for the package, put the pencil down by the telephone and used it later when Mrs. Fields called. No, she hadn't noticed the cup at any time. No, she hadn't especially noticed what the boy looked like.

Dismay stabbed at her. Suppose they traced the boy and he got into trouble? She picked up the package and looked it over carefully. All it told her was that it came from one of the largest department stores in the city, but that was enough. The store must make dozens, hundreds, of deliveries every day. She wouldn't have to give the exact time that the boy had come. Or, better yet, why not take the package away with her, along with the china and the pencil? She could say that both boy and package had disappeared together, and the Mitchells would assume the package had just been an excuse for getting entry to the apartment. Things like that happened all the time.

Later she could mail the package back to the store, and they would send it out again, taking for granted that some minor mistake had been made in the delivery. That way, the boy wouldn't be involved at all. She wouldn't even describe him as a boy. He could be a little short man, wearing a hat. It would be so obvious to everyone what had happened to the cup, and no one the worse for it. She would keep her job, the Mitchells would get their package a few days late and the cup would just have disappeared.

Her story was clear now, all the loose threads tied up. She found a piece of brown paper in the kitchen and wrapped the package, the pencil and the china bits together. It didn't even make a very large bundle, and she could take it out under her coat. After thinking about it for a moment, she went and got her coat out of the closet and put it on the kitchen chair, bringing the folds around to cover the bundle neatly.

It was going to be all right. She wouldn't plan any more. She would clean the apartment till it shone.

She got together all the things she needed—the vacuum cleaner, the mop, two nice clean dusting rags. There wasn't an inch of the apartment that escaped her. Her broom attacked the closet floors. She took shoes and boxes out and replaced them in strict rows. The chromium fixtures and the green tiles in the bathroom sparkled, and she was grateful that her back ached, because it gave her something to think about besides the cup.

Twice she rehearsed carefully in her mind what she would say, and it all sounded right. It wasn't until she was down on her knees in the kitchen, scrubbing the linoleum, that she found herself praying. It wasn't quite a prayer, just a voiceless asking. *Make it be all right*, she kept saying inside her. *Please make it be all right.*

The pain in her back worked up inside her head, and by the time she finished the floor she was so dizzy that she had to sit down. She stayed still for a while, and after a bit she began to make sense and realized she'd had nothing to eat. She went over to the refrigerator and opened its big white door. Inside was a salad, all ready on a plate, and two sandwiches in waxed paper and a bottle of milk right in front where she'd see it. That was nice of Mrs. Mitchell.

She took the things out and put them on the table and tried to eat, but the bread stuck in her throat, and finally all she had was some of the milk. She scraped the salad carefully off the plate and put it into the garbage container along with the sandwiches, pushing them way down to the bottom so that they wouldn't be noticed, and Mrs. Mitchell wouldn't worry.

That was different from hiding the cup. Hiding the food meant saving Mrs. Mitchell's feelings; hiding the cup meant saving herself. She pushed the thought way down in her mind. There were still the things to be ironed.

She got them off their racks. The blouses were too dry, and she had to sprinkle them again, and that took time, but she ironed them as if they were for a royal family. The microscopic tucks lay flat under the iron, and the pleating stood up in crisp fans. She hung the blouses on cushioned, scented hangers from Mrs. Mitchell's closet and laid the other pieces out on one of the beds. A professional couldn't have done them more carefully, and she hoped that Mrs. Mitchell would be pleased.

It was almost three when she finished the last piece and put the ironing board away, and she realized that the doorman hadn't come, after all. Perhaps Mrs. Mitchell had decided that the new cleaning woman could be trusted. She had a moment's warmth from the thought, and then she felt a stab that was like real pain because Mrs. Mitchell would be wrong, even though she wouldn't know about the cup.

It was no use thinking about that. She went around the apartment, going over it carefully to make sure that everything was done. She had polished the windows from inside and as much outside as she could reach; she had cleaned the mirrors and the ash trays, plumped up the sofa pillows, straightened the magazines in their rack. Her thoughts had a crust over them, keeping her from anything except the cleaning.

When she heard Mrs. Mitchell's key in the lock, she stood still and didn't feel anything at all.

Mrs. Mitchell came in, carrying the fur scarf and a news-paper. She looked a little tired, but she gave Jessie a pleasant nod before she went over to the sofa, took a cigarette out of the silver box and sat down, lighting it and inhaling smoke with a satisfied sigh. From where she was sitting, it wasn't likely that she would notice the wall bracket, but suddenly it seemed to Jessie that the shelf where the cup should have been screamed aloud its emptiness.

Fear had a spongy feeling. She said, "I finished the cleaning, ma'am."

Mrs. Mitchell nodded again, then glanced around the room and reached for a pillow to put behind her back. "It looks love-ly, Jessie. I expect you want to go now. I'm afraid I've kept you a few minutes late."

Jessie wanted to run, to be out of the apartment before Mrs. Mitchell's approving eyes looked in the wrong place. She said, "It doesn't matter, ma'am. Oh, there was a call from a lady, a Mrs. Fields. I wrote the number down. She said would you call her back, please."

"She's always calling," Mrs. Mitchell said. She sat up straight, shook out the handsome fur and ran her hand over it. "The apartment looks beautiful, Jessie."

Jessie said, "You have such pretty things," and then caught her breath because that might make Mrs. Mitchell think of the cup.

She didn't, though. She just said "Thank you" and reached for her pocketbook, opened the catch and took out a billfold. She counted off some bills and held them out to Jessie. "Is that right?"

Jessie didn't count them. She just nodded and said, "I'll be going now," and then she turned and walked straight out to the kitchen. Her hands were shaking as if she had fever again. She picked up the bundle she'd wrapped and put it inside her coat, holding it tight against her with her arm. It wouldn't show at all.

Her story was very straight and very clear in her mind. Maybe they'd never ask her at all about the cup, but if they did she had the sentences ready in her head: "When I came back, the man was gone. I thought he'd just made a mistake and got the wrong apartment."

It was a perfectly straight story. She just didn't want to have to tell it now, with Mrs. Mitchell's eyes looking at her. She put her hand up against her cheek, holding it as if there was pain there. If only she was going home to Dave instead of to an empty room. If he was there, she could tell him about the cup, have him to comfort her.

She must have stood there, staring at the blank kitchen wall, for a full minute before she let rise to the top of her mind the knowledge that had been there all along. If Dave was home, she couldn't tell him. About breaking the cup, yes—that would be all right. Anyone could break a cup.

But she couldn't tell him, ever, about what she had done afterward.

She closed her eyes, but not for very long. When she opened them again, she reached inside her coat and took out the brown paper bundle. Her fingers trembled, untying the knot, but finally it fell apart. The heavenly blue color of the cup gleamed up at her. She took out the little package from the store and put it on the table. She took out the pencil and laid it beside the package. Then she picked up the brown paper with the cup fragments on it and, carrying it carefully, she walked straight into the living room.

Mrs. Mitchell glanced up from the newspaper she was reading. She had slipped on a pair of heavy-rimmed glasses, and Jessie couldn't see her eyes, but she could hear the quick catch of Mrs. Mitchell's breath as she saw the broken pieces.

Jessie didn't wait for any words to be spoken. She said quickly, "I broke this, ma'am. It was an accident." It was a silly thing to say, because of course it was an accident. No one broke a beautiful thing on purpose.

Mrs. Mitchell didn't say anything for a long time. At least, it seemed like a long time, but maybe it was only a few seconds. When she spoke, there was a kind of coldness in her voice. "What happened? Were you dusting it?"

Jessie shook her head. "I . . . picked it up to look at it. It was so pretty. I didn't mean——" She tightened her mouth at the corners the way she'd taught herself to do.

Mrs. Mitchell got up from the sofa. She took the brown paper out of Jessie's hands, the paper and the broken pieces, and she put them down on the table, staring at them hard. "It can't be mended," she said.

Jessie said, "No, ma'am."

Mrs. Mitchell looked at her, and Jessie looked back, trying hard not to show how frightened she was. And then, all of a sudden, the coldness went out of Mrs. Mitchell's voice, and she sounded quite different. "Don't worry, Jessie," she said. "It's all right." She stirred the pieces with the tip of her finger. "It's just something I picked up once in a secondhand shop. I thought it was pretty, like you did."

Jessie said, "Mrs. Mitchell——" In another minute, folding her lips wasn't going to help any. She could feel the tears behind her eyelids.

"Don't look like that, Jessie. It isn't even valuable. Anyone can have an accident." She gave the brown paper a sudden push, shoving it away from both of them. Neither of them spoke for a minute, then Mrs. Mitchell said briskly, "Can you come next week at the same time?"

"Yes," said Jessie. She wanted to say something more, but even that one syllable nearly choked her.

"That's fine." Mrs. Mitchell's voice sounded absent, as if her mind had gone off somewhere. "I'll expect you."

Jessie nodded. She pulled her coat tight around her, and then she gave Mrs. Mitchell a quick soft look and went fast to the door, pulling it open and closing it behind her.

There was such a loud singing in her heart that it didn't seem possible Mrs. Mitchell couldn't hear it. It was the first singing there had been since Dave had left, because if one miracle could happen maybe another could too. She had something to go on now, and it was like a promise.

After the door closed, Mrs. Mitchell stood in the middle of her living room for quite a long time. Finally she reached out and picked up one of the broken pieces of the cup. It was a wide triangular piece, and all the lovely colors showed on it— deep blue, warm blue, pale clear blue, and at the bottom no blue at all.

She remembered the cup being in her grandmother's house, and how she had loved it. She remembered the day it was given to her, how old it was and how beautifully made. She remembered how she had put it up there on its shelf, even before the rugs were down, when the apartment was new.

The cup was broken and could never be mended. She didn't try to explain to herself the impulse that had made her tell Jessie it didn't matter. All she knew for certain was that her grandmother had been the kindest person she had ever known, and that her cup which was so lovely mustn't be allowed to hurt anyone.

"I'll keep just this one piece," Mrs. Mitchell said aloud to the empty room.

WALLACE ADAMS said he would walk the rest of the way, and his friend, his good friend Newhouse, nodded briskly and reached across him to open the car door.

Wallace said, "Thanks for the lift. It makes it easier for Helen when I can let her have the car."

"Oh, sure." Newhouse's voice was placid, and he lifted a hand from the wheel, absent and friendly.

Wallace said, "Well, thanks again," feeling the pleasant solidarity of neighbor and neighbor, then turned and started up his own driveway. Behind him, the big car murmured into gear and slid away.

The road curved up to his house, placid and dignified in its green tide of lawn. The spires of delphinium were too high for the design, and mad with loveliness. The roses spilled over from their regulated supports and choked the air with sweetness. Wallace thought: Mine.

The front door of the house flew open with a bang and a shout, and a leggy, brown-skinned ten-year-old catapulted himself down the steps. Wallace braced for a welcome, and the young shooting star that was his son raced down the drive and flung himself at his father, his straw-thatched head boring devotedly into Wallace's midsection.

"Hey!" said Wallace protesting, but he hugged the fledgling body against him for a moment, feeling the bones and the lightness and the squirming, confident possessiveness. Then he undid Tommy from his belt and held him off for a look. There was an impression of sunshine and brown knees and unplanned nose.

"You're early," Tommy accused, leaping beside him.

"Mr. Newhouse gave me a lift."

"He's fat," said Tommy, a trifle unjustly.

"So're you," said his father, spreading the unjustness around.

Tommy gave a hoot of derision and hiked up his shorts. "Mother's in the living room, and Vee's still upstairs, putting her face on."

"Is Vee going out again?"

"She's going out with that Jim Hutchins." Tommy's voice mimicked soprano. "He's so-o-o handsome."

Wallace gave a half-hearted smack to the seat of the sailcloth shorts. "Don't tease your sister, son." He frowned, trying to place Jim Hutchins among the solemn, smooth young faces of Vee's friends. He must be Cliff Hutchins' son, so he was all right.

Tommy bounded ahead, opened the door and yelled, "Hey, Mother! Dad's home." Wallace followed him into the living room.

Helen was standing by the mantelpiece, self-possessed and beautiful in apple-green linen. Her amber-blond hair was high on her head, accenting her cheekbones and the pretty, square line of her jaw. He kissed her and said, "Hello, darling."

Helen pulled away gently. "Wally dear, it's hot."

He said, "You look as cool as a cucumber," and then felt remorse at sounding so uninspired, but his tongue was always uneasy and shy. He caught a glimpse of himself in the glass above the mantel and thought penitently that, after all, his words fitted him. The face that looked back was ordinary and middle-aged, with its light brown hair receding from a narrow forehead.

Helen smiled at him. "You're early."

"John Newhouse gave me a lift."

"Oh? Katherine called up this afternoon."

"Katherine Newhouse?" He was vaguely surprised. "Bridge party?"

"No. She wanted to talk to me about—something." There was the faintest shadow on her voice. "I'll tell you after dinner."

"I'll go and wash. Tommy says Vee's going out again."

She nodded and looked pleased. "That nice Hutchins boy." She walked across the room to pick up a magazine from the arm of a chair. "Wally, it's so nice to know the children are really meeting the right people. I love it here. I feel so—settled."

He did too. American roots went down quickly. It must be the light, rich soil of the country that had turned so eagerly under the pioneer plow. Hey, thought Wallace, I'm getting poetic. But the idea pleased him, and he went upstairs playing with it. The roots really were as deep as in Europe, because the ground had welcomed them. *My country, 'tis of thee.* He looked out of his bedroom window. *My piece of country.* It was beautiful beyond words. Whistling, he went off to wash his hands.

Vee came downstairs as they were finishing dinner, and Wallace looked up at his daughter with quick pleasure. Her honey-brown hair was soft on her shoulders, and she was wearing some sort of silky blue dress. She might have been painted by Renoir's sweet brush, and at seventeen she was any man's dream of springtime. He felt the quick jealous clutch of fatherhood and eased it with the knowledge that Vee's escort was Cliff Hutchins' son. He grumbled, "Going out again?" meaning that Jim Hutchins was a lucky youngster.

Vee dropped a respectful kiss on his bald spot. Across the table, she said, "Mother, I've gone."

"Don't be too late. You look sweet."

Vee said, "Yes, don't I?" and left them in a fragrant, silky gust.

Helen stood up with her coffee cup in her hand. "Shall we go out on the verandah, Wally? It's cooler out there."

She had something she wanted to talk to him about. He followed obediently. The light was just beginning to leave the air. The color that had tipped the spikes of delphinium, the deep crimson of heavy-headed roses, the uninvited glow of dandelions in the lawn dimmed and mellowed.

He lighted Helen's cigarette, then his own, and sat back lazily in a white-slatted chair. Through half-closed eyes he could see the tiny claws of woodbine clutching at the stone pillars. The fading air just touched his cheek. His heart lit up with love, and he felt a strong, deep peace. A man needed his acres, and it was not altogether a sense of property. Vaguely and genuinely, he wished this for all men.

Helen said suddenly, "I told you Katherine Newhouse called this afternoon."

"M'mmm." He tried to sit up straighter in deference to the subject, but the chair had a lazy back.

"It was about Mr. Benson. He'd just been talking to her."

Wallace nodded. Benson was the local real-estate agent, a small, tubby man of great cheerfulness.

"He'd just gotten an offer on the Stiles place," said Helen.

"Oh." Wallace sat up straighter, charmed. New neighbors. He had considered buying the Stiles place himself, but it had been a little larger than their needs. "Thought of taking the place ourselves," Wallace's mind murmured complacently, speaking to other men, "but it didn't quite suit." He then ceased from wandering and paid attention to his wife. "That's fine. It'll be nice to have someone living there."

She stubbed out her cigarette. "It would be nice," she said, "but these people won't do."

"Why? Can't they finance it?"

"They're Jews."

"Oh," He sighed. He had been pleased when Helen spoke of new neighbors, and now they wouldn't do. It was too bad. After a moment, he said, "Why did Katherine call *you*, Helen?"

She got up and crossed to one of the stone pillars, leaning against it. "That was what I wanted to talk to you about, dear. Mr. Benson told Katherine that it's very hard to move such big properties, and he wanted to be sure he was doing what everyone wants him to, if he says no." She spread her pretty hands.

"So Katherine thought that it shouldn't be just John and herself who told him. She thought we should get together somewhere, all the leading members of the community, and—well,
actually what she said was that she thought our house would be
a good place."

"Why *our* house?" Wallace asked.

She was a lovely shadow of the dusk. Her voice was smiling.
"Because we're the newest ones here, and the Newhouses like
us. They know we think the same way they do."

He hunched forward, staring at the verandah floor, uncomfortable and resenting it. He had been sitting there quietly,
wishing all mankind well, and he felt a dim dislike of Benson
for involving him in this. After a little while, he said, "You
know anything about these people?"

Helen's shoulders moved up lightly. "Not a thing."

The habitual line between his nearsighted eyes narrowed a
little. "Do you know their name?"

"No, I don't."

It didn't matter—the name, whatever it was. They were not
suitable neighbors. But his discomfort deepened.

Helen went on. "I told Katherine she could ask whoever she
wanted to. We'll just serve cocktails."

He sighed and cast around for something to anchor his mind
on. "Arthur Hearn will be coming, won't he?" If Hearn came,
it was all right. The entire development had once been the
rolling acres of the Hearn family estate, and Hearn, cool and
caustic and alert, set the community pattern, without caring
whether he set it or not. What suited Hearn's assured mind
should suit any of them.

Helen said, "I hope so, but I think he and Mrs. Hearn are still
in Canada. It doesn't matter. We know how they'd feel."

Wallace nodded. "Well—"

Helen crossed in back of his chair and leaned over to put her
cool cheek against his for a moment. "It's awkward, of course,

dear," she said, "but we have to consider our neighbors. It's just a matter of business, like zoning a residential district against night clubs or something."

"People aren't night clubs," he said thinly.

"No, of course they aren't." Her voice was disarmingly quick. "But you know what I mean. It isn't just these people. It's what it starts. They bring their friends. They're—pushing." She sounded gentle and reasonable.

He nodded again and put up his hand to draw her closer. This was her home and their children's, and those three—so infinitely precious to his vulnerable heart—must have what they wanted. His own role was safely passive; it was the Newhouses who had suggested this meeting. He said, "When are they coming for our famous cocktails?"

"Day after tomorrow. Saturday. You're sweet, Wally."

It was dark now as he turned and reached up his arms to her. She responded for an instant, and he forgot the dim confusion she had waked in his mind. This was all his, his love to hold and the soft night to hold her in.

For a moment, neither of them spoke, and then she gave a little shiver against the cool air. "I'm going in, darling." The door opened to light from the hallway, and closed again behind her.

He sat there, looking out at the darkness and listening to the small night noises. A cricket was tuning its tiny violin of sound somewhere in the soft grass, and from beyond, there was the sleepy twitter of a robin protesting the dark. After a moment's listening, Wallace got up, hands in pockets, and walked slowly down the steps and onto the grass.

Around him, the night bloomed, tender and blessed.

He was thinking of Saturday. Saturday had a sharp edge in his mind. He pushed it back and tried to listen to the robin, and it overrode the bird's gentle complaint with its own dull obbligato. Wallace hunched his shoulders up in sudden irritation.

He was being childish. All that was involved was a simple, legitimate agreement between neighbors—people who had bought their homes in a district which would stay as they wished. These others, these people who wanted to buy the Stiles place, need never know that a door had been deliberately closed in their faces.

He stared miserably into the darkness.

But what if they did know? What if they were, in fact, rather dreadfully used to it? How did it feel to be shut out, because of your name, because of your race?

"Hokum," said Wallace Adams, aloud. He and his neighbors had bought and paid for certain things. There was nothing to be ashamed of in wanting to keep the identity of their own community intact. Helen saw the values much more clearly than he did. She had said, "We have to consider our neighbors."

We have to consider our neighbors.

How did it feel to be shut out? What was it like to find there were two sides to a wall, and to be on the wrong side? How would he feel if it were himself and Helen and their children?

He had a sudden, frightened glimpse of blinded cruelty, of human hands cupped to hold security, of men walking a road that narrowed and narrowed.

His mind leaped to safety. Good God! He was making mountains. It wasn't that important. The whole thing was perfectly straightforward and simple. It had always been understood that the district was a restricted development. Restriction, exclusion. What were the walls of a man's own house but restriction and exclusion? What was a property line? You were bound by the rules of your own society.

He remembered, with satisfaction, how friendly John Newhouse had become. He remembered that it was to Helen that Katherine Newhouse had turned. He remembered that Vee was out dancing with the nice Hutchins boy.

That was what he wanted for his family, that sureness. He

had no right to disturb their peace with impractical abstractions. By Sunday morning, the whole thing would be over, pleasantly. He wasn't being anti-anything in his acquiescence. Put on a business basis, he was protecting his investment. Put on a human basis, he was safeguarding his family.

From what?

He stopped at the edge of his lawn. *From what?*

His mind stiffened, pushing away the question. He retreated into the safety of his own world. He was only an ordinary, middle-aged man with a family—an ordinary, middle-aged man, standing solemnly in his garden and indulging in dramatics.

It was all tremendously unimportant. He told himself it was unimportant.

The bird's lament had stopped. The night was quiet. Wallace crossed the lawn and walked slowly up his front steps.

Cliff Hutchins and his wife were the first to arrive, the Tom Brents just behind them. Cliff's hearty voice shouted a greeting for everybody, as the men followed their formal patterns of hand-shaking, and the women touched cheeks with bridge-table affection. Wallace excused himself to mix their drinks, glad of a task which took his mind off the purpose of the meeting and made it possible to cling to the role of passive host.

Helen joined him briefly. He looked up from counting glasses, and said, "How many more?"

"Just the Atkinsons and Madge Hennessy. And the Newhouses, of course."

He said, "They know why they're here?"

"Naturally."

Naturally. He mixed a Scotch and water for Cliff Hutchins and carried it over to him. Cliff gave one of his rather hearty, meaningless laughs and said, "Quite a crowd," sounding gratified. Wallace looked at his guest and disliked him. He disliked his laugh and his light blue eyes and his big pudgy hands. For a passive host, Wallace felt unreasonably quarrelsome. If he had been drinking himself, he could have put it down to the liquor, but he had not been drinking. He said inanely, "Beautiful summer."

They discussed the weather, unable to get away from each other, until the arrival of the Atkinsons with Madge Hennessy churning behind them. Madge dropped her gloves and bag on the nearest chair, pulled off her hat and fanned herself with it briskly. "I like this room," she announced, and added, with apparent inconsequence, "When does the jury sit?"

It would be childish to pretend he didn't know what she was talking about. Wallace said stiffly, "We're waiting for the New-houses."

"Oh. Of course."

He gave her a sharp look, but her broad face was as placid as a cow's. "Court's in session," she said suddenly, jerking her head toward the door. He thought: She's enjoying this, and despised her for it. If an unpleasant thing had to be done, it might at least be done decently. He excused himself and crossed the room to shake hands with the Newhouses, more than a little flattered by the genial warmth of the big man's welcome. John Newhouse made the room seem suddenly crowded and important. There was the usual hum of greeting, an edging forward of chairs. Wallace said, "What's yours, John?"

"Rye, I think." Newhouse glanced at his watch. "Hope you people don't mind holding the meeting up a little. There's a chance Arthur Hearn will be coming."

Helen made a soft little sound of pleasure. Wallace said, surprised, "I thought he was in Canada."

Newhouse smiled. "He was, but I happened to know of a business matter he might be checking on personally, so I called his office. They said he flew in by private plane this morning."

Helen said, "Oh, that's wonderful, John."

Newhouse nodded gravely. "He was out when I called, but

I explained to his secretary that this meeting concerned his property interests, and she said she was sure he'd do everything possible to get here. But of course he might be late. He's a busy man."

Wallace looked down at the floor. The little flicker of pleasure he had felt because the sought-after Arthur Hearn might be a guest in his house died out abruptly. Property interests. Enough big guns were lined up already for that imperishable cause; Wallace hoped Hearn wouldn't come.

The guests waited, their talk desultory. Conversation in the room lifted, then dragged out. Newhouse glanced again at his watch, then shook his head and walked over to the fireplace, where he stood with an elbow on the mantelpiece. From that position, he dominated the room. Wallace, finding himself next to Madge Hennessy, with an unclaimed glass in his hand, shifted his feet uneasily. Madge patted the arm of her chair, and he set the glass down on the floor and perched reluctantly beside her, feeling clumsy.

Newhouse cleared his throat and looked benignly around the room. "I'm sorry to have kept you waiting here. We've been hoping that our good neighbor, Arthur Hearn, could be with us." There was a little innocent patter of applause at the name, promptly hushed. "However," said John Newhouse, "I don't think we should wait any longer. And of course we know he would feel as we do about this meeting." He straightened his shoulders against the mantel. "I don't think this need take much time. You all know why we're here."

There was a polite hum of assent. Everyone was very polite. John Newhouse went on. "You all know that Benson has had an offer on the Stiles property. The—people involved don't seem to be suitable." He gazed around him calmly. "I think we're all agreed on that?"

Wallace stared down at his feet. If he wanted to say anything, he knew this was the time to say it.

Newhouse's competent voice continued. "We felt the pleasantest way to handle the matter was simply to appoint a committee to see Benson and express our wishes." He gave a small, deprecating laugh. "It all seems rather formal, of course, but actually the matter should never have come up. As you all know." He looked at them paternally. They all knew.

Wallace was conscious that the palms of his hands were sweating and clammy. John Newhouse's voice deepened a little. "The reason for this—formality is that we wish to establish a clearer precedent in Benson's mind. We are all property owners here. We chose our lovely district for its neighbors as much as for its land, and we naturally want to maintain it. We are thinking in terms of the future, as well as the present."

Wallace thought: He's talking too much.

The words went on, firmly. "I think a committee of three would serve us best," said John Newhouse. "And I would like to propose our host as the chairman."

It was a moment before Wallace realized whom he meant. Then his heart gave an uncomfortable little jump, and he looked across at Helen. She was looking back at him, proud and eager over this confirmation of their position in the community.

When he heard his voice say "No," it was almost as much of a surprise to him as it was to his guests.

Newhouse's heavy eyebrows went up slightly. "I know you're a busy man, my dear fellow, but you and Helen have our interests so much at heart—"

What in God's name had Helen committed him to, in her talks with Katherine? All he wanted was to be left alone. He said unhappily, "I just don't feel that I want to—" Helen was looking at him incredulously.

Newhouse's voice was as pleasant as ever. His eyes were a little hard. "Aren't you with us?" he said.

Wallace folded his arms across his chest, because his heart

was pounding like a schoolboy's. Something harsh and permanent in him said, *No*.

He got slowly to his feet, sliding off the arm of his chair. He felt stupid, standing, like a youngster called on to recite, but he couldn't stay perched there. They were all waiting for him to say something. He hunted rather desperately in his mind for some graceful way out, a way that would neither alienate him nor make him responsible for what was done later. A comfortable way, which would insure his neighbors' good will and his own self-respect.

"Well?" said John Newhouse, heavily.

Wallace said, "No, I'm not with you."

There was a slow, sluggish silence in the room, unstirred for a moment because it was unaccepting. Only, his words were an echo, and echoes stay. Newhouse's voice was suddenly harsh. "This is rather unexpected," he said. "I thought we could assume—"

Wallace kept his eyes carefully away from his wife. "I know," he said. "Everybody assumes. That's just the trouble. I'm sorry, John, I—" He tried to find the words for his protest. But what does the sheep say when it leaves the herd?

There was another short silence, while Newhouse looked at him expressionlessly. His voice when he finally spoke was untroubled. "Well," he said, "we seem to have made a mistake in our choice of chairman. I'll propose another name."

Helen said quickly, "John, I'm sure Wally didn't mean—"

Her voice brought instinct back, superseding reason. Wallace tried to soften what he had said. "I only meant that we ought to know more about these people." He sounded humble, and he hated it. "I only meant—"

John Newhouse told him what he meant. "You only meant," he said politely, "that our wishes and yours are not the same. The—welfare of our community doesn't interest you. I don't think we need trouble you for any other explanation, my dear chap." My error, said the bland tone of his voice. I thought you were one of us. My error, my dear chap, my error.

Newhouse glanced around the room. "As for knowing all we need to know about Benson's clients—"

Wallace interrupted bluntly. "What *do* we know about them? Except that they're Jews?"

It was too blunt, too harsh. But he had named it, and the conspiracy of silence fell apart. It was no use pretending any longer that this was a gentlemanly affair of business. The real reason for the meeting was out in the open.

John Newhouse looked at him, and through him. His voice was the voice of the well-bred host, covering a guest's unfortunate social blunder. He said firmly, "We are all agreed. We are here by agreement."

It was as easy as that. Newhouse's deep voice reassured them. The word "Jews" might never have been said.

And, abruptly, Wallace Adams was very angry. He knew that anger could only weaken his position, but he was not, for the moment, a reasonable man. He was an angry man. He was sick with anger.

It loosened his tongue, that mute instrument which had never fully told Helen he loved her, or the children of his cherishing. This was love too, and, if they hated him for it, it was still love.

He said, "All right. I agreed to it. But I don't want to agree to it any longer. I don't see what right we have to keep anyone out, when we don't know anything about them. If they're undesirable as people, it's reasonable. But you're telling me these people are undesirable as Jews."

Newhouse put his broad shoulders back against the mantelpiece. His eyes were opaque, but his smile was still very patient. "I think I'm only being realistic, my dear fellow. These people may be very nice, but it's what follows. If we once drop our—agreement—"

"Why not drop it?"

He was ignored, the way a child is ignored. "It makes too difficult a position for everyone, including the newcomers. They bring their friends, their relatives—"

Wallace said, "I bring my friends, my relatives. That's what a home is for."

Newhouse's voice rose. "I have an interest in this community. I intend to protect that interest."

The room was very quiet. Anger beat its wings in the air between the two men. Wallace said, "I don't want any part of it. If it's nothing else, it's damn bad manners."

Newhouse snapped. "I don't think my etiquette is part of this discussion." His face was brick-red. "After all, if it comes to manners, I'm here as your guest."

He couldn't answer that, couldn't say it was Helen's invitation, not his. After all, he had acquiesced, and that was the root of the whole matter. People like himself, who, believing one thing, accepted another. He looked down at his hands and was vaguely surprised to find that they were shaking.

Newhouse pushed his advantage. The flush died out of his face, and he said calmly, "You're overexcited, Wally. After all, there are other homes for these people to buy. Let them live in their own communities. We don't ask to come into their lives, do we?"

Wallace had no answer. All the sympathy in the room was flowing away from him like water. There was almost a deliberate cruelty about it, and he was afraid to look at his wife. And yet he knew he was right.

He heard Newhouse say smoothly, in the assured voice of the majority, "I withdraw my suggestion about the chairman. We are all agreed, except Wallace—"

Madge Hennessy's brisk, deep voice cut into his sentence. She sat forward in her chair. "John, you'd better count me with Wallace."

Newhouse looked at her; Madge stared back. A sudden hope lightened Wallace's mind and heart.

Madge went on, implacable as a tank. "I'm for letting the people buy the place." There was a heavy silence. "I don't really know," she said, "why Jews shouldn't live as neighbors with—what is that old-fashioned term?—Christians."

For just an instant, there was a hollow look about Newhouse. Then abruptly, he picked up the reins of control. He said coldly, "Two is hardly a majority. I think the rest of us are in complete agreement." He looked around the room. No one spoke, and Newhouse nodded in satisfaction.

The sense of property was safely in the saddle again. The wan little hope of brotherhood had fallen at the first fence. Wallace's hands hung slack at his sides.

A voice from the doorway said, "Meeting not over, is it? Sorry I couldn't get here before."

The room turned as a unit. Helen rose instantly, the quick, welcoming hostess. "Mr. Hearn!" she exclaimed. "I didn't hear you come in."

"The door was open, my dear. I just walked through." Arthur Hearn nodded across at Wallace, turned to Newhouse. "Hello, John. I got your message rather late. How's the meeting going?"

"Fine, Arthur, fine." Newhouse's manner expanded perceptibly.

Hearn crossed the room, held Helen's chair for her and took up a position behind it. Cliff Hutchins half rose, offering his own chair, and Hearn waved him back.

Newhouse said, "I'm glad you could come, Arthur. We're just choosing a committee chairman."

"Committee for what?"

Newhouse explained, easily. "Just a group of three, to call on Benson."

"Oh." Hearn nodded. "Well, don't let me interrupt. I understand it's merely a matter of protecting our property interests here?"

"That's right." The two men looked at each other casually, over the heads of the group, understanding each other. New-house went on, elaborating. "It's very simple, Arthur. Benson is anxious to sell the Stiles property to clients we consider undesirable. We're being formal about this meeting because we want Benson to realize just how we stand."

Hearn said, "Naturally," approving.

Newhouse looked pleased. "Of course, we'd be delighted if *you'd* take the committee chairmanship yourself, Arthur."

Hearn said, "Certainly. Glad to."

Relief in the room was almost animate. The final touch of sanction blessed the meeting. Wallace's hands tightened, each on the other. Let it go, he thought. Let it go. The majority rules.

Newhouse dropped his hands, safely relinquishing the reins. "You want to choose your own committee, Arthur?"

Anger had drained out of Wallace, and he closed his eyes, waiting for Hearn to make his choice. He had done what he could, and it would never be enough.

He thought suddenly: I will not let it go. He heard his own voice, dogged with the tired patience of defeat. "Mr. Hearn."

"Yes, Mr. Adams?" Hearn was quick, courteous, just faintly impatient.

Wallace pressed the knuckles of one hand into the palm of the other. He said slowly, "John hasn't explained everything, quite. He hasn't told you that he offered me the chairmanship, and I turned it down."

Newhouse said abruptly, "We've been over that, Wallace."

Wallace ignored the warning. "The only thing we know about these people," he said, "is that they're Jews. We don't know anything else about them at all."

Hearn said, "That right, John?" He frowned slightly.

Newhouse glanced resentfully at Wallace, then shrugged in acquiescence.

Hearn said, "It's always been understood that this district is restricted." The brief anger that had touched Newhouse's face smoothed out completely. Wallace looked at the two of them, impregnable, sure of themselves, their world the only world. He had tried twice, and he had lost twice.

Hearn went on. "Restricted, that is, against undesirable people." He looked at Newhouse. "They've got money, I suppose? They could finance a property as big as Dick Stiles' place?"

Newhouse looked slightly surprised. "Well, of course. But that's beside the point."

"Not to me it isn't," Hearn said briskly. "I'm very much interested in the cash angle. We don't want that property bouncing back on the market again. Looks bad for the neighborhood. People start thinking a district is running down when you can't sell the houses in it."

Newhouse put in sharply, "They'll think it's running down even more if we let—" He stopped, and Hearn finished for him.

"If we let Jews in?" He said the word "Jews" as if it was just a word. "That depends on the Jew. I know a lot of Jews I'd be glad to have for neighbors."

He looked around the room. His manner said, more plainly than words, that what was good enough for Arthur Hearn was good enough for any of them. No one spoke. The heads that had turned toward him turned back to John Newhouse. Newhouse hadn't moved, but the fingers of his right hand, casual against the mantelpiece, pressed down so suddenly that the knuckles showed blue-white.

Hearn went on. "Seems to me what we need to know about these people is what they're like, and what their background is. That's what this committee ought to be finding out." He nodded at Wallace. "I should think you'd be pretty good at the job, Mr. Adams. If you'd care to serve with me, I'll be glad to have you."

Wallace said, eagerly, "Certainly. On that basis."

Hearn raised his eyebrows. "What other basis is there?" He studied the room, his eyes resting briefly on Cliff Hutchins, then moving on. He looked at Tom Brent. "How about you, Tom?"

Wallace glanced at Brent and saw him struggling self-consciously to his feet. "Why—yes. Yes, of course. Glad to." His voice was suddenly very small and hurried. "I never liked this business much, anyhow."

Perhaps none of them had liked it much, thought Wallace. They had only wanted the assurance that they were right not to like it. He looked quickly, anxiously at Helen and saw that she was smiling. Mr. Hearn had given his approval; her own husband was on the committee. She was pleased, he knew, for the wrong reasons, but it didn't matter. She was his Helen, and he smiled back at her.

Hearn's voice picked up the meeting. "Fine," he said. "That's settled then." His voice was easy, crisp, disinterested. "Wallace, Tom— I'll give you a ring, and we'll get together to see Benson. Great pleasure, Mrs. Adams."

He moved toward the door. There was a general stir in the room. The meeting, as a meeting, had suddenly ceased to exist.

John Newhouse, with his hands thrust deep into his pockets, stood unyielding against the mantelpiece. The group he had called together broke up into people, but he didn't see them. He was staring straight ahead, at nothing.

Wallace felt a sudden and intense pity. The lost, he thought, are not the outcasts. The lost are those who cast them out.

THE OLDER ONES

Q FOR QUITCLAIM

MR. PICKETT, who had had oatmeal for breakfast and was feeling as alert as a beagle hound, bounded into his office, said a cheery "Good morning" to Miss Truesdale and breezed on through to his own room, untroubled by the fact that Miss Truesdale had not responded.

He put his briefcase tenderly on his desk, withdrew himself from his topcoat and bowler hat, hung them up neatly and sat down, planting his fingertips on the blotter in front of him and breathing deeply. "Ha!" said Mr. Pickett, in tribute to the oatmeal inside him. He then took a good look at his desk and frowned.

There were no letters on his desk. It was curious, this morning of all mornings, when he was so well lined and prepared to sweep aside the trivia of business detail. It was hard on a man, since letters must have come. Letters always came to the firm of Hatcher, Pickett and Bohn, Attorneys at Law.

The deduction was inescapable. Miss Truesdale had failed to sort the morning mail. Mr. Pickett planted a thumb firmly on his push button and gazed at his letter opener, a thin, daggerish-looking affair inscribed, "Compliments of Jos. Treeb, Insurance of All Kinds."

155

The door did not open. Miss Truesdale did not appear. A baffled man, Mr. Pickett rose and went forth on a scouting expedition. The outer office was still and lonely and empty. The electric clock on the wall gave a mournful hiccup, jerked its minute hand and informed Mr. Pickett that it was nine-thirty.

Mr. Pickett turned and trundled back to the executive rabbit warren, selecting a door inscribed chastely with the legend: "Mr. Hatcher." He opened this and popped his head through. "John!" he said.

Mr. Hatcher, a thin man with a face like an intelligent cold chisel, glanced up, weighed his words carefully and said, "Good morning, Mortimer."

"Good morning," said Mr. Pickett. "Have you got Miss Truesdale?"

"No," said Mr. Hatcher broodingly. "Nor have I any letters."

"She isn't in."

"I deduced that."

"Well, well," said Mr. Pickett, mystified, but still cheery. "Must've stepped out."

"Ah," said Mr. Hatcher.

Mr. Hatcher's door forthwith popped open again and the rest of the law firm came into the room. Mr. Bohn was tall, dark, youngish, and wearing his favorite necktie, which was red and which Mr. Hatcher deplored. "Hail, gentlemen," he said cordially. "If you're looking for Jean, she's got a bad cold and won't be in today. She telephoned to ask if it was all right, and I said sure."

"Jean?" said Mr. Hatcher, being willful.

"Miss Truesdale."

"And you assured her it would be all right?" said Mr. Hatcher, cross-examining the witness.

"She was sneezing like a banshee," Mr. Bohn said. "I couldn't, in common decency—"

Mr. Hatcher was not mollified. "I need Miss Truesdale today," he said indignantly. "I must have her. Metcalf may be coming this afternoon, and you know what that means."

He sounded severe, and his partners looked at each other and nodded. Hatcher, Pickett and Bohn had been hard at work on Mr. Metcalf for six weary weeks, dealing with a personality that would have put a cactus plant on its mettle, and Mr. Metcalf still held the upper hand. All the attorneys asked of him was that he would sign a quitclaim deed and go away. Perversely, Mr. Metcalf did not sign the deed, and stayed. Once a week, at least, he came in to annoy them with his elusiveness, then departed, saying "We shall see" from under his rather too natty fedora.

"It is," said Mr. Hatcher aloofly, "most inconsiderate of Miss Truesdale."

Mr. Pickett, still full of the oatmeal of human kindness, surged to their secretary's defense. "Come, come, John. It's not so bad. We can get a girl from an employment agency."

"I will not," said Mr. Hatcher, "have a strange woman cluttering up the office when Mr. Metcalf comes in. Things are quite difficult enough."

There was a short silence of men thinking. "It appears to me," said Mr. Pickett hopefully, "that we could manage by ourselves for one day. I could sit outside and answer the phone. I was planning to go over those Internal Revenue papers anyhow. I can do that anywhere."

Mr. Hatcher, an orange-juice-and-coffee man, lacked his colleague's sense of inner security and was inclined to take a dark view. "What about typing?"

"Put it off till tomorrow if you can," said Mr. Pickett quite cheerily. "If it can't be put off, we'll type it ourselves. I believe all the typewriter keys have letters on them. . . . Excuse me. I hear Miss Truesdale's phone."

Miss Truesdale's desk was littered with the morning mail,

scooped up by Mr. Bohn and tossed there on arrival, and Mr. Pickett, in grabbing for the phone, which was shrieking tiresomely, knocked most of the letters onto the floor. He ignored them spaciously, picked up the instrument and said, "Hello." He then remembered his manners, cleared his throat repentantly and substituted, "Hatcher, Pickett and Bohn, good morning."

"Give me Hatcher," said a voice.

"One moment, please," Mr. Pickett caroled competently, took a look at the push buttons on Miss Truesdale's desk, and pressed the one marked "Hatcher." Nothing happened. He found another family of buttons on the other side, also tidily named, and pressed "Hatcher" there too. There was a moment's silence, then Mr. Hatcher's voice said, "Yes? Hatcher speaking."

Mr. Pickett, feeling rather Olympian, waited confidently for his two voices to merge. Mr. Hatcher said, "Hello, hello. Hatcher speaking." Silence, like a beautiful white dove, continued to spead her gracious wings.

"Hello-hello-hello. Are you there?" Mr. Hatcher's voice rose slightly. "Is anyone there?"

"I am, John," said Mr. Pickett brightly. "Your man seems to have gone. He was on a moment ago, and now he's gone."

Mr. Hatcher said accusingly, "You pushed the wrong button."

"I did nothing of the kind," said Mr. Pickett. "I pushed the one marked 'Hatcher.'"

"Ah," said Mr. Hatcher. "Well, he's gone, at any rate. . . . Are there any letters for me?"

"I'm sorting them, John."

"Ah." The conversation expired, owing to lack of stimulus, and Mr. Pickett put down the phone, got down on the floor and began to retrieve the morning mail. The phone lay quiet for a moment, and then rang again. "Um-m-m," said Mr. Pickett,

who had found a letter of his own and was reading it interestedly on all fours. "Just a minute." He then remembered who
he was and bounced back into his chair. "Hatcher, Pickett and
Bohn, good morning, oh, hell," said Mr. Pickett to the phone.
He was still on the Hatcher line. He pushed the top button
hastily, drew a blank and pushed the next one.

A voice, crackling in his ear, said, "I want Hatcher. I was
cut off."

"Yes, sir," said Mr. Pickett, made a swift resurvey of all the
buttons, pushed "Hatcher" on his left and buzzed "Hatcher" on
his right.

"Yes?" said Mr. Hatcher, who had apparently been crouched
to spring.

"I've got your man for you again, but he seems to have gone.
Wait a minute while I push the other button." He pushed the
button he had started out with and was greeted by the tranquillity of the ether. He switched back to Mr. Hatcher rapidly.
"Are you there, John?"

"I am," said Mr. Hatcher succinctly. "Stop playing games."

"There's something wrong with these buttons," Mr. Pickett
decided. "Hang up and I'll ring you back." He hung up himself
and leaned over the desk, thinking deeply. Then he picked up
the phone again and pushed "Pickett," remembered that Pickett
was out, pushed "Bohn," and was about to reach for the Bohn
buzzer when his junior partner's voice said "Hello" in his ear.

Mr. Pickett jumped. The only thing he had been at all clear
about was the buzzer system for getting his partner's attention,
and now even this seemed to have betrayed him. "How could
you answer me before I buzzed you?" Mr. Pickett demanded
indignantly.

Mr. Bohn's voice said, "I'm sorry. I was making a call, and
I pushed the wrong button. Jean's mentioned that to me before.
I'm really very sorry. Did you want something, sir?"

"No, thank you," said Mr. Pickett politely, and hung up.

He returned to sorting the mail, and silence fell for the space of three seconds. Then the phone rang again. The voice this time was bordered with black passion, and it still proclaimed a desire to be connected with Mr. Hatcher, coupled with an unflattering character sketch of the blankety-blank idiot who was answering the phone.

Mr. Pickett, now two hours distant from his comforting breakfast, said, "Yes, sir. Just one moment, please," in a humble voice, put the telephone gently down, rose and tiptoed out of the room.

He came back with Mr. Hatcher, who sat down at the desk and made the connection direct. Mr. Pickett, hovering, continued to sort the mail.

"Yes?" said Mr. Hatcher. "No," said Mr. Hatcher. "Yes, indeed," said Mr. Hatcher. He then put his hand over the mouthpiece and announced hoarsely that it was Metcalf on the wire. Mr. Pickett lost interest in the mail. "He's coming in this afternoon," said Mr. Hatcher, keeping his partner *au courant* with the situation. "About the quitclaim. Have you got that copy, Mortimer?"

"No," said Mr. Pickett promptly. "It's in the files, I imagine."

"Find it.... Yes, Mr. Metcalf. Certainly. Two-thirty will be splendid." Mr. Hatcher hung up, breathed deeply and said, "He's coming in. Help me find the quitclaim, will you, Mortimer? And that letter we had about it from Bayard and Holmes. Metcalf's coming in."

"You said that," Mr. Pickett pointed out, and bounded across the room to the filing cases. "What do I look under? B for Bayard or M for Metcalf?"

"B for Bayard, I should think," said Mr. Hatcher. He then added profoundly, "or M for Metcalf. Here, I'll help you. You take B."

Mr. Pickett took B, Mr. Hatcher took M, and time marched on. After a while, Mr. Pickett said anxiously, "Could it be under

Q for Quitclaim?" and Mr. Hatcher, murmuring, "Manchester, Markham, Masters," waved a silencing hand. He then said, "Middleton" rather grimly and added, "You might just get Bohn out here. The fresh approach——"

Mr. Pickett vanished rapidly and returned with the fresh approach, who was carrying a pile of papers—H for Harwood—under one arm.

Mr. Bohn amiably put his own papers on top of the morning mail and plunged into the files.

The best that could be said for their search was that it solved the problem of the telephone, since the whole firm was now in one place and the intercommunication system was automatically outwitted whenever the telephone rang. It rang at regular intervals. In fact, it was a distinct surprise to Hatcher, Pickett and Bohn to find how many calls they got in a morning. Normally filtered through Miss Truesdale, all kinds of telephone pals now reached them, including a racy bit of dialogue between Mr. Bohn and a woman who wanted to discuss her table linen with a laundryman by the name of Hepfelman.

By the time a gently perspiring Mr. Bohn had made it clear that he was neither Mr. Hepfelman nor Mr. Hepfelman's brother-in-law—a character named Mr. Engelhardt who sometimes obliged when Mr. Hepfelman was out—his senior partners were in an advanced and deteriorated state of nerves.

"Something about table napkins," said Mr. Bohn, hanging the telephone up quietly. "She says they're written down in black and white on her own laundry list, but judging by the prima-facie evidence I'm inclined to think Mr. Hepfelman has the legal rights of the case on his side. . . . Did you find the deed?"

"No," said Mr. Pickett and Mr. Hatcher palely. Mr. Pickett added, "Do we have Miss Truesdale's telephone number, Mac? I'm afraid we shall have to call her."

"We have it," said his junior partner unhappily, "but she

takes her calls downstairs at the building superintendent's phone, and there's a nasty draft in the hallway. But, of course, if you think——"

"No, no, of course not. Wouldn't dream of it. Might develop pneumonia or something." Mr. Pickett winced at the thought. "Wouldn't there be some sort of a separate file on the whole case somewhere? John——"

"I don't know. When I want a file, I just ring her and she brings it in. . . . There's a letter here from Bayard and Holmes, but it's about that unfortunate affair with the street-railway people. What are we going to do? We can't just let Miss Truesdale stand about in a draft when she's sneezing."

They looked at one another helplessly, then Mr. Bohn snapped his fingers, causing Mr. Hatcher to skip like a high hill. "Why not just draw up another quitclaim, sir?" said Mr. Bohn brightly.

Hatcher and Pickett regarded Bohn with respect, genuinely glad that it was their junior partner who had solved the problem. It gave him standing. Mr. Pickett said he thought he had a quitclaim form on his desk, and, deeply stirred, he trumpeted off to get it, returning a moment later in a subdued mood to announce that he had spilled ink on it last Tuesday, and anyway it was a warranty, not a quitclaim.

His report was received in silence, followed by a general return to the files, which already bore an intimate resemblance to Times Square on a New Year's morning.

A lengthy and earnest search followed, spasmodically interrupted by the telephone bearing clients who wanted action. With their minds riveted on the Metcalf problem, none of the attorneys was in a mood for clients, and there was a distinct and rather peevish feeling that business as usual was an interruption of business *in extremis*.

This policy got carried rather too far when Mr. Pickett absently signed an admission of service on a complaint brought in by a small but bossy law clerk from the office of Brooks, Hanlon and Glaser. Mr. Pickett accepted it with great efficiency, shoved the law clerk out the door and handed the document to Mr. Bohn to enter on the calendar.

Miss Truesdale herself could not have done it better. There was, therefore, no reason for Mr. Bohn to give a startled yelp, except for the trifling complication that the complaint should never have been delivered to them at all. It was intended for Wylie, Wylie, Thyrkelson and Wylie on the next floor of the building, and there was a short and spirited interlude during which Mr. Bohn ran a relay race against the elevator service and won, catching the law clerk by the tail of his coat.

Mr. Bohn returned, panting, to find his senior partners triumphantly waving a covey of blank quitclaim deeds, which had been traced down to Miss Truesdale's bottom drawer, in company with all the other legal forms, and neatly indexed.

"Laus Deo," said Mr. Bohn fervently. "Who types the dear little thing?" The question was rhetorical, as he was the youngest and most defenseless. He took the cover off the office typewriter, looked at the mechanism pessimistically and reached out his hand for the deeds.

"Two carbons," said Mr. Hatcher automatically. "See here, my boy, we've got to hurry. It's afternoon already."

"What about lunch?" Mr. Bohn inquired. He retracted the question immediately, realizing that it was definitely not old-school-tie, and grunted his way manfully through the process of getting three deeds and two carbons into the roller. He then found that he had put them all in upside down and said, "*Damnum absque injuria*" under his breath, with the accent on the first syllable. Mr. Hatcher, who disapproved of profanity, but could hardly take offense at legal terms, clucked in a thwarted manner.

"It's not as if Metcalf will sign this anyway," said Mr. Bohn gloomily, correcting his error in direction. "Shall I date it today or next week? If I date it next week, we can use it when the big lug comes around again. Or how about next month?"

Mr. Hatcher said he did not like to see pessimism. "Date it," he said, "today. We can type a new copy for next week."

His junior partner started to say something, thought better of it, and, with his teeth gripping his tongue, began to type the date. He then said "Oops" in a hurt voice and stopped.

Mr. Pickett leaned over his left shoulder, Mr. Hatcher over his right.

Mr. Hatcher said, "Tsk."

The date read "the %TH day of JUNR."

"That's very odd," said Mr. Bohn.

"You hit the *R* instead of the *E*, my boy," said Mr. Pickett. "And the percent sign instead of the 'Five'. It might have happened to anybody."

"It did not happen to me," said Mr. Bohn between his teeth. "I admit the *R*. That was mostly bad aim. But the 'Five' I hit. Look." He pointed it out on the typewriter, hit it again and it came out "%." "See?" he said, halfway between triumph and despair.

"The key says 'Five' and 'percent,' " said Mr. Hatcher, doing some detective work. "I believe you're typing with the capitals."

"Oh," said Mr. Bohn. He then pressed the tabulation key, causing the entire carriage of the machine to shoot madly across the page and Mr. Hatcher to leap nervously. The bell on the machine went "Ding," followed by a hush.

"H'm'm," said Mr. Bohn, strain making him monosyllabic. He pushed another shift and got a back space. He then began taking the plain rubber caps off the various keys scattered around the edges and was eventually rewarded by finding one marked "Shift Key." This he hit and something fell gratifyingly. He hit the 5. It was 5, and not %. They all beamed at one another.

It took another ten minutes for Hatcher, Pickett and Bohn to find an eraser, mainly because Miss Truesdale incomprehensibly kept hers in the desk drawer, the last place a lawyer would look for an eraser. There then arose a warm legal discussion as to the matter of alterations and erasures on legal documents, which was automatically closed when Mr. Bohn, attempting to move the deed in the typewriter so that he could get at his percent sign, ripped the page across.

Mr. Pickett, who had been on the non-Hatcher, or losing, side of the argument, cheered up enormously and rushed up a set of replacements. Mr. Bohn patiently assorted his carbons and put the whole thing back in the typewriter again, planting a large blue thumbprint on one corner of the deed. "*Locus sigilli*," said Mr. Bohn, thinking on his feet. He then began to type the date again, and this time it came out "the 5th day of june," which Mr. Hatcher and Mr. Pickett both agreed was close enough, but that next time Mr. Bohn should remember the capitals.

Mr. Bohn promised that he would try to do better and bent anxiously above the deed. "Metcalf with an *e*?" he inquired after a moment. Mr. Hatcher said no, Metcalf without an *e*; and Mr. Bohn said, oh, that was too bad, but they could erase it later. He got the party of the first part and the party of the second part safely in, plowed through the good and valuable consideration, and then demanded the property description.

Mr. Hatcher was ready for him and began to recite. " 'Commencing,' " said Mr. Hatcher happily, " 'at a point in the west line of Lot Twenty-eight distant fourteen hundred and ninety-five point ninety-five feet south from the northwest corner——' "

Mr. Bohn, who by hard work had got as far as the second *m* in "commencing," asked him please to wait. "Gently, John, gently," said Mr. Pickett.

The telephone rang. "Tell 'em we don't want any," Mr. Bohn grunted, looking around for the *e*.

"It's for you."

"Oh," He got up, sat on the edge of the desk and became involved in the statute of limitations with a lady client who was unable to see why a fine old legal formula like that should work in any way except in her favor.

Behind his junior partner's back, Mr. Hatcher stabbed tentatively at the keyboard, got the *e* Mr. Bohn had been seeking and shot through "—ncing" in a mad rush involving not more than sixty seconds. Carried away by this successful offensive, he really settled down to work.

Mr. Bohn hung up thoughtfully and returned to his duties to find that his superior had written "at apount 9n the qest line." Mr. Hatcher got up and said, with careful nonchalance, that Mr. Bohn might as well finish the typing, since he had started it. He also said he thought typewriters should be planned on a more scientific basis.

Mr. Bohn said, "How true," as his mother had raised him carefully, and sat down again. Mr. Pickett said anxiously, "Would you like a drink of water, my boy?" and Mr. Hatcher, still dictating, said, "'Of Lot Twenty-eight distant fourteen hundred and ninety-five point ninety-five feet south——' "

"Please," said Mr. Bohn faintly. By the time Mr. Pickett returned from the water cooler, the deed had progressed as far as "distant," with Mr. Bohn considerably cheered by the discovery of the symbol / for striking out unwanted letters, of which he had several, all involuntary.

"'Fourteen hundred and ninety-five point ninety-five,'" said Mr. Hatcher. About a minute later he said it again, as Mr. Bohn appeared to be in a coma. Mr. Bohn, in the tones of a man betrayed, said, "There is no Figure One on this damn machine."

Both his partners agreed that there must be, implying that Mr. Bohn was merely being difficult. "There is no Figure One," said Mr. Bohn. He pushed his chair back from the desk, planted both elbows on his knees and gave himself over to a survey of the keyboard, with his colleagues breathing helpfully down his neck. After a few moments, he had them on his side. There was no Figure One.

"Use an *i*," said Mr. Pickett gallantly.

Mr. Bohn used an *i*. The results was "i495.95 feet." "It might be considered a defect in the deed," said Mr. Bohn plaintively. "How about a capital *I*?" He went back and produced "I495.95," which was officially regarded as an improvement but still left Mr. Bohn unsatisfied. "Jean uses a Figure One," he insisted, rather stubbornly.

Mr. Hatcher said that their secretary was a remarkable young woman, but did Mr. Bohn know that it was already two o'clock, with Mr. Metcalf due at two-thirty? Mr. Bohn's typing finger—the index one—returned meekly to its post.

Mr. Hatcher cleared his throat. "'South from the northwest corner of the east one half of the northwest one quarter——' You can write one half out in full," he said kindly.

Mr. Bohn, however, had just discovered "$\frac{1}{2}$" on his machine and had no intention of wasting anything so pretty. "The . . . east . . . $\frac{1}{2}$ . . . of . . . the . . . northwest . . . $\frac{1}{2}$——"

"Northwest quarter, not half," Mr. Hatcher interrupted. "The quarter's on top of the half. Doesn't that mean you use your capital key again? Here." He held the shift key down for Mr. Bohn, neither of them having discovered the shift lock, and Mr. Bohn patiently went back. Unfortunately, he miscalculated his distances—and the result was "the northwest $\frac{1}{2}\frac{1}{4}$," which Mr. Pickett, in a moment of misguided humor, said was an entirely new note in legal description.

He got a joint look implying that he was being frivolous, to which he responded by repentantly holding out the eraser, which had been put in his custody. Mr. Bohn undid his necktie and the top button of his shirt, and Mr. Hatcher mopped his brow. "Northwest quarter—then what?" said Mr. Bohn.

"'Of Section Twenty-four, Township ——'" Mr. Hatcher paused tragically. "'Township One hundred eleven,'" he said. "If you use the capital *I* for that, my boy, you'll have a Roman Numeral Three. Which I don't think conveys the description at all satisfactorily."

Mr. Bohn glared at the keyboard and muttered darkly to himself. Mr. Pickett said hesitantly, "You could write it out. One hundred eleven, you know."

"True, sir," said Mr. Bohn respectfully, finding unexplored depths of wisdom in his partners. He clenched his tongue between his teeth again, typed out "One Hyndred elven" and swore gently.

Mr. Hatcher, peering over his shoulder, said with infinite tact that the intent seemed to be clear and that time was pressing. "'Range Twenty-three comma then south——' Have you been putting in any commas, Mac, my boy?"

Mac my boy admitted regretfully that he had not. He then typed "Range 23?", having shifted again under the fond impression that all punctuation demanded this rite. Mr. Pickett held out the eraser without being asked.

"'Then south to a point distant two hundred eighty-nine point twenty-five feet——'" Mr. Hatcher went on, dictating at the considerate speed of a snail backing up. "'Then north parallel——'" There was a moment's silence. "I think you've spelled that wrong, my dear fellow."

"P-a-r-a-l-e-l-l." Mr. Bohn frowned. "It does look odd." He rubbed his nose crossly with the back of his hand, then brightened up. "Well, what the *l*?" he said, added "Joke," apologized manfully, was about to observe that the legal intent again appeared clear enough, and then gave an excited yelp.

Mr. Hatcher bit the words "parallel with said east line" in two and jumped.

"Look!" Mr. Bohn trilled. "The missing Number One. It's the *l*, as in 'parallel.' I knew it had to be somewhere. I can write a hundred and eleven now—see?" He wrote "111" after "parallel" in his excitement, said abjectly that he was sorry, but he had been carried away, and marked the figures out with his treasured stroke line.

Mr. Hatcher said kindly that it was quite natural to have been deeply moved by the discovery, but that they must keep to the text. He then went on with his dictation, Mr. Bohn in laborious pursuit. They came at last to a triumphant close, and Mr. Bohn put in his last period and gazed admiringly at the deed.

"A trifle smudged," he admitted, "but authentic."

Mr. Hatcher—a man who had no faith in electric clocks—took his own timepiece from his vest pocket. "Mr. Metcalf," he observed, "is usually prompt."

Mr. Bohn, who was suffering from reaction after the thrill of the chase, said gloomily that it wouldn't do much good if he was prompt. "He won't sign the deed anyway, and there's no use kidding ourselves. That old pickle ——" The door opened.

Mr. Bohn nearly bit his tongue off. Mr. Hatcher and Mr. Pickett came to attention. Mr. Metcalf entered the room. Mr. Metcalf was a large man with two chins, both of which stuck out pugnaciously. He wore his hat as if he had had a fight with it, and his eyes had the tender, maternal glint of a rock pile. His suit was steel-gray to match them. His tie was orange and brown with zigzag stripes, and he had chosen the pattern because he liked it.

Obviously surprised to find the entire firm of Hatcher, Pickett and Bohn in their front office, Mr. Metcalf stopped on the threshold, then came all the way in.

"Well, gentlemen!" he said.

"Good afternoon, good afternoon," said Mr. Pickett. His cordiality bounced like india rubber off Mr. Metcalf's facade, and he retired, deflated.

Mr. Bohn sat silent for a moment, twiddling with the typewriter keys, then glanced dubiously at the deed, which was still in the machine. The blue smudge where he had planted his carbonized thumb seemed to have spread. The use of the stroke line, which had seemed to him so masterly, now appeared excessive. His honest attempt to correct the spelling of "parallel" shrieked aloud of crass ignorance.

"Er," said Mr. Bohn, unresourcefully.

Mr. Metcalf swept them with a contemptuous glance. The room, owing to the divide-and-conquer system they had used on the files, was not looking its best. Mr. Hatcher and Mr. Pickett were not looking their best. Mr. Bohn was definitely looking his worst, and his surreptitious efforts to reorganize his necktie came too late. "Incompetent," said Mr. Metcalf's look.

Mr. Hatcher, the Mr. Hatcher who could reduce a witness to ashes, cleared his throat. "We—uh—our—uh," he said. "That is, Miss Truesdale —— We have just been preparing the quit-claim for your signature, Mr. Metcalf."

"So?" said Mr. Metcalf, clearly amused by their youthful optimism. "Want me to read it again, eh?" He gave a half-formed, wholly repulsive chuckle and held out his hand peremptorily. Three hearts sank as one. This was ritual. Mr. Metcalf always read it again, with tantalizing carefulness. Sometimes he even read it through twice before he graciously handed it back and said his little speech, which began, "Well, gentlemen, I hardly feel justified ——"

Thinking unthinkable thoughts, Mr. Bohn rolled the deed out of the typewriter, removed the top copy and handed it silently across to their visitor. Mr. Metcalf accepted it with a faint smile.

Mr. Bohn—no flowers, by request—gently removed the top sheet of carbon, preparatory to laying the deed copies out decently. The paper under the top carbon was blank.

Mr. Bohn gave a shriek like a damned soul, causing his colleagues to spin around. "Where in hell is the copy?" Mr. Bohn wailed, feverishly flinging aside the second piece of carbon paper. Beneath that, too, lay an untouched deed.

Hatcher, Pickett and Bohn looked at Bohn, Pickett and Hatcher. It was only too plain that evil influences were at work. A man has a right to expect a carbon to produce a copy. It is an immutable law of nature.

"I don't understand it," whispered Mr. Bohn, half awed, half shattered.

Mr. Metcalf, with the original of the quitclaim in his hand, gazed at them for a moment in silence. Then he turned the quit-claim over. On the back of it, written in reverse and looking like a wild Russian folksong, appeared the missing copy.

"You put your carbon paper in upside down," said Mr. Metcalf.

There fell upon the office of Hatcher, Pickett and Bohn a deathly stillness. The three partners stayed quite quiet, waiting for the explosion. "Incompetent" would be the mildest term that Mr. Metcalf could employ. If he terminated their legal relationship in one sweeping exit, there was nothing they could do. They merely avoided looking at one another.

Mr. Metcalf had turned the deed over again and was staring at it. "Who typed this thing?" he demanded. Mr. Bohn blushed, answering the question. Mr. Metcalf gave a snort, crossed over to Mr. Bohn, put his hands on the back of the chair and gave it a jerk. "Get out of there," said Mr. Metcalf.

Mr. Bohn got.

Mr. Metcalf sat down, pulled the machine toward him and looked around. "Give me three blank deeds," he ordered.

Mr. Bohn gave.

With impressive confidence, Mr. Metcalf took the deeds, shuffled them with the carbon paper and slipped the result into the carriage. "The shiny side of the carbon paper," he said, "goes down, not up." He gave Mr. Bohn a severe look, and Mr. Bohn said "Yes, sir," meekly.

Mr. Metcalf dusted his hands together briskly, then poised them above the keyboard. "First, the date," he said, pressed something, agilely moved the roller into place and, copying from the deed beside him, typed the day, the month and the year in rapid, neat succession. Mr. Pickett, bending over Mr. Metcalf's right shoulder, sucked in his breath with admiration. "Party of the first part," Mr. Metcalf went on spiritedly, his fingers frolicking over the keys. "Uh'm—no *e* on my name, young man."

"No, sir," said Mr. Bohn in an awed voice.

"Parties . . . consideration . . . and description." He screwed around to eye the junior partner again, having encountered Mr. Hatcher's "at apount ǫn the ǫest line." "What's this supposed to be—a point in the west line?"

Mr. Hatcher cleared his throat defensively. Mr. Bohn said, "I socked the wrong keys." Mr. Hatcher put a fatherly hand on his junior partner's shoulder.

"Ha," said Mr. Metcalf, and began to type. There was a moment during which the only sound was the rhythmic click of the keys, as tidy letters and figures raced across the page. There was not even a check in speed at "111."

"You're typing without looking at the keys," said Mr. Bohn, his voice cracking as it had not done since he was sixteen.

"The touch system," said Mr. Metcalf with commendable modesty. "Nothing to it at all, my boy."

"Amazing." Mr. Hatcher's voice was reverent.

Mr. Metcalf nodded amiably, continuing his exalted performance through "seventy-five acres, more or less" and plunging into "subject to encumbrances." He then pushed something and rolled the page up to peer at the closing paragraph. "'In witness whereof,'" he read, "'the party of the first part has hereunto set his hand and seal the day and year first above written.' You legal boys use very fancy language. Just check this description with me, Bohn."

They all checked, four heads in a huddle. To the end, Mr. Metcalf's performance had been flawless, not a comma misplaced. Mr. Metcalf withdrew the deed from the typewriter with a flourish that, in Mr. Bohn's hapless hands, would have torn it in two, laid it out on the desk, withdrew the carbons and presented to their view one perfect original and two copies, innocent of smudges, revisions or errors.

"There," said Mr. Metcalf, eying his handiwork with fatherly affection. He gazed at the deed thoughtfully. It seemed to lack something. A beautiful and exquisitely rounded manuscript, it still needed one final touch. Mr. Metcalf took from his vest pocket a large black fountain pen, and with a few flourishing strokes he completed his masterpiece.

"You boys can witness this, no doubt," said Mr. Metcalf.

He handed the signed document to Mr. Hatcher.

Mr. Hatcher took it with hands that shook slightly. Mr. Pickett, for once, was silent. Mr. Bohn gulped.

Mr. Metcalf, who knew a tribute when he saw one, said modestly, "Nothing to it at all. I do most of my own typing."

Hatcher, Pickett and Bohn stared at one another. Mr. Metcalf reached for his hat. The telephone rang.

Responding to his morning's training, Mr. Pickett picked it up and pushed the wrong button with his customary and infallible precision. "Hello?" said Mr. Pickett.

"You pushed the wrong button," said Mr. Metcalf promptly.

This was unanswerable. Mr. Pickett said helplessly, "I don't understand these things."

Mr. Metcalf put down his hat and took the phone away from Mr. Pickett. He punched the proper button, said "Hello" briskly, and nodded at Hatcher. "For you," he said. "Want to take it in your office? I'll switch it over." He waved Mr. Hatcher out of the room.

Mr. Hatcher departed, tenderly clutching to his heart the cherished document with its precious signature.

"Now, watch this carefully, Pickett," said Mr. Metcalf. In a simple, direct and masterful manner, he proceeded to push, switch and buzz, making the connection. Mr. Hatcher and the voice on the wire spoke to each other. "There you are," said Mr. Metcalf, and hung up.

"You know all about the buttons too," said Mr. Pickett in a thin, enchanted voice.

"Nothing to it," Mr. Metcalf said happily. "Here, I'll explain in detail. The top button represents ——"

Over his head, Mr. Pickett and Mr. Bohn gazed at each other.

Mr. Metcalf continued to expound the theory and practice of button-pushing. He was very happy. As a rule, he didn't care much for lawyers, but these people were charming.

MISS MAGGIE DOONS AND THE
WICKED CITY

Miss Maggie Doons rubbed her nose with the back of her hand and went to the calendar that hung above the kitchen sink.

She didn't want to know the date. It was Monday, and therefore washday. It was August, and therefore hot. These she knew. But the calendar had a picture, and wherever she went, the picture called after her. It was a photograph of a city at night, with lights pinpointing its luscious dark and skyscrapers cutting into the clouds. It was New York.

Maggie shook her head at it. It was a sinful, wicked city, well she knew, no place for a hard-working little scrapbag of a woman, and it was a foolish thing to hanker after, but there it was. She wanted to see it. It was full of cutthroats and foreign characters; it had dark and crooked streets in a place called Chinatown, thieves and murderers on the Bowery, and rich scandals in its gleaming palaces on Park Avenue. She knew, because she had seen movies and she heard things, and it was her own mother who had stayed on Ellis Island (in a bad temper, no doubt, but corrupting the officials with her eyes) and later had set foot on that great lane called Broadway. Broadway, where there were more lights than the stars, and where they would as soon slit your throat as look in your eye.

She stood there a moment, looking yearningly at the calendar, and then she turned and looked around the kitchen.

It was a fine big kitchen, and there was a tender Scotch tidiness in the way the red-striped towels hung on their racks and the saucepans marched on regimented hooks, but a body could have been in it too long so that the polished shine on the saucepans meant only elbow grease gone a-wasting, and the dear little darns in the towels meant tired eyes. Inside Maggie, her Scotch father said approvingly that anything worth doing was worth doing well, even after ten years of doing it in someone else's house. It was Maggie's Irish mother, from Kilkenny, who cocked her arms akimbo and upbraided her for being a wisher, a longing woman, and still staying in the same place.

Maggie sighed, and at the same moment the washing machine gave a sigh of its own and stopped swishing its suds about. All the clothes sank to the bottom of the tub and huddled there crossly. Maggie looked at the washing machine without any love for it. She would have to go and tell Mrs. Meacham that it had stopped again and that they would have to have the man in, and Mrs. Meacham did not like hearing these things.

Maggie sighed again, then jumped as the swinging door burst open and Master George Meacham waltzed in breezily. She wiped her hands hurriedly on her apron and said, "Where's your ma, Georgie?"

"In the living room." George located a handful of cookies,

then sat down on the kitchen table to chew. George chewed continuously. Maggie closed her eyes against the sight of his chewing, then she opened them and marched through the swinging door.

Mrs. Meacham was sitting on the rose-spattered chintz sofa beside a bag of golf clubs, and she was nursing a niblick with real affection. Her legs, stuck out in front of her, were short and rather stocky, and her tweed skirt had hiked up. Hard-bodied and healthy, she sat on the roses and hummed.

"Ma'am," said Maggie from the doorway.

"Oh, it's you." The humming stopped. "What's the matter now?" She looked at Maggie without welcome, light blue eyes displeased.

"It's the washing machine, ma'am. It's stopped again."

"Oh. Well, call up the man in the village."

"But the wash, ma'am—"

"Finish it in the tub, of course. Good heavens, Maggie, you can figure that out for yourself without bothering me."

Maggie nodded. She *had* figured it out for herself, but there had been a little hope that Mrs. Meacham would say the clothes could wait until the machine was fixed. Scrubbing was hard on a person's back, what with the dirt on George's socks and the required whiteness of Mr. Meacham's shirts. She said hopelessly, "Yes, ma'am," and turned to go out.

Mrs. Meacham's voice halted her briskly. "Oh, Maggie. Mr. Meacham's office wants him to take his vacation, starting next week, so we'll be going to the shore. We'll leave next Monday." Out of a vague, goodhearted impulse, she added, "It will make a nice change for you."

It would make a nice change, indeed. Instead of a washing machine that didn't work, she would do the clothes in the sink. Instead of her sunny kitchen, she would have the cabin's make-shift one, with the old iron stove that fought her biscuits and saddened her cakes. Something stirred in Maggie. It dated back a long way, and in more vigorous times it had been named the Irish Rebellion.

"Ma'am," said Maggie, frightening herself by the sound of her own voice, "I'm not going to the shore with you this year."

Mrs. Meacham's sandy eyebrows rose. "You're not what?"

"Not going with you, ma'am." Maggie's voice got firmer; that was Kilkenny, out on a limb. "I'm planning a little trip, Mrs. Meacham," said Maggie. "I'm vacationing in New York." She had said it, what for ten years had lain there in her mind like a singing. She was perfectly appalled.

Mrs. Meacham was perfectly unperturbed. She laughed good-humoredly. "Good heavens, my dear woman, I never heard such nonsense. You'd be lost in New York, quite apart from wasting all your money. It's lovely and cool at the shore, and of course you'll come." She patted her niblick briskly. "Now, go and call the washing-machine man, and tell him to hurry for once. There's no reason we should wait."

The Meachams never waited. It was the family motto. Maggie looked at Mrs. Meacham, and her little spurt of revolt lay down like an obedient puppy. "Yes, Mrs. Meacham," said Maggie. She hid her hands in her apron and hurried back to the kitchen. Whatever had possessed her, to be talking such nonsense? Her, with her good job!

George was still in the kitchen. He had spilled milk on the floor, and it lay in a white puddle, which he poked casually with a dirty shoe. "Wipe that up, Maggie, will you?" said Master George, stuffed and lordly.

Maggie reached for a cloth. The calendar caught her eye and winked at her.

Very suddenly, with a sort of gentle fierceness, Maggie folded up the cloth and put it away. She looked at George, then at the clock. Mr. Lillis, at the bank's savings window, would be surprised to have Miss Doons asking to draw out her money, but he would not argue about it. Banks are not privileged to raise sandy eyebrows at people.

You're mad, said Mr. Doons inside her. *You're the beat of my heart*, said Mrs. Doons tenderly.

Maggie went upstairs, and there, in her neat plain room, she wrote a short note. It said, "Dear Mrs. Meacham and Mr. Meacham. I am going to New York. I hope you have a nice time at the shore. I will see the man about the washing machine on my way to the train. Faithfully yours, Maggie Doons."

She put a few clothes into her suitcase, which had not been farther than the shore for ten years, and went downstairs. George had gone, and the milk was drying in a sticky film on the floor. She hesitated a moment, moved toward the cleaning rag, then stopped and shook her head.

She put the note on the table, weighted it with the bread knife, went softly to her calendar, took it down and tucked it under her arm.

Then Maggie Doons nodded to herself and stepped out the back door.

New York was a far-off place, no less than five hours. Obedient to the instinct of escape, she had taken the first train out of the village station, and this maneuver had complicated the lives of ensuing stationmasters, so that she shuttled back and forth until her feet were rightly set on the paths of wickedness. She sat quiet on the train at last, with her hands holding each other for company and a terrible thrill where her lunch should have been. The train wheels clicked away, and first she was very alert and excited, and then she was very sleepy and excited, and by and by her head fell back against the cushion and her eyes closed and her mouth opened.

That was how Maggie Doons came into Grand Central Terminal, rushing into the wicked city through a great black tunnel and not even knowing it. The train shook all over, and it woke Maggie, who sat up with her mouth dry and her insides in a fine state of nervousness and her hands grabbing for her purse, which was still there and only by the grace of God when you thought of it, the world being what it is to travelers.

The conductor came down the aisle, and when she asked, he assured her that it was indeed New York. It was hard to believe, because all she could see was a maze of panting trains, but when she had gone up the steps and found herself in the bright cathedral they called a railroad station, with people swirling around her like leaves on a millpond, she knew this was New York all right, and might the Lord forgive its sins because it was very beautiful and very gay.

She knew, in a bemused way that the first thing to do was find a nice hotel room and settle herself, but the moment she stepped outside the station, Maggie Doons was a lost woman. Hither and back she trotted, coaxed by wonderful sight and sound, entranced by the lavish strangeness and all the people. Bright bits of girls went chattering by on long stems of legs with their gay skirts like a wink, and each such a small enchantment that Maggie felt a dim impatience because only an occasional young man turned with a wistful look. She would have liked for one to turn all the way around and go back to take an elbow.

"Now, where would I be getting such ideas?" said Maggie to herself wonderingly, impressed to find that New York was already lowering the Doons principles. Ah, it was a wicked city, this one. She saw a policeman standing on a corner, a big man, with his hands spread on his hips. He looked bored, and Maggie marveled, because how could a policeman in New York ever look bored, with thievery sprouting on every corner and doubtless a murder or two down the block?

She shuddered deliciously and marched on until she came to a sign that said "Fifth Avenue," where she turned to walk down a street Saint Peter might have planned, with great, glassed-in stores and windows with lovely wax ladies posturing in fur coats, being cool in there, no doubt, although she could not bring herself to go in and see, her purse being an unwary creature.

For a long time Maggie walked, and after a while she left Saint Peter's beautiful way and walked straight into the Other Gentleman's lane with its sign saying, "Broadway." Maggie drew a long and happy sigh. Here was wickedness itself, and it was on this very road that her mother had walked, with her little arched feet going fast and her heart keeping up with them. That was a long time ago, but sinfulness was a fine enduring thing.

She went up the street. There was a shop with baby turtles in it, and a shop with music coming out, and a beautiful shop where you could climb onto a high white stool and drink orange juice out of tall glasses. There were movie theatres with strange, huge pictures of ladies and gentlemen, and there was a place called a shooting gallery, which fixed Maggie in her tracks until a policeman went past and never even glanced in.

The street led her like a flute calling, but there is a limit to all of us, and it begins in the feet. Maggie's shoes suddenly stopped fitting her, and at the same time she became aware of a deep yearning inside, which was a yearning by the clock and had to do with dinner.

She remembered passing a little sandwich shop, and she turned and went back to it. The shop had booths where a person could take off her shoes, and, with her feet resting peacefully and a large ham sandwich standing up to her and a steaming cup of coffee next to it, Maggie was a happy woman.

She took her time. She took it so spun out, in fact, that she was not prepared for what Broadway had done in her absence. The sky had gone almost dark in a trail of misty amethyst, and the little man-made lights had crept out while she had been sitting with her coffee. Yellow they were, and pink and red and green and a bright electric blue, and they ran up and down her mother's street, winking and chasing their tails in streamers of brilliance. Around the theatres they rushed, and their colors were a shock and a bliss to the eye. They stabbed yellow from the office buildings, and red and green from the traffic lights, and white from the street lamps, and between and over and around they sent out sparkles like a great handful of gems. She stood on the street, clutching her suitcase, and she was hard put to it to keep her feet decorous on the pavement.

Finally she drifted back to the earth and remembered she must find herself a hotel to stop in. This was accomplished daringly by asking advice from a stranger, and the stranger Maggie picked was a yellow-haired lady in a tight black dress, who called Maggie "dearie" with great happiness and affection. The lady's cheeks were a very gay sort of red, and her lashes stuck out in fine merry points like little daggers, and a critical party might think she was a bit free in the use of her blue eyes when they chanced to light on something in trousers, but for Maggie's taste she was a fine, bright woman and most helpful. She gave Maggie the address of a hotel which she said was a real nice place if you locked the door, dearie, and then she even put Maggie on the right bus and waved her goodbye.

The hotel was a bit small and the lobby of it was very dark, but Maggie knew trustingly that it was good place, else the yellow-haired lady would not have sent her there. Safe as a nesting thrush, she unpacked her suitcase, put on her cotton nightgown and climbed into bed, knowing that the great city lay just outside her window. She fell asleep within the minute, and she slept without dreaming, for why would a person dream when waking would be the best dream of all come true?

She opened her eyes to bright sunlight and the dream still there, with the traffic purring and growling outside and the wicked, gay city going about its wicked, gay business. She dressed in her neat black suit and her placid small hat, and then she left her room with the key held tight in her hand, it being the first key which had ever been completely her own.

There, beyond the hotel door, lay the town. Maggie stepped through the lobby and out into the world, knowing, with a fast-beating heart, that beyond lay all the wickedness a body could ask for. All she had to do was look for it.

She looked. It could not be said of Maggie Doons that she did not search earnestly and well, because she did. She went into small streets and big streets; she looked into strange faces and heard all the tongues of Babel. She walked through the intricate, tiny maze of Chinatown's Mott and Pell Streets and listened to the sweet singsong of Oriental voices, and she even came upon a sign with "Bowery" unblushingly on it. There were drunken gentlemen there, to be sure, and their clothes were a sight to behold, but the raggedness of them only stirred in Maggie's thin fingers an instinct to sew, and you could not name as wickedness what was only a sad kind of failure. There were drunks in Kilkenny too, without a doubt, and New York's most eager guest had expected better things.

Could it be that New York's sins were too carefully hidden, or was it that Maggie Doons failed to have the seeing eye? It was far too soon to tell, and she went back to the lights and glitter of Broadway, where the rather undressed ladies gleamed from great signs and the lights twisted like snakes.

There was a movie house so bright it was like a fire, and Maggie bought a ticket and went in, to be swallowed up in a great darkness. The movie was a Western one, and it might well be she could have seen it in the Meachams' village on one of her rare nights off, so she stopped looking at the screen with all its galloping horses and exploding guns and she looked instead at the people around her. There was a young pair in front, for instance, wound well and tight in each other's arms, but the village had such young people too, and where was the wonder in two young folks doing a bit of loving? They seemed happy, not wicked, and with a sigh Maggie concluded that was what they were.

A little wistfully, she rose from the leather seat and went back to her hotel.

Three days she had like that, three mortal days, each ending with her hotel room and not one bright bit of sin to be recounted and admired. On the third night she came upon the lovely sight of the East River, lying gray and wide under a hot sky, with the lights of a spiderweb bridge stabbing down into it and a great moth of an airplane flying over. Maggie stood and stared for a long, rich time, and if she had come to New York to be glimmered by the beauty of things, she could have gone back to the Meachams with a full content heart. But beauty she had seen before, there being such things as spring apple blossoms in the Meachams' yard, and other such things as a full moon picking up the branches of a tree to paint it against the white shingles of the Meachams' house, and even such things as a fresh golden baking and the crisp froth of egg whites in a blue bowl.

She left the river at last and walked down a thin little street, where there were so many people that she felt there must be some wickedness, too. But the heat had laid a heavy hand on the city, and the people had only moved out from their crowded cracker-box rooms to find a little relief. There were fat, spreading ladies sitting on front steps, and thin tall boys in still groups under the street lights. There were listless babies in perambulators, and men playing cards. Harmless and aimless, hot and tired—she could have found all this in the little village she had left behind her. It was a hard thing to come all the way to a big and glamorous city and then to find in it your own home town.

She did not know that New York had her on its mind.

She did not know it even when, the next afternoon, on a small side street, she came upon her rather special fate. It hardly looked like fate; it looked more like three little boys, in stringy shirts and overworked pants, wrestling over a bottle of soda pop. The

littlest boy, who was blue-eyed and dirty, had temporary possession, and he backed away from his young bandit friends and into
Maggie. He said, "Sorry, ma'am," and kept on backing, watch-
fully. Maggie thought of Georgie Meacham, for whom apolo-
gies did not exist, and her heart warmed toward this young
man, hoping he would keep the bottle.

Possession and politeness did him no good. There was a sudden grab, and the soda pop was out of his custody. He gave a
brief yelp and dived for ownership again, but the biggest boy
held it out of reach and laughed at him. The third boy yelled
suddenly, "Throw it to me, Tommy. Throw it over here."

Tommy threw, and the littlest boy leaped despairingly at
the same moment, deflecting his aim. There was a warning howl,
then the crash and tinkle of a bottle of soda pop soaring through
a first-floor window.

Perhaps you have seen baby partridges when the mother
clucks at them that danger is coming, and how they suddenly
crouch and vanish in the stillness and the leafiness of their
woods. That was how it was with Maggie's three young men.
One moment they were there, shocked speechless, and the next
moment the sidewalk had swallowed them up, with the blessed
assistance of two ashcans. Maggie stood alone, but only for a
moment. A window shot up in the stricken building, and a
screaming female voice demanded the exact whereabouts of the
hand that had thrown the missile.

Maggie stood, tranced and staring. Wrath surged in a riot,
and all around heads came popping forth like a Punch-and-Judy
show. Behind the ashcans, the culprits lurked silent, and the
cans quivered faintly like fields of wheat with a storm passing
over.

A big voice behind Maggie said, "What's going on here?"
and Maggie turned to find one of those fine figures in blue she
had so much admired on Broadway. The policeman settled on
the loudest screamer, which was the first lady, and from her

wails he sorted out the crime. He turned to Maggie. "Ma'am," he said politely, "did you see who threw the bottle?"

Maggie looked at the ashcans and thought of the little bit of a blue-eyed thing and his skinny little friends. All she had to do was point and the brass-buttoned Law would take action.

"Ma'am?" said the policeman patiently.

She drew a deep breath. "I threw it, officer," said Maggie Doons grandly.

He looked at her in a disbelieving way.

The screaming lady shrieked passionately, "You'll pay for it. You'll pay for it! Officer—"

The policeman pushed his cap back and scratched his head. "Why, ma'am?" said the policeman to Maggie. "Why did you throw the bottle?"

"I wished to," said Maggie.

"Oh, hell," said the policeman, quietlike.

That was how it was that Maggie Doons saw the inside of a station house. It was an old, dignified place, full of gentlemen in uniform and a couple of characters who were presumably dregs of humanity, else what would they be doing in the charge of these grand boys in blue? Maggie looked admiringly at the sweating young policeman, who now had her in custody, with the broken-window lady tramping along behind him in a financial frenzy.

The policeman at the desk, who was addressed as Lieutenant, looked up from the big green book in front of him. "What happened, Joe?" he asked. Joe told him briefly. The Lieutenant heard him through, then eyed Maggie wearily. "Will you pay for the broken window, ma'am?"

She regarded him with thoughtfulness. It would be wrong for her to pay for the window; she had not broken it. The little partridges hiding behind the ashcans would be well away by now. Maggie shook her head.

The Lieutenant turned to the lamenting owner of the window. "You want to enter a complaint, ma'am?" Her head bobbed up and down in an impassioned affirmative, and the Lieutenant turned back to Maggie, pen in hand. "Name?" he said.

"Miss Maggie Doons," said Maggie.

"Address? Age?" He entered them neatly. "Any friend you'd like to call from here?" He fixed his gaze hopefully on the undeniable respectability of Miss Doons' hat.

"A friend?" said Maggie unbelievingly. She caught her breath. "Oh, but there is only the Meachams. The people I work for. You would not be calling the Meachams, surely?"

"Not if you don't want us to," said the Lieutenant. He glanced at the big station-house clock. "But it's a bit late to get you into court this afternoon, and unless you want to put up your own bail, we'll have to hold you for night court."

"Bail?" said Maggie, wondering what fine new thing bail would be.

The Lieutenant explained about bail. Maggie was not interested. She was on the sure moral grounds of one who does not intend to pay out cash for an offense not committed. Besides, she was happy where she was. More than happy, she was fascinated. Surely, if one was going to meet up with real wickedness, she had come to the right place.

"No bail," said Maggie firmly.

The Lieutenant shrugged his regret. "All right, then," he said. "You'll both have to appear in night court."

"Me, too?" said the lady of the window.

"Sure, you too."

The lady settled her hands on her hips. "And when do I get my boys their suppers and into bed?" she demanded. "You cops! First you let people break my windows for me, and then you keep me up all night making complaints, and never a thought for my family."

The Lieutenant mopped his brow. He seemed to be feeling

the heat. "Can't be helped, ma'am. If you want to make the complaint, you've got to stick with it." He glanced at Maggie.

But Maggie's mind was off in a trance, and she was gazing dreamlike at the lady. "Your boys?" said Maggie.

"Three," said the lady shortly, clearly wishing she had six to make the tale more pitiful. "Three, and it might as well be a regiment, the life they lead me. It's all very well throwing bottles through windows," she added bitterly, "but you never think of the trouble you cause."

"Three little boys?" said Maggie.

"Three little boys. Not that I could expect an unmarried female to understand—"

Three little boys. And a soda-pop bottle. Three little partridges.

"Mister Lieutenant," said Maggie.

"Yep?"

"Mister Lieutenant, I think I've changed my mind. I'll pay for the window." She opened the catch on her purse and looked delicately at the lady. "How much would it be, then?"

The lady looked surprised. "Eight dollars. Maybe ten. Besides the worry."

Maggie nodded her head soberly. There was the worry too, of course. "I'll give you twelve," she said. Twelve was too much, and Mr. Doons in her head was calling her impractical, but perhaps with the extra the lady would buy her three little boys a bottle of soda pop apiece, and then there would not be all the fighting. And even maybe a pair of pants for the littlest blue-eyed one. She counted the money out on the desk.

The lady snatched at it.

The Lieutenant looked at Maggie. "Okay," he said. "She's withdrawing her complaint. You can both go."

The lady had already gone, moving like a quick breeze, but Maggie lingered, gazing around her with yearning and hopefulness.

The Lieutenant, who had started writing on the police blotter again, looked up and smiled at her. "Something else we can do for you, ma'am?"

Maggie nodded. Her voice was small, but it was urgent. "Mister Lieutenant," she said, "the—the gentlemen over there. Did they do something bad?"

The Lieutenant glanced toward the corner. "Eviction case. We're waiting for the landlord."

"Oh," said Maggie wistfully. She had hoped they might be cutthroats in a small way, and they were not. It was very hard. In the whole station house there was just herself and the policemen and two people come about an eviction. She pressed closer to the desk. "You must be very busy men here," said Maggie prayerfully. "This is a fine, wicked town, is it not?"

The Lieutenant gave her a long, thoughtful look, then he nodded his head. "I suppose it is," he said. "There's about one homicide a day, and last year there were over ninety thousand felonies reported."

Maggie looked back at him gravely. He was not telling her the truth, of course, because where could there be a town that was that bad? People would have no time for their ordinary business. But he was a fine kind man to be telling her such a magnificent story. She said goodbye and started for the door.

The Lieutenant said, "So long, ma'am, take care of yourself," before he turned back to his work.

Maggie walked down the steps of the station house, thinking hard. The Meachams wouldn't be gone to the shore yet, but, the way things were, she might as well go home. She had been to the one sure place and it had cost her twelve dollars, but now she knew that New York was not a wicked town at all. She would go back to her own kitchen and hang the calendar on the wall again, and when she looked at it, there would be much to remember. There would be the lovely lights on the East River, and the friendly good people under the hot street lamps, and the yellow-haired lady, and the kind policeman, and the dear riot that was Broadway.

Well, it would be a treasure to save up in her mind against the days when the washing machine would not work and Georgie tracked up the kitchen floor.

The back door of the Meachams' house was unlocked, and Maggie came through it and put her suitcase down in the middle of the kitchen floor. Nothing had changed, except that the neat crisp place she had left now had the frantic, lop-eared look of an alley cat. Dishes were piled, unscraped, in the sink. The saucepans were burned, the towels were dirty, and a pool of water leaked stealthily from under the refrigerator.

She was standing there, looking at it, when Mrs. Meacham came through the swinging door, with George behind her. "Maggie!" said Mrs. Meacham in a wrath that was diluted with relief. Maggie knew the relief for what it was. The Meachams would eat better now.

Maggie said, "Yes, ma'am. I came back early."

"I see you did," said Mrs. Meacham frostily, "and about time." She stood staring for a moment, her mouth tight. Then she said, "Well, the less said about it the better, I suppose. Get your things off and start straightening up. You've caused us a great deal of inconvenience." She waited for Maggie to say she was sorry, but Maggie stayed silent, and after a minute Mrs. Meacham turned on her heel and left.

George remained, staring. George was chewing again. His shoes were dirty, and he had tracked up the floor. "I want some cookies," he said suddenly, and his voice snapped its fingers at her.

Maggie looked at him. And if she wanted to, she thought, she could be telling Master George a thing or two. Maybe she had not found the wickedness she had gone to look for, but she had been in a fine great city, the biggest of them all, and she had seen many things beyond the Meachams' little back yard.

And then, suddenly, a beautiful brave light came down from the ceiling and shone around Maggie's head. Oh, it was wrong she was about the wickedness! It had been there, right under her questing nose, and she had paid no attention. In all that beautiful, respectable city there was one piece of real sinfulness no one could argue with, and who should know it better than Maggie Doons, because she was that piece? It was Maggie Doons, was it not, who was taken to the police station house in custody of the Law? It was Maggie Doons, was it not, whose name was immortalized in black ink on a police blotter?

She looked at George, and scorn rose within her, blissful and luxurious. Had the Meachams ever been arrested, then? No. What policeman would have them?

She fixed her eye on George, and she spoke. "Get out of here," said Maggie. "You'll have your cookies when I've a mind to it." A child he was, unused to the ways of the sinful, and perhaps she should not have spoken so. But when she opened her mouth again, the words were still, "Get out!"

For a long moment George gazed at her. Then he turned and scuttled away.

Maggie drew a deep breath, then she bent down and opened her suitcase. From its neat interior she drew out her calendar and hung it reverently in its accustomed place, then stepped back to admire New York's lights. Oh, a fine wicked town it was, after all! A demoralizing town, from which even a stranger could not depart without her name being written, beautiful and lasting, on a police blotter.

She gazed for a moment at the lights, then she nodded her head firmly, picked up her suitcase, and started to climb the back stairs.

With her heart as light as an Irishman's coattails, Maggie Doons went up to change her dress.

ESCAPE

THE road lay exactly as Matthew had remembered it, brown-rutted and narrow, and the bushes along it tangled with wind. There were no flowers at all, although it was summer, and what grass there was clung to the ground in stubborn, tufted mats.

He had taken the train out and then the bus, the long way that he and Cathy had once come, and then he had walked up from the sea village, leaving behind the brown huts and the bright gardens and the neat people. He had supposed he would be very aware of Cathy—in fact, he vaguely thought he had come to find her again—but she was dead these twelve years, and there was no ghost keeping step with him.

The road began to rise sharply, and when he came to the next bend, the strong westering light of the sun shone full in his eyes and the black edge of the overhanging cliff was silhouetted just ahead of him. Beyond that there was nothing except sky and gulls and the heavy sound of the sea.

He walked to the rim of space and looked over, straight down the drop of sheer cliff to the rocks more than a hundred feet below. The rocks glistened as the waves pulled back and bared them for a moment like teeth, then vanished under the heavy surge and pouring of water with only spitting amber froth left to hiss on the shingle. There was a sucking sound each time a wave slid back from the shore, and then there came the heavy crash and pound of an incoming breaker, and after a moment the noises began to hurt his head and he turned away from watching.

He stood for a moment with his back to the sea and looked around him, although there was nothing but flat, bare space to look at, a few weeds, and to one side of the road's end, a straggle of brown bushes, dense and woolly like grazing sheep and giving shelter, perhaps, to birds or small animals.

He spread his coat and sat down, a short distance back from the cliff. It was twenty years since he had come here on a picnic with Cathy, and it was all just as it had been then; but in spite of the sameness, or perhaps because of it, he was quite unable to conjure her up. He could remember that she had been wearing a yellow dress and some kind of band to keep her hair out of her eyes, but they were just pieces of a picture and not Cathy.

What he could see much more clearly was himself, sitting stiffly on the other side of the picnic basket and going over phrases in his mind so that, when he asked her to marry him, he would be sure to use the right words. None of the sentences came out the way he wanted them, and it began to look as if he would sit there dumbly forever.

Then she had poured coffee from the thermos bottle into a tin cup, and when she had handed the cup to him, he had taken it awkwardly and spilled coffee onto the clean napkin she had laid out for a tablecloth. He had sat there watching the brown stain spread and feeling terribly ashamed of his clumsiness. And then, because he loved her so and had wanted everything to be exactly right, he had said, "Oh, Cathy," in a kind of groan and turned his head away.

She had got up instantly from the grass and gone straight to his side, and it was that moment that came back to him now, twenty years later, so that her ghost visited him absolutely. He was sure the memory was right, because it was so exactly like Cathy, who went to people instead of waiting for them to come to her.

He had had his eyes closed, remembering her there. When he opened them, she was gone, and the sun was shining full in his face and too strongly.

After a moment, he drew his knees up and hunched over, leaning his forehead against them, a small gray man, past middle years, a little foolish to be sitting there shelved between burning sky and pounding sea. He felt a slight sickness, perhaps from the sun or the exertion, or from remembering. He said, "Cathy?" experimentally, but she was truly gone, and he had very little hope that she would come back again.

He looked down at his hands.

They had never been a worker's hands; they were narrow palmed, not tanned, swollen now and bent at the knuckles. They had been good hands for a teacher, gentle with books and capable with a pen, and he had never meant them to stop being a teacher's hands. Cathy had been deeply proud of his profession and had made highhearted plans for promotion, not so much because she was ambitious as because she wanted everyone to appreciate him. She was incapable of buying so much as a bag of groceries or a new hat without weaving in some remark about his students or the number of papers he had corrected the night before, and she had once turned quite pink with pleasure when a bank teller had prematurely granted him a Ph. D. and called him Doctor.

When she had died suddenly, within the space of a day, saying how foolish it was to be sick like this and worrying about whether he had had his lunch, he lost more than he could bear to lose. He lost his own faith, and although he tried stubbornly and with a kind of desperation, he couldn't learn how to go on without it. It seemed impossible to do anything right.

He told himself prayerfully that it was the shock and that time would cure him, and perhaps time would have but it was never given. The school could not afford patience, and the first warning came when the Dean had him in for a private interview, called him Matthew heartily and spoke of pulling oneself together and not letting our youngsters down.

He had left the Dean's office, frightened and ashamed and determined to do better, but the shadows gathered and he couldn't fight against them. There were no more interviews with the Dean, but when his contract expired, he was told that it would not be renewed.

Now he sat still, on his patch of land above the sea, staring at his hands. It all seemed an endlessly long time ago, and in the years between, there was nothing worth the remembering.

He had always meant to go back to teaching, but the fear of failing again in the only work he cared about kept him from applying for a position, and he finally took a job in a book-keeper's office. His neatness helped him with the straight red lines and the black mathematical figures, but the close columns made his eyes ache and he couldn't afford new glasses. The mistakes he made were from trying to hurry, not carelessness, but they were still mistakes, and he wasn't being paid to add up errors at the foot of a ledger page. He had lost that job, as he had lost all the later ones, and it seemed as if he had disobliged the world by not being able to make a living in it.

He tried very hard to keep his self-respect, and he knotted his broken shoelaces together and learned to conceal the frayed cuffs of his shirt sleeves when he was applying for work; but the people who interviewed him always saw through to the empti-ness beyond, and so did the clerks at stores where he asked for credit, and the landladies who wanted two months' rent in advance.

He was getting old, and he had to try too hard; the work you pleaded for, you could never get. He wondered what Cathy's faith would make of him now. His last job had been as cashier in a tiny restaurant, and he had thought he was safe for a while in the wire cage that sheltered him between morning and night. The laconic "Out of Business" sign on the restaurant's door had cut him off abruptly, without warning. His rent was paid only to the first of the month.

That was yesterday. Tomorrow he would have to start look-ing for another job. They would ask him his age, his experience;

they would promise to keep him in mind, and then they would forget him. The time between jobs would be longer than ever; the jobs, briefer. The rooms he rented would be successively shabbier. The loneliness, the knowledge of failure, and the emptiness would lie down beside him at night, wake with him in the morning. He was no longer sure that the living was worth the fear.

This time he said, "God?" the way he had said, "Cathy?"— experimentally, not irreverently. He had never been a religious man, but if there were something outside that could fill the well, he would like to know. He wanted a reason.

The bland sky withheld any sign. The sheep-shadows of the bushes were lengthening, and the wind had died down. He was completely alone, with the cliff.

He released his thoughts slowly, knowing where they would lead. He believed in nothing, almost he was nothing, and so nothing would be lost.

An inexpressible relief filled him. All he had to do was walk to the cliff and, at the cliff's edge, not stop. He wondered if that was why he had chosen this place to come to, an exit so close at hand, but whether he had come consciously or unconsciously was of no importance. He was here. He would never force a door to death, but this one was open. Ten yards of walking, no more than a man might stroll to his own gate at the foot of his garden path, and the giant fist of the sea would close about him.

The place held its breath. He felt very small and infinitely safe. There was a kindness, almost a peace, about coming to it so easily. He had never been especially brave, and now bravery was not even going to be required. It made him feel curiously welcome.

He got to his feet and started to walk to the cliff, not hurrying, but not walking slowly either, like any man keeping any appointment.

He was level with the brown bushes before he saw what he

hadn't seen before, a small gray shape that might be a rock or an animal. Then it moved, and he realized he was looking at a child.

It was a small boy, very small, intensely quiet. There was no way of knowing how long he had been there, settled back on thin haunches and staring. He was holding some sort of toy in one hand, a bit of wood shaped roughly like a boat, and he had a pale, flat face like a goblin's, and a small goblin smile. His shirt could have been white once, but it was gray now, and his little short trousers were gray and held up nicely with a bit of string.

Matthew stared back, and the peace he had felt began to fade. He had been so comfortably near the end, and now there would be this delay while he sent the child away, and afterwards it might be harder.

Harder, he thought, but not really any different. He had made a pact with the cliff, and the place would see he kept it. In the end, it would all be the same.

He said, "Go away. Go home," the way he might have said it to a strange dog. The child didn't move, and he said it again, louder. The goblin stayed there, so still it might almost have been a patch of sea fog that had drifted in and settled down to become a haunt.

"Go away! Home!" His voice was shrill and louder than he meant it to be. The goblin smile never wavered, but the child held out its toy.

Matthew said, "No," quickly, beginning to be angry, but the child stayed there with its fixed, meaningless smile and the little wooden ship floating on its hand, the hand moving rhythmically to make a private ocean.

Matthew drew in his breath sharply. He would *not* be interrupted. He studied the little crouched thing for a moment. Perhaps, for some reason of its own, the child wanted him to have the toy. He would take it, and the little boy would go away.

He said, "Well, give it to me. Come here and give it to me."
He might as well have talked to the bushes.

His heart was beating too hard. He felt a little dizzy with
the need to have the child go away, to leave him so he could
escape to the peace and the nothingness that were all he wanted.

He shouted, standing there, his hands clenched into fists. The
game between the child and the boat went on, placidly. The
shout wheeled up around the gulls and fell back against the
ground.

"Please go," said Matthew, whispering suddenly. "Please go."
After a moment, he reached into his pocket and found what
he wanted—a silver half-dollar, a bright cartwheel of bribery. It
was enough money to buy a meal, but he wouldn't need money
any more, and he threw it toward the child. It struck the boat
and glanced off. The child pounced, like a ferret.

It's always money, Matthew thought. The teachers talked,
and the wise men spoke. The best things in life are free, they
told you, and then they grabbed. They were the world, and
the child was They.

His mind was beginning to stumble. There was a pressure
inside his brain, and yet it wasn't a pressure. It was like sea fog
drifting in, and he knew he must hold out against it because
it would come between him and the deep peace, the surrender.

He watched intently, passionately.

The child stood up.

The sea fog began to drift and part. It would go now.

The child stood there, the goblin smile still on its lips, the
dark eyes peering from the pale face. It began to talk. The
hands clutching boat and money began to move, swiftly, importantly, in a clownish pantomime. The small fingers patted
the half-dollar in quick little pats, the mouth chattered.

It was a full minute before Matthew realized what was
wrong, that the chatter had no sound, that the mouth opened

and closed without words. He felt a kind of numb horror, knowing why the child hadn't run away when he had shouted at it, hadn't come when he called. It was a deaf-mute.

If he had needed a sign outside his own heart to tell him it was a world to escape from, the child had given it to him. The cliff was absolute innocence now; the small island of life on which he stood was sick and infected.

The child had dropped to its knees again. It put the shining coin onto the boat, took it off, put it on. It patted its possessions, talked to them. Without any sound.

Matthew turned to the cliff. In a moment he would be running to it. The child would not look up from its play, and if it did, it would see nothing, except perhaps, for a moment, a man flying like a gull. It would go back to its play, its closed-in, shuttered world.

He told himself the light was fading so fast now that the line between cliff and sky was almost gone. Shadow and substance were becoming one. The child would not see.

But suppose it did?

Suppose, for one moment of awfulness, it saw a man in flight, and knew the difference between man and gull?

Matthew pictured it running to the edge of the cliff to look over, wanting to see where the man had gone—the kind man who had given it the shining toy that rode so proudly on top of the boat.

He saw the child staring down at the sharp rocks, and at the dark water licking against the thing sprawled across them.

And then he saw it running desperately from the cliff. He saw the little boat flying to the grass, the silver half-dollar spinning on the ground. He heard the child screaming its terror.

But it wouldn't scream. It couldn't. It had no voice.

It would see and never be able to stop seeing. It would try to tell someone, and it would not be heard. It would be locked up, forever, alone with what had happened.

He prayed that the child would not see; he prayed to be allowed to escape. He knew that he must get to the cliff now or not at all. If he didn't, it would all start over again—the fear and the loneliness, the empty, indifferent world. He could never come back here, coldly, with a plan formed.

And still he did not move.

He knew the moment was passing, the possible moment when escape was still a reality. He thought he could hear the great wings of the promised darkness rushing past him, like a wind. There was an instant, a wrenching moment of despair and longing, when he could still have clutched and been borne up and cast over and freed.

He shivered. The exit closed. The rush of wings was only the sound of a sea beating on rocks. He was in bondage again, a small, used-up man, standing high on a plateau, with everything ahead that he had thought to leave behind.

But he could not hurt the child.

He stood and looked at it now, seeing the small head and the pale flesh in the twilight, and the little bones. It was busy with its toys again and didn't look up, and after a moment Matthew turned away.

His coat was lying on the ground where he had left it. He picked it up and put his arms through the sleeves, settling the collar at the back, the way he would the next morning when he went out again to look for work.

He said goodbye to the child, knowing it could not hear, and then he started to walk down the hill, on the narrow road that led away from the cliff.

He was not thinking about the cliff any longer. He was thinking about the high place above the cliff, the dead dry bushes and the old grass and the child playing there. He found he was thinking of it as a good place.

It was a small, warm island of safety, and yet nothing had really happened to change it. All he had done was to reach out toward a child and give it the only gift he could, the negative gift of no bad dreams. He had kept the child from harm, and he had cherished it.

For a moment he wanted to turn back to the warmth and the reassurance he was leaving behind. And then he knew suddenly that a man could make a lighted room for himself anywhere in the world.

"And his banner over me was love," he thought, without being able to remember where the words came from.

He began to walk faster. The road ahead was not so dark, after all. He would be home before long.

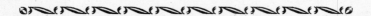

THE VEXATION OF BARNEY HATCH

THE big bell clanged in the church tower, and all the pigeons gossiping on the roof flew up in a violent state of nerves, as if the Day of Judgment had come upon them.

This created a fine rumpus of snow-gray wings in the snow-gray sky over Barney Hatch, but it confirmed him in a private theory that pigeons were not quite right in the head. The church had been around for more than a century, and the bell gave its great shout every hour, which meant that twenty-four times a day for over a hundred years the pigeons or their ancestors had been blowing their tops. Barney was not mathematically an able man, but even he could see that the thing had got out of hand.

A panhandler himself, Barney had a certain professional sympathy for pigeons, birds with an eye to the main chance and an alert capacity for spotting likely crumb-droppers.

He stared down at them now, bobbing and clucking around his shoes, and rubbed his nose thoughtfully with the back of his hand. His nose was cold, and he rubbed it some more, turning it from a melancholy blue to quite a cheerful red, but his mind was on neither the pigeons nor his nose. Barney Hatch had a project, and the project required cash.

Not a large fortune, but a sum of that size affectionately known as tidy. This project was going to cost three dollars and forty-nine cents, and since he had only forty-seven cents in his pocket he still needed three bills and two pennies. The trouble was that time was running short, tomorrow being Christmas Day and Christmas Day being the cause of the whole thing.

Christmas was all over the city—wreaths in doorways, tinsel and red ribbon and holly berries bursting out at odd corners, a piny, citrony, maddening jumble of sights and smells, tugging and nudging like a persistent cat at an ashcan. It had roused in Barney a sudden determination to do some celebrating himself for once and to join in the general exuberance of warmth and good cheer.

The very notion of a celebration had automatically pointed his toes toward the nearest liquor store, and he was engaged in a conscientious survey of the stock of whisky in the glittering window, with an eye toward economy, when the gold seal on a front-row bottle winked at him. It was a fat bottle, nicely shaped to accommodate the hand, and in addition to the gold seal it had a fancy label and a scarlet ribbon in a Christmas bow around its neck. It was plainly a bottle designed for good cheer; and judging by the price, its contents had been knowingly distilled.

On the other hand its price was outrageous.

Barney's struggle with his good sense was brisk but brief. After all, a Christmas treat was a Christmas treat, and what good was a celebration unless it was done right? He thought about the glow there would be in a bottle of good whisky like this one, and how the glow would last and spread and get deeper and wider. Nothing in the world could give you a glow like that, one you could count on, and a whole bottle to himself would very probably produce the finest glow in the history of man.

All he had to do was raise the money.

Contemplating the financial aspects now, among the cooing, huffing pigeons, Barney did comforting sums in his head. After all, it was Christmas, a time when any competent panhandler can count on a certain amount of soft-headedness among his clientele. Estimating, he decided that six suckers at fifty cents each would just do him nicely. He raised his eyes from the improvident birds and took a good look around.

A man went by, briefcase in hand, a rolled-up newspaper under one arm. A literate gent, well-heeled. Barney got his feet moving fast and performed a sort of flanking movement. Barney smiled an ingratiating, a calculating, smile. He said, "Sir," like a cooing dove, imagining for a moment that the man would press a five-dollar bill into his hand, touched by the general lunacy of Christmas.

The man stepped neatly around Barney, said, "Left my wallet home," and departed. Barney said, "Yah!" to the tails of the gentleman's overcoat. Left his wallet home! He'd be as apt to set sail without his trousers as without his money.

Expressing dissatisfaction in a low mutter, Barney left the pigeons and the church bell and tried another street. A lady in a squirrel neckpiece gave him a dime and a lecture, leaving him with two ninety-two to go and a bad taste in his mouth, which came not from remorse or shame but from biting the dime.

Business seemed suddenly to have turned sour, but the gold-seal bottle hovered in the air above him, slightly to one side of his right eyebrow. He walked up one street and down another. The professional shamble became quite sincere, his feet hurt, he had never had such a bad day. One would think, with Christmas practically ready to pounce, that people would be digging deep into their purses and handing over dollar bills with warm enthusiasm. Lock and key on 'em, Barney grumbled to himself. Lock and key on every purse and wallet in town. The whole city dizzy with Christmas and good will, and what did he get? Ten cents from a squirrel neckpiece, with a lecture thrown in.

He walked through a transported grove of pine trees on a street corner, little fat trees and tall lean trees, all waiting for the tinsel and the star and the fancy trimmings that were nice enough when you had four walls to wrap around them. "Knick-knacks," said Barney scornfully. "Jinglejangles." And he thought of the knickknack and the jinglejangle of a gold seal on a whisky bottle. He thought of waking up on Christmas morning and taking his first drink, savoring it in a gentlemanlike manner, not gulping, the whole bottle to go through and the whole day to go through it. He thought of how he would admire the label and the seal and the Christmas ribbon before he pulled the cork and had himself his first Christmas drink, spreading warm and bright.

He walked on, and the gold-seal bottle kept just one step ahead of him, out of reach, an air-borne promise. He stopped outside a department store, its windows shimmering and quivering with light and glitter, people rushing inside, where it would be nice and warm, with their purses gaping, and then coming out and quickly closing the purses again so the loose change wouldn't catch cold.

Barney swore. It began to look as if he was going to spend Christmas with fifty-seven cents and no gold seal, no cork, no different from three hundred and sixty-four other days.

He stepped into the doorway of the store, out of the way of the wind. He thrust his hands deep into his pockets and glared at his reflection in the store window.

A fat man with a busy face came lumbering out of the store. He stared up the street, down the street, and then he stared at

Barney. His eyes narrowed like he was doing sums on his fingers, and he shook his head and sighed. "You want a job for a couple of hours?" said the man.

Barney looked back over his shoulder, figuring the man was talking to someone behind him, but there was no one there. He wasn't used to being offered jobs, and a wary look came into his eyes, because you never know about offers. Like a dime, the thing to do was take a bite of it and see if it bit solid.

"How much?" said Barney.

"Dollar fifty an hour."

Two hours at a dollar fifty was three bucks, and he only needed two dollars and ninety-two cents. Profit, eight cents. He was rich. "Okay," said Barney.

"Thank goodness," said the fat man with real sincerity, and added, "You're skinny, but we can stuff you."

"Eh?" said Barney, recoiling.

"Come on, come on." The man took his elbow and piloted him into the store and down the crowded aisles.

"What you hiring me for?" Barney asked plaintively. "What you want to stuff me for?"

"Santa Claus, of course." The man's voice implied that any fool should know that. "Ours has gone home sick. We called the agency, but they can't get the substitute here until one thirty. Line of kids a mile long, yapping and yelping. Mothers getting so mad they'll yank them out of line and go somewhere else. They go somewhere else, *we* go broke. How we going to pay our taxes?" He glared at Barney.

Barney was not tax-conscious. He was, however, conscious that he had no wish to play Santa Claus for a mob of children. His instinct warned him to escape while escape was still possible, and he was about to take its advice when—in a rather peremptory manner—the vision of the gold-seal bottle appeared in the air above him. Barney relaxed.

His escort pushed him through a doorway into what appeared

to be a dressing room. A scarlet suit, furred and benevolent hung from a hook. "I'll help you get dressed," said the man, calmer now that he had caged his Christmas spirit. "On account of the pillow."

Barney took off his coat and thought hard about the money he was making. Even with two pillows under his belt, there was something faintly melancholy about his shape. He tested the pillows against slippage. "What do I have to do when I get out there?" he said nervously.

"You sit in a chair by the Christmas tree," said the man, frowning at Barney's front, "and you talk to the kids and you give them each a lollipop."

"What do I say?"

"Promise them anything they ask for. Especially if it's in the store."

"I don't know what's in the store."

"Promise them anything."

This pie-in-the-sky approach seemed slightly sinister. "When do I get my money?" said Barney, leaning toward the mirror and tying on his beard. It was a splendid beard, long and white and fluffy, but self-esteem was not going to hinder self-interest.

"Oh, that." The man scribbled something on a piece of paper. "Give this to the cashier when you leave. You come back here and give the new man your suit (and I hope to God he's got more shape than you have) and then you can get your money and be on your way."

Barney grinned and took another look in the mirror. There was something not quite right about the beard; it looked more like some strange white thicket behind which he was lurking. And his nose had faded, being indoors. Still, he looked more like Santa Claus than he looked like anything else, and when the business was over and done with he would be three dollars richer.

Patting his front with a certain anxiety, Barney let himself be shepherded back through the store to where a glittering Christmas tree touched the ceiling and a small jungle of assorted children milled about, shouting their boredom and their lack of faith.

Barney had an impulse to run, but his guide, perhaps sensing it, shoved him briskly into the thronelike chair and anchored him by putting a small child on his knee. The infant was fat, fair and female, and Santa Claus regarded her with marked distaste. He then thought of the three dollars and pulled himself together enough to inquire what the little lady wanted for Christmas.

The little lady sounded off like a clockwork mouse, her list of vital necessities having apparently been ready for days and her memory excellent. When he took her off his knee and forgot to give her a lollipop, she demanded that too, and Barney had to admire the tough grip she had on the situation.

In about ten minutes he was pretty well into the swing of things, the Santa Claus racket being somewhat easier than expected. If a toddler wanted a grizzly bear in his Christmas stocking, all Santa had to do was pat his head, promise a den of bears and hand him back to his mama. This grandiloquent largess with no responsibility speeded the passage of the two hours, and Barney had just promised a little girl with pigtails that she would have curly hair for Christmas when the small boy turned up.

He was a very small boy, even smaller than the other children, and he looked out of place in the line among the well-brushed, neatly dressed household creatures who were patrolled by parents. His hair, if it had been combed at all, had been combed by his fingers. His pants were too short and his coat sleeves too long, his face was dirty, and he stood with his hands thrust in his pockets and his chin sticking out.

Barney recognized him. He was a street sparrow, and wherever else he might belong, he didn't belong in the warm, rich aisles of a big department store.

The boy stood and stared at him, and Barney stared back. There was something about this kid's stare that was different from the others', and it took a moment for Barney to place it. Then he realized that the boy was looking at him as if he were real. The other children had looked at him as if he were a handy device for registering propositions.

He felt a vague embarrassment, very foreign to him. He rubbed his nose with the back of his hand, causing his whiskers to lurch sideways. "Well, my little man," he said, because that was more or less what he had been saying for almost two hours, "and what do *you* want for Christmas?"

"What I didn't get last year," said the boy. He looked at Santa Claus long and hard. "What you promised me last year and I didn't get."

Barney pulled his beard back into position and tried to think of some way of counteracting this very unfavorable propaganda. Several children in the line were giving him rather cool up-and-down looks, and Barney wished no complaints made to the management before he pocketed his money.

He said with false cheer, "Well, well, we'll do better this year, won't we? Just what was it you wanted?"

"You know," said the small boy quietly. "The harmonica."

It was a long word, but he didn't miss a syllable. It took Barney a moment to identify a harmonica as the small musical instrument which was played like corn on a cob. "Must've slipped down to the bottom of my pack," he said cleverly. "Imagine that happening!" He gave a conciliatory, unsuccessful chuckle. The boy regarded him calmly but with unnerving watchfulness.

"Well, you'll get it this year for sure," said Barney defensively.

"You said that last year."

"I *told* you. It slipped down to the bottom of my pack. Here." He handed over a green lollipop. "Take this and go away and be a good boy. If you aren't a good boy, you won't get anything for Christmas at all." Even as he said this, it struck him as a revolting philosophy, but it was backed by tradition. He said hopefully, "Two lollipops?"

The boy shook his head and backed off. "No, I don't want them. I want the harmonica."

The line behind him was growing restive, and there was a faint murmuring of parents. "Go *away*," said Barney.

"Okay. I'll see you later."

Not if I see you first, thought Barney, and turned with considerable relief to his next customer. The clock told him he had ten minutes to go, and then the world in a gold-seal bottle would be his.

When the clock hand moved into place, Santa Claus' eagerness to quit his duties was such that he nearly dumped the last child on the floor. In the dressing room his replacement was waiting calmly, a cozy gentleman with a twinkle in his eyes and a curve like a robin's under his waistcoat. The beard and his red suit merely confirmed that here was Santa Claus. Barney frankly admired him and hoped the small harmonica-seeking boy would turn up in the line again, pitted against a Santa who would know how to deal with him.

Whistling, he sought out the cashier's desk, and in a few minutes he had exchanged his white slip of paper for three pretty green ones, underwritten by the Treasury of the United States.

He now had three dollars and fifty-seven cents. He would walk slowly to the liquor store; he would stroll, savoring every moment. The very magnificence of the gesture would lay out a red carpet for Christmas. It would be glorious.

Floating on a cloud of anticipation, Barney Hatch walked out of the department store and into the street.

"There you are," said the small boy, rising at his elbow.

Barney leaped and came down quivering, like a spring stretched too far. For a moment he thought he must still be wearing his whiskers, but a hand to his chin reassured him. Case of mistaken identity, he told himself quickly; probably looked like the kid's grandpop. Privately he didn't think he looked like anybody's grandpop, but the alternative was even more fantastic.

The boy took hold of Barney's coat and gave it a good sharp tug, endangering a vital button. "Come *on*."

"Scram," said Barney, resorting to simple English. "You've got me mixed up with someone else."

"No, I ain't."

Barney stopped in his tracks and stared down at the top of the head that needed a haircut. "Who do you think I am?"

"Santa Claus," said the boy.

He knew he shouldn't have asked. He couldn't even figure out how the kid had been able to spot him without his beard and his furred suit. He said, "Look, kid, I saw your friend Santa Claus just a minute ago. He's in the store. You go back in the store and you'll find him there under the tree."

"That ain't Santa Claus," said the boy.

"It is so," said Barney indignantly.

"It ain't."

All right, it ain't, thought Barney. "You shouldn't say 'ain't,'" he said to the boy. "Santa Claus is up at the North Pole. He don't get into town nowadays."

"Yes, you do."

"Listen," said Barney, "you're making me very nervous. Go away or I'll call a cop." He looked up the street in a threatening manner, and his eye lit on the happy sight of a fine specimen of a Santa Claus, halfway up the block, standing by a phony chimney and ringing a bell. Barney put a hand on the boy's shoulder and gave him a fervent push. "There's your Santa Claus, up there. See, I told you you'd got the wrong guy."

"That ain't Santa Claus."

"Geez," said Barney with some passion, "can't you get a new record? What makes you think the guy up there ain't Santa Claus?"

"Because *you* are," answered the boy.

Barney shook his head hard, feeling life getting complicated, and then he had a bright idea. He surrendered suddenly. "Okay," he said, "so I'm Santa Claus. How'd you guess?"

The boy shrugged. "I don't know—I just did."

Reindeer fur got shed on my trousers, I suppose, thought Barney with some bitterness. Aloud, he said, "Well, it was real smart of you. I'm sort of anonymous, you know. That means nobody knows I'm in town." He put a hand on the boy's shoulder, and the boy squirmed away. "Now, look, son. That guy in the store, the one that's wearing my costume—well, he's one of my special assistants."

"Yeah?"

"Yeah." Barney felt exasperation crawling up inside his collar. What was the matter with modern youth anyway? No faith. He said, "Yeah," twice more, just to make things clear. "Well, he handles the musical-instrument side of the business, see? So you go back in the store and tell him I sent you, and everything will be okay. See?"

"No."

"Whaddya mean *no!*"

The boy said stolidly, "You promised me my harmonica last Christmas, and I didn't get it. I've waited a whole year." He looked up suddenly. "I've gotta get it this year, I've wasted a whole year when I could've been playing. You *promised* me."

Barney's voice rose. "I wasn't even around last year!"

The boy just looked at him, in the patient way children look at grownups who make silly remarks. Barney began to feel haunted. A man might as well try to get a wad of chewing gum out of his hair as this little squirt. For a moment, he toyed with the idea of turning tail and running, but there is nothing that attracts a policeman like a running object.

The situation required something more subtle. Barney heaved a sigh. "How about your ma and pa buying a harmonica for you?" he said hopefully.

The boy's eyes slid sideways. For just a second Barney was sorry he'd asked, there being so many homes in the world where stockings never hang at Christmas time. Then he cheered himself with the thought that the kid had probably long since driven all his relatives into the loony bin with his persistence, and so he was able to hurl his bombshell without a qualm. "I didn't bring no harmonicas with me this trip," he said crushingly. "You're out of luck this year."

"You c'n buy it."

The mere suggestion of parting from any cash caused a cry of anguish to rise to Barney's lips. He said in one outraged defiant breath, "See here, you! You're too old to believe in Santa Claus, and furthermore there ain't no Santa Claus," and then he waited stoically for the expected broken heart.

It failed to materialize. The boy nodded calmly. He said, "Like you told me, you have to be anonymous." He called it "anon-y-mouse," like something a cat would be watching for.

Barney sighed heavily and stroked the end of his nose. He was not an expert on harmonicas, but he was pretty sure you could buy one at a dimestore toy counter. Take away one dime from his cash on hand, it would leave him three forty-seven, only two cents short of his ticket to Christmas Day. If he couldn't make a two-cent touch in the next couple of hours, he deserved to be read out of the panhandlers' club anyway.

He sighed again. "All right," he said glumly. "Where's the nearest dimestore?"

The boy started to say something and then changed his mind. He took Barney's hand, not in the least trustingly but plainly to prevent his escape. They walked down two blocks, one over, turned sharply into a grubby side street, and stopped in front of a store.

"Hey," said Barney. This was no dimestore. This was a kind of store Barney knew inside and out: a pawnshop, and not a classy one. Its fly-specked dusty windows were piled high with objects as miscellaneous as a junkman's dream: old tired medals on faded bits of ribbon; an alarm clock with no hands; a china lamp with a Cupid base and dirty blue ruffles; a handful of painted brooches; a snuffbox with no lid; a silver mug inscribed 1887-1907; a stuffed and lopsided owl.

"There," said the small boy. "There, by the owl."

Barney looked. A beat-up tarnished harmonica lay in a satin-lined box. The lining had been red once, but the sun through the window had faded it to pink like a raspberry stain, and there was a big dent in the harmonica's side. It looked like a long time since anyone had played it or wanted to.

A connoisseur of old age and unwanted objects, Barney figured a quick guess that the harmonica had been lying there anyway five years. It was a weather-beaten shipwreck washed up on a pawnshop beach. Junk, really junk.

Barney looked down at the head just under his elbow. "Is *that* what you've been yammering about?"

The head nodded. Its nose pressed against the windowpane. "I told you about it last Christmas. That was when you promised—"

Barney bit the tail off an expletive, calling down a justified imprecation on some previous hired Santa Claus who must have been throwing out promises like confetti. He stared at the harmonica and worried the tip of his nose. It was hard to know with pawnbrokers; this one might charge as much as a quarter.

"Been there a long time," he said. "Wouldn't you rather have a nice clean harmonica from the dimestore?"

The small boy said scornfully, "They're just toys. This is a real one."

Real like his Santa Claus was real. Two pieces of junk. "This is awful old. Been there years."

"Don't hurt it," said the boy. "Not if it's a good one." He moved back from the window a little, unconsciously cupping his hands as though the instrument already lay in their grubby palms.

The most the pawnbroker could possibly charge for that piece of junk was fifty cents. Fifty cents was an awful thought; fifty cents was outrageous for a skinny piece of music-making tin. But on the other hand the essence of a pawnshop was bargaining, and no one knew this better than Barney Hatch, who, in his day, could have bargained a sparrow out of its beat in the gutter. Starting at fifty cents, he would begin to work downward. The dent in the harmonica, the dust, the years it had been there with no one wanting it, the tarnish, even the pathetic satin lining of the box. Mentally Barney talked the price down to thirty-five cents.

Thirty-five cents was still too much. At the thirty-five-cent level he would begin to apply sentiment. It's Christmas, ain't it? Here's a little boy believes in Santa Claus. Here's a moldy old harmonica, no good to anyone, taking up space. No class to a piece of junk like that. Make it twenty cents, we'll take it off your hands.

Twenty cents. That was the sky.

"Awright," said Barney dismally, and pushed the boy through the door. The shop was full of shadows. The fattest shadow detached itself and came forward. "Want somep'n? Oh, it's *you*."

"Me?" said Barney.

"Nah. The kid." The man had a flat face like a moon. "Comes here all the time. Nose sticking right through the plate glass." He looked at the small boy, from whom, suddenly, a quiver of electric current seemed to be flowing. "Listen!" said the pawnbroker, outraged by so much intensity. "I'm not gonna haul that thing out of the window for you again. I told you last time—"

The boy said, "He's going to buy it for me." He said it quite quietly. The songs of all the golden trumpets must have come from somewhere else.

The pawnbroker looked at Barney sharply. "That right? You gonna buy it?"

"Got to look it over first," said Barney. He reached into his pocket, past the cool crackle of his beloved dollar bills, and found a quarter, which he rubbed tenderly between his fingers. When it came back to him, it would be shrunk to a nickel. A sad end for a lovely object.

The pawnbroker waddled toward the window, talking to himself. "Gives me the creeps, that kid does, staring inna window all the time. Comes in, says, 'Can I see it again?' I got nothing to do but run around hauling the thing outa the window. Been there so long, fits so nice."

"Spoils the window," said Barney, sensing conflict.

"Props up the owl," said the pawnbroker, sighed heavily and justified his gloom at once by removing the harmonica and causing the owl to fall onto the China cupid-lamp. "You see?" he said with a kind of melancholy pride. He blew dust off the box and the harmonica, waddled back and planked the box down. The small boy put his chin on the counter and stared so hard it looked as if his ears might fly off.

Barney reminded himself that twenty cents was an outside price.

The boy's dirty paw reached up, and one finger touched the

deep dent in the side of the instrument. "Don't touch!" said the pawnbroker crossly.

The boy put his hands in his pockets, because, uncaged, he could not be responsible for them. Barney kept thinking about the twenty cents; the old harmonica was so busted up it probably couldn't even carry a tune. "Piece of junk, ain't it?" said Barney, very loud and affable. "Pay you to let the kid cart it away, huh?"

The pawnbroker gave a short, unpromising laugh.

Barney shrugged; he had not expected the gambit to work. "Whadda you want for it?" he said casually.

He had expected the pawnbroker to hesitate, sizing up his customer's affluence according to immemorial pawnbroking custom. The pawnbroker did not hesitate. He said crisply, "Three bucks."

Barney gave a wild, incredulous howl. "Three bucks! You're outa your mind."

"Take it or leave it," said the man. "That's the price."

"You're outa your mind," said Barney.

There was a small bubble of sound down at counter level. The kid had reached up and taken the harmonica into his hands and was now rubbing it tenderly against his coat sleeve. The pawnbroker said, "Put it down!' with weary irritability.

"Bet it don't even blow," said Barney indignantly. "Piece of junk. I'll give you two bits for the piece of junk."

"It blows," said the pawnbroker, unmoved.

"Bet it don't." Barney was wondering what had got into him to make him offer two bits when his outside limit was twenty cents. This crazy three-bucks talk must have addled his brain.

"Blow it yourself," said the pawnbroker coldly.

Barney stretched out his hand. The small boy pulled away and put the harmonica to his own lips. There was a small breathy sound, wheezy like an old organ, as the little instrument breathed out the dust of the window, breathed in something new. Then it piped, a sweet little pipe like a bird in a meadow, following a thread of tune, a tiny melody that went up and down, miniature but recognizable.

"Don't breathe so light," said the pawnbroker fretfully. "Makes it sound like a sick cat. You've got to fill your lungs."

"Ain't used to me yet," said the small boy in the smallest of whispers.

"Where'd you learn to play a tune?" said Barney.

"Fella taught me once." He volunteered no more. His eyes were enormous; his hands were cradles. He talked gently to the harmonica.

The pawnbroker and Barney looked at each other. "Thirty cents," said Barney. "That's my last word."

"Listen." The pawnbroker leaned across his counter, master of all his objects. "You hear how good she plays? Six years inna window and still as sweet as a bird."

"No volume," said Barney.

"Get the dust outa its innards and some breath into the boy, you'd get plenty of volume. Three bucks, nothing less."

"Who," said Barney rhetorically, "do you think you're kidding?"

The pawnbroker waved a hand. "A dollar a year I take off. Last Christmas, she was four bucks. This Christmas, three. Next Christmas, two. See you next Christmas, Santa Claus."

The kid's head jerked up. Barney leaped like a flea. "Don't call me that!" he yelped.

The boy looked at the pawnbroker with interest. "How'd *you* know who he was?"

"Who?"

"Him. Santa Claus."

"Listen!" said Barney hysterically.

"He's anon-y-mouse," said the boy pleasantly. He lifted the

harmonica to his lips again, and this time the tune didn't sound so thin any more but almost like a real piece of music. Over his cupped hands, his eyes were as bright as a squirrel's.

"Three bucks," said the pawnbroker.

"Talk sense," said Barney.

The pawnbroker shrugged, then turned to the kid. "Gent ain't gonna invest," he said indifferently. "Give her here. I'll put her back in the window."

The kid backed away, the harmonica held tight. He looked up at Barney. "You promised."

Barney glared at him. Maybe the whole thing was a racket; maybe the kid and the pawnbroker were in cahoots. Only a sucker would be expected to pay three dollars for a piece of junk, even if the piece of junk did have a tune inside it.

Barney Hatch was smart and Barney Hatch was getting out, his money tight in his pocket, his Christmas Day all spelled out for him, the glow of his own private bottle of good whisky just around the next corner.

"Thirty-five cents," said Barney coldly. "Not a nickel more."

"Three bucks."

"Thirty-five cents."

The pawnbroker said to the boy, "Put the harmonica down, kid. The gent ain't interested." He spread his hands on the counter, watching the boy, and after a minute he said, "I told you, put it down."

The boy, moving so slowly he hardly moved at all, put it down. He reached up and placed the shiny little piece of junk, value three dollars, on the counter, and then he opened his hand and let it go like it was a baby rabbit or something. Then he touched the dent in it with one finger, like smoothing a baby rabbit's ears. The pawnbroker took it up and put it back in its box and snapped the lid down hard.

The kid looked at Barney.

It all of a sudden became very clear to Barney that he didn't have to stand there in a dirty old pawnshop with a skinny little kid staring at him. He pushed his hands down deep into his pockets and felt the lovely, crackling reassurance of his money, and that did it. He spun on his heel and left the shop, and he walked down the street in such a hurry that you would have thought there was a pack of angels snapping at his heels.

He didn't stop and he didn't look back, and he turned a corner so fast that he bumped into a fat lady with a lot of packages who gave him a huffy look like her mouth was full of pins. He didn't pay any attention. The corner he was turning was the corner by the liquor store, and the one thing that was clear in his mind was that he was going to convert his dollars into Christmas and convert them quickly.

There, in the window, was the bottle he had picked out, gold seal, fancy label, red Christmas bow, and, inside it, Barney's passport to Christmas. He could imagine its glow, spreading and comforting, making the twenty-fifth of December something to remember. Just looking at it made him feel better.

He reached into his pocket, taking out the bills, smoothing them, putting the change on top. Three dollars and forty-nine cents, the price of a good bottle of whisky, only forty-nine cents more than a cheap, beat-up harmonica in a satin-lined box.

Barney made a cross sound. He hadn't intended thinking about the kid. He looked at the whisky bottle again, it not being shaped like a harmonica at all. The kid must be used to waiting by now; he could wait another year. It would learn him not to believe in Santa Claus. Kids had no business going around believing in Santa Claus anyway. Probably just a gag. Who believed in Santa Claus?

Suppose this kid did?

Well, then, it was high time he stopped believing. High time he grew up!

Barney looked down at the dollar bills and the loose change, and then he looked past them, at the whisky bottle. Kids like that one never grew up; they didn't have to. They were born old. What Barney knew about people not caring, what the whisky bottle knew, that was what the kid knew too.

Today, just in case he'd forgotten his lesson, the kid had learned it again.

The whisky bottle glittered in the window. The gold seal shone like a star. Barney swore. Barney said, "The hell with it," and a passerby gave him a shocked look which Barney didn't see.

He turned on his heel and he started walking fast, walking back the way he had come. The last couple of blocks he ran, because the kid might be gone.

The kid wasn't gone. He was standing there outside the pawnshop window, hugged up close to the glass, waiting for next Christmas. The hand that Barney put on his shoulder was rough. It was rough the way Barney marched him into the store. It was rough the way he slammed down three dollars on the pawnbroker's counter and the way he said, "Get that junky thing outa the window again." It was a roughness like shattered glass, like a broken whisky bottle.

The pawnbroker scooped up the money first. Then he went to the window and took the satin-lined box out and put it in front of Barney. Barney pushed it over with one angry hand, not looking at the kid.

The kid didn't ask. He knew it was his. He put out both hands, and it almost seemed, though it wasn't possible, that the harmonica jumped up into them. He turned his back to the counter, and he pressed his shoulders against it. He held the harmonica up to his mouth, but his hands were shaking, and the silly little tinny thing wabbled and shook too.

He put his hands down level with his chest, the harmonica tight and safe in his fingers.

The pawnbroker brushed some imaginary crumbs off the

counter. The room was getting dark with twilight, and outside the wind was worrying the big window, trying to get at the stuffed owl and the china lamp and the silver mug.

Barney stood in the middle of the pawnshop and listened to the wind. If it had come into the shop and laid its cold finger on his shoulder, it couldn't have told him more plainly what a fool he'd been. Money gone, whisky gone, Christmas gone. The Christmas that would have been a real one, the Christmas that would have kept the cold out.

He hunched up his shoulders. The pawnbroker and the kid were both looking at him, and suddenly their staring made him angry. What did they have to be gaping at him for? Kid had his harmonica, pawnbroker had his money, everybody was sitting pretty except Barney Hatch.

He opened his mouth to shout his anger at them, but the kid spoke first. "I'm awful sorry," the kid said anxiously. "I didn't say thank you." After a moment, he tried again. "I c'd play a tune for you," he said hopefully. "Only I don't know but the one."

The pawnbroker leaned abruptly across the counter. " 'Tisn't suited," he said firmly. "Don't you know any Christmas tunes, like—" he thought for a moment "—like 'Hark the Herald Angels Sing'? That's a good tune."

The boy shook his head. "I don't know it. I never heard it."

"Imagine that," said the pawnbroker wonderingly. "Imagine that." He straightened up from the counter and drew a deep breath, and from inside him there came a sort of rumble. The rumble was just a little bit off key, but the herald angels were clearly on their way.

For a moment the kid listened with his head tilted on one side, and then he cupped the harmonica and put it to his lips. At first he had a little trouble making the tune come right, and then it began to grow until the harmonica was singing glory to the new-born King as if it had been silent for six years just for this moment.

The pawnbroker beat one hand on the counter, keeping time, and the chorus of Christmas angels came up so fine and strong that the dust danced on the pawnshop shelves.

Barney stared. Very slowly, all through him, there began to spread a glow, warm and golden and quite unmistakable. It was the glow he had planned to buy for three dollars and forty-nine cents, the glow he had thought came only in a bottle.

He stood there, listening, and he let it warm him. Outside the wind shook hard at the window, wanting to come in out of the cold.

Date Due

JUL 1 2		
AUG 1 1		
NOV 19 '58		
NOV 24 '58		
DEC 1 '58		
FEB 2 0 61		
MAR 2 - '61		
JUN 9 - '61		
OCT 6 - '62		
JUL 2 9 '63		
OCT 2 - 1965		
MAY 5 '69		
DEC 2 8 '83		
MAY 30 '85		
SEP 2 6 '85		
FEB 9 1988		

PRINTED IN

C 1

Chute

Blue cup.